Praise for Christine d'Abo's *30 Days*

"Well-developed and engaging characters, major and minor, lead to conflicts that feel both realistic and fresh, and difficult subjects are handled with empathy and gentle humor. Romance fans will delight in this sweet and spicy expedition."

—*Publishers Weekly* STARRED REVIEW

"Christine D'Abo crafts a rare treat in *30 Days*, a book that's equal parts sexy and heartwarming, fun and deeply emotional. Bravo!"

—*New York Times* bestselling author J. Kenner

30 Days

Christine d'Abo

KENSINGTON BOOKS
www.kensingtonbooks.com

KENSINGTON BOOKS are published by

Kensington Publishing Corp.
119 West 40th Street
New York, NY 10018

All Kensington titles, imprints, and distributed lines are available at special quantity discounts for bulk purchases for sales promotion, premiums, fund-raising, educational, or institutional use.

Special book excerpts or customized printings can also be created to fit specific needs. For details, write or phone the office of the Kensington Special Sales Manager: Kensington Publishing Corp., 119 West 40th Street, New York, NY 10018. Attn. Special Sales Department. Phone: 1-800-221-2647.

Kensington and the K logo Reg. U.S. Pat. & TM Off.

eISBN-13: 978-1-61773-955-2
eISBN-10: 1-61773-955-3
First Kensington Electronic Edition: August 2015

ISBN-13: 978-1-61773-954-5
ISBN-10: 1-61773-954-5
First Kensington Trade Paperback Printing: August 2015

10 9 8 7 6 5 4 3 2

Printed in the United States of America

For Mark. My one and only.

Part 1

The Proposal

1

So, the thing about me being a widow at the ripe old age of thirty-five was that no one knew what to say or how to act around me. My couple friends still invited me over to their parties, barbecues, and the like, but the conversations always drifted into the land of awkward. *Oh you look great. I haven't seen you since Rob . . . since the funeral. Did you do something to your hair?*

The few single friends I had tried to pull me into their world. I didn't quite fit with them though. While they were clubbing or barhopping trying to find the perfect guy, every time I met someone my brain automatically compared him to Rob. I wasn't *still* looking for that special someone—I'd found and lost him.

Being a widow is not quite the same as being divorced. I'd been quite happy being married, having regular, boring sex with my amazing husband, followed by eating cold pizza in bed while we watched the hockey game. It was what I'd always wanted. *He* was who I'd always wanted.

Seriously, fuck cancer.

As a result, I found myself on my own more and more. It wasn't a bad thing, really. I'd been with Rob since I was nineteen and we'd been friends long before we'd officially started dating. We'd grown up together, had the same interests, same fears. Hell, we used to speak in nothing but punch lines, only to dissolve into giggles together when no one else in the room knew what the hell we were talking about. Not having him by my side had forced me to slowly become a singular entity instead of a plural.

Being on my own was . . . strange. Rob had been gone nearly two years and I still found myself turning to say something to him at the weirdest times. Though over the past month that started happening less frequently. I couldn't tell you exactly how I felt about that. Guilty? Oh my God yes. But I knew it meant I'd finally started to move on. I hadn't told anyone about my mental shift. Instead, I found myself going to this quiet place in my head, speaking less, observing more. It was different. I guess I'd become different more out of necessity than any real desire to change.

We'd known his time was coming to an end and took the last month of his life to simply enjoy each other. It was on one of our various trips to the beach that he handed me The Envelope.

"What's this?" My fingers were damp from the ocean spray and sticky from the ice cream I'd just finished. "If this is some death letter thing, I can't read it."

He grinned at that. "Naw, it's not sappy or anything. But yes, it's for after I'm gone."

"Rob—"

"Lyssa, listen to me. I promise you it's not what you think." He huffed, puffing out his shallow cheeks. "How many guys have you slept with?" The breeze moved his shirt and the sun made his brown eyes sparkle. If he had any hair left it would have blown from his forehead. My heart ached to run my hands through his hair once more. "And if you say more than one I'll promise not to be pissed."

"Don't be an ass. You know you're the only man I've ever been with." We'd talked a lot about that after we'd gotten married. Rob had a small measure of guilt that I hadn't had a chance to sow my oats. Somehow he thought because of my limited dating experience I would get bored or grow to resent him.

The idiot.

"That's my point." He took my hand and pressed the envelope into my palm once more. "Don't open this until you're ready. Hell, you might not want to open it at all. Just . . ." He gave my hand a squeeze, but for the first time in a long while, he couldn't meet my gaze. "I know you said you didn't think you'd want to be with anyone else."

"I don't." The thought made me ill.

"Baby, you shouldn't be alone. You have too much light and love inside you. The thought of you being on your own, of not having anyone to share in the joy you have to give? No. I know you. There will come a time when you'll realize that you're ready to move on—"

"I won't."

"—and I know you'll feel guilty about that. You'll ignore the feelings for as long as you can, thinking that you don't need anyone. Then something will happen. You'll see someone and in that beautiful brain of yours you'll be all *nice ass, dude,* and that will be it. You'll cry about it but you'll realize you're ready."

"Please. I wouldn't cry." Because it wouldn't happen. Ever. "Not over a nice ass."

He chuckled, finally looking me in the eye. "You'll cry. But then you'll remember this conversation and know that I was right. So I'm going to say *I told you so* now. Then I want you to take this envelope and open it."

"Rob—"

"It's about sex."

I stood there with my mouth open. "What?"

"Just some ideas I had for you about sex when I'm gone. Getting back on the horse. Riding the cowboy. That sort of thing."

I wasn't ready to think about him being gone, let alone wanting to have sex with someone else. "I don't want to talk about this anymore. Seriously, shut up or I'm going to punch you."

"Okay."

He didn't let me forget about the envelope. He tried to get me to talk about it, but I would always cut him off. When I shoved it into a pile of papers in the closet, it found its way back onto my dresser. That box in the basement of papers that was older than me? Materialized on top of my desk. The recycling bin? Back onto the counter. I could have continued to play that game, but then Rob took another turn for the worse and all thoughts of envelopes and what they contained were the last things on my mind.

The cancer won.

And I was suddenly alone.

It really wasn't as bad as I'd first assumed it would be. I thought a lot about Rob, and missed him terribly for the better part of the first year. I functioned, worked, went out, but that was more of an automated response than actual living. There'd been more tears than I ever thought possible. My chest ached and my stomach churned. When I didn't feel ill, my mind wandered. I couldn't pretend to have any focus. My friends and the people at work never called me on my distraction.

Then I started to emerge from under the darkness and began to live once more. I still missed Rob, thought about him daily, but the tightness in my chest eased. That's when the guilt kicked in. At least he'd already told me it would.

I stopped going out to our friends' homes for a while. They'd begun to get used to me as a singular—Alyssa—and not a plural—Rob and Alyssa. With their ease came my anger that they were all still couples. Their lives hadn't been shattered and swept away without their permission. They'd smile, laugh, and all the while I wanted to scream at them.

So I stayed away.

It helped. I was able to catch my breath, cry, hit things, and slowly my brain adjusted. I could be allowed into public once more, no longer a danger to happy couples.

One thing that helped was changing up my routine. I'd rearranged all the furniture in our condo, painted the walls, even put up some new pictures. Rob would have hated them. I wasn't a fan myself, but it served its purpose. I started going to a new coffee shop half a block farther away from our building. I saw new people as I went, had to train a new barista named Len, smiled at a street performer who always played the same three songs on his guitar. It was good.

By the time the beginning of June rolled around, the tension had bled from my shoulders. It had taken me nearly two years, but I knew I was going to be okay.

That was when it happened.

A new guy moved into the complex.

Our building was a renovated school, each unit composed of three converted classrooms. Rob loved that we had a working water fountain just outside our front door. For fun, we'd mentally labeled the condos by classes. We were English because of the sheer number of books we had. Mr. and Mrs. Le Page were French, the Chin family were Home Ec and on and on. The new guy had moved into Tourism, the condo owned by some company that let their out-of-town employees stay there for extended periods of time. It was just down the hall on the side opposite our place.

No, *my* place.

And he had a nice ass.

I knew this because my first sight of him was him bent over, pushing a large box through his front door. His jeans were stretched tight as his long legs worked against their load. I don't know how long I stood there, but it was enough that I hadn't unlocked my front door and he must have felt my gaze on him. He looked over his shoulder and smiled.

My body shivered. Even with the distance between us, I felt the intensity of his gaze.

Then I heard Rob's chuckle in my brain, that little one he'd give me when he knew he'd won an argument. I had to get in before I looked even more the idiot. I waved to the guy and immediately fumbled with my key. I knew he was watching me, which made the entire process of opening the door a monumental task. *Click, whoosh, bang* and I was safely inside. I pressed my forehead to the door and contemplated the probability of dying from embarrassment. Given my current state, upward of forty percent chance of death.

The bastard *did* have a nice ass.

It was in that moment that I remembered my conversation with Rob at the beach and his envelope. I was guilty, but that guilt wasn't nearly as strong as it had once been. With my hand pressed against the wood, I pushed away and slowly made my way to the bedroom. The envelope had taken up residence in my underwear drawer—I knew Rob would approve—deep beneath my panties and socks. I hadn't thought about it for quite some time, but rather than feel sad about the prospect of opening it, I had a strange tingle of anticipation.

I held it in my hands as I sat on the edge of the bed. The stains from my ice cream–coated fingers were still on the envelope. Chocolate with fudge. I ran my thumb across them.

Nothing else adorned the front of the envelope, no indication of what may be inside. I huffed, then licked my lips before I finally slipped my finger beneath the edge and tore the paper open.

Hidden inside was a single piece of paper wrapped around a bundle of index cards. I ignored the cards for the time being and spread open the paper. I took a moment before I could read the note. This was something new from Rob and my heart broke a little bit more. Those invisible fingers squeezed at my chest.

Alyssa.
I love you. I know you love me. I'm glad you're ready to move on and start having some fun once again. I also know you well enough to realize you'll only go so far before you stop. Don't

*do that. And for God's sake, don't get into a serious relationship
right away either. I always thought you hadn't taken enough
time to figure out who you were as a person before we hooked up.
We jumped into being a couple and lucky for us we worked and
it was awesome.*

*You always said you never regretted being with me so young,
but you also didn't date anyone else. You didn't sleep with anyone else. I took that experience from you and I always hated that
you didn't get to explore. I wanted to give you my permission to
go out there and experiment. Have fun. Fool around and don't
feel the least bit guilty about it.*

*I thought I might also offer you some suggestions on how to
get started.*

Humor me, okay.

*I've had a lot of time on my hands recently. When you weren't
here, I started this little project. I call it Alyssa's 30 Days of Sex.
Please don't have sex thirty days in a row because I'll be jealous.
Not really. If you can do that, go for it. Seriously though, jealous.*

*Anyway, even if you don't use any of these cards, I had a lot
of fun imagining you enacting them. You'll read them and think
OMG boy dreams! That's cool. They are. Change them up if you
want.*

*Even when you weren't with me, you made me happy. I'm
going to stop now before I get sappy. Go get laid and enjoy the
kinky sex.*

Love you, baby.

Rob

I laughed. It was such a Rob thing to have done. I had no difficulty picturing him coming up with ideas for his cards while
going through his chemo. Come to think of it, that explained
most of the Internet pop-ups I'd been forced to clean off his laptop after he passed.

Sex cards. He wrote me freaking sex cards. I fell in love with
him all over again. My best friend and lover was giving me advice

on how to hook up with other people from beyond the grave. The idea was a mix of weird and sweet, the perfect descriptor for him.

My fingers shook as I flipped through the cards. Tears filled my eyes, but I couldn't stop myself from giggling. If he were still here, I would have punched him on the arm for confusing the hell out of me. I kept laughing as I flipped through the stack. He didn't actually expect me to do some of these? Threesome. Public sex. Get tied up. Have sex with a vibrator in my ass.

Actually, that one sounded interesting.

Eventually I went back to the first card and looked at it closely. On the top of each one he'd printed *30 Days of Sex,* and directly below it, the day it represented. This one had *One* written across the top and only one word written in his messy scrawl in the middle of the card. While it appeared to be the simplest to complete, I had a few doubts about starting on this insane game.

Masturbate.

That was something I'd forgone doing for so long I wondered if my body remembered how.

Light was fading outside and it would be time for bed soon. Memories of Rob and the new guy with the nice ass were bumping around in my brain. My nipples grew sensitive and rubbed against the padding of my bra as I shifted back on my mattress.

This wasn't a big deal. It wasn't even really sex. Not really.

Masturbate. I could do that. Totally.

Some of the other cards though, Rob might have overestimated my taste for adventure. But at the very least I could do this one thing. I picked up the Day One card, set the others on my nightstand, and walked out to the kitchen to get something to eat.

It was only one thing. I didn't have to do everything in the pile. Hell, if I only ever did this one, it would be a change for the positive.

I used to love sex. We'd enjoyed each other, explored and had fun whenever we could. We hadn't been ready for kids, but that didn't stop us from practicing every moment we could. The more I thought about it, the more I realized I missed it. I was tired of feeling empty and alone.

I could do this.

Leaving my dishes on the table, I took the card and went into the bathroom. If I was seriously going to attempt this, then I was going to do it right. That meant preparations.

Water rolled across my body, making my fingers glide across my skin easily. I took my time and used a facecloth rather than my normal loofah. The shower had never been a place where I'd pleasured myself, but I knew if I was going to make this work, if I was going to take Rob's cards seriously, then like the other things in my life I needed to change up my routine.

So no relaxing in the bed where we'd once had so much fun.

After I'd finished with my quick wash, I dropped the facecloth on the holder and proceeded to wash my hair. I'd always had this thing about my head being touched, fingers being dragged across my scalp. There used to be a time when a trip to the hairdresser would result in me getting so turned on that I'd jump Rob the moment I walked through the door. Unlike every other occasion over the past two years, I took my time and let my nails move across my skin until I shivered.

The soap bubbles slipped down my neck and fell into piles on my chest. I moved a hand to push the suds across my breasts, my nipples already hard as I touched them. For a moment there wasn't the tingle of pleasure I used to feel whenever I'd touch myself. Again, I caressed the peak, pinching and rolling the sensitive skin between my finger and thumb.

It was hard to turn my brain off and simply feel. I pushed aside my emotions, the loneliness, everything and allowed my body to be the boss. I scraped my nail across my nipple, flicking it twice hard.

A gasp escaped me before I realized it was coming. My pussy pulsed and for the first time in forever I was aroused. God, it *had* been forever. I hadn't allowed myself to feel anything beyond anger and grief for far too long. It was as though I'd opened up a window and a strong breeze had blown through the numbness of my mind.

I hated when Rob was right.

Turning around, I rinsed the soap from my hair and put in the conditioner. The slick fluid was perfect for what I wanted to do. With my back to the shower spray, I pressed my fingers to my clit, circling the swelling flesh, and tried to relax into the sensations.

It felt nice.

I pressed my other hand against the wall to steady myself and closed my eyes. Flecks of water splashed across me, but I ignored them. My world was focused down to the space between my thighs, the place where only Rob had been, and my growing need to feel something pleasurable. I set a simple rhythm, something that had always gotten me where I wanted to go before. For a brief time it worked. It became harder to breathe and my body shook. I pressed harder, even took the chance to slip my fingers into my slick passage, remembering what it was like to have Rob press into me.

As soon as his face floated up into my mind the arousal I'd felt slipped away. One moment I was climbing the mountain to orgasmland and the next I'd crashed back to reality.

"Shit." I pressed my forehead to the wall. That was anticlimactic.

And that thought got me giggling. Then I started to cry.

Okay, maybe I wasn't quite ready for this. I rinsed the conditioner from my hair and turned the water off. The towel was warm and dry wrapped around me, offering me a small measure of comfort for my failure.

2

Nikki invited me to go to the farmers' market with her the following Saturday morning. The summer air was already warm despite the early hour and I'd been forced to pull my hair up into a bun. I loved my sister for so many reasons, but right now it was her ability to make me laugh that was winning me over.

"Dude, oh my God, look at this." She picked up a cucumber the size of an arm and started waving it around. "You could kill someone with this. Or have a really pleasant night in." She turned to the vendor and handed over her money. "This baby is mine. Hello, my darling. I shall take you home and make sweet, sweet love to you." She kissed its tip.

"You're such a pig." But the thought of my sister doing the nasty with a cucumber got me thinking about my own dilemma. Though I wasn't about to follow her lead and buy my date from a farmer.

"What's wrong?" She bumped my arm as we walked through the thinning crowds. "You were all smiling there and now you're not. I need my baby sister happy."

"I'm happy." No, I wasn't.

"No, you're not. Don't try to pull that shit on me. I'm a

trained professional and know when people aren't telling me the truth." That was the downside to having a psychologist as a sister—she always knew when something was wrong with me.

She hooked her arm in mine and pulled me over to a coffee vendor. Only once a large black coffee was firmly in my grasp did we find a table to rest. Nikki patted my hand before she guzzled down half of her drink.

"I don't know how you can drink that when it's still hot."

"I'm a freak." She grinned. "And you're trying to deflect the conversation. What's up?"

My family had made it a point not to bring Rob up with me anymore. They would talk to me about him if I started the conversation, but that was it. I never knew if it was because they didn't want to upset me, or if they didn't know what to say.

"This is a bit weird." I'd started carrying Rob's last letter to me since I'd opened the envelope. While I didn't break down into tears anymore, I still felt a bit adrift. Having Rob's words close to me somehow made everything a bit easier. Nikki didn't say anything when I pulled the note from my purse and slid it across the table. "It's from Rob."

Her eyes widened. "And you just found it now?"

"Not really. He told me about it before . . . at the beach. He said it was for a time when I thought I was ready to move on."

Nikki had loved Rob like a kid brother, even though she was only two years older than him. He'd been around so long we teased him about changing his last name to Wood instead of me changing mine to Barrow. "And are you? Ready to move on."

She sounded skeptical, which really wasn't surprising. Nikki had once claimed that Rob and I gave her hope that she'd find her soul mate someday. She was currently on the hunt for husband number four.

"I'm never going to forget him. And no, I'm not sure about getting back out there. But this isn't so much about dating as it is about sex."

Nikki cocked her eyebrow and carefully picked up the letter. "Should I be reading this?"

"Would I give it to you if you shouldn't?"

"You totally would. Perv. Oh my God, he gave you sex cards."

I burst out laughing at the look of horror on her face. "You do know that I've had sex, right? Many times."

"Shut up. Eww." She carefully set the note down. "Dare I ask what was on them?"

"Not unless you want to be scarred for life." This was good, being able to talk about this and not feel the urge to cry. "I'm not about to start dating, but . . ."

"But you . . ." Nikki gave my hand another squeeze. "You're ready for something. He's right, you know. You should get out there and have some fun. Sex doesn't have to be about love. It can be about needing to feel something. To be touched. To get all those happy endorphins running through your brain so you don't kill someone."

"Been awhile for you, too?" I grinned at her when she stuck out her tongue. "I know. You're right and Rob's right. I just can't help worry that I'm going to suck at sex. I knew what he liked. He knew my body and what got me off. We figured all that shit out together. I can't imagine trying to find someone new and learn all that over again."

That had been the crux of my problem. Maybe it would have been different if I had dated before, had been intimate with another person, but that wasn't what had happened. My life had been flipped on its head. I could either continue to live a solitary life with my head and heart stuck in the past, or I could do what Rob wanted me to and take a step out into the big world on my own.

As much as I wanted to remain loyal to him, I was lonely.

"You know what? I think you should do it." Nikki leaned back and looked over at the passing crowd. "I mean, you and

Rob were perfect together. He's also right that you shouldn't jump into another relationship right away. We could have some fun, hit the bars, do a singles' cruise, anything that will get you out there in the path of some hot guys. I wouldn't worry about figuring out what they want. Most will tell you ad nauseam."

Rob hadn't. He'd been surprisingly quiet in bed throughout our marriage. "His first card was something simple, but I haven't even been able to do that."

"What did it say?"

Shit, I really didn't want to be having this conversation in public. I took a breath and ignored my rising discomfort. "He told me to masturbate."

Nikki blinked several times. "You mean you haven't been?"

"No. Sex wasn't exactly on the top of my list in the past while."

"I know but . . . seriously?"

I rolled my eyes. "I know this is hard to believe, but I don't normally have sex on the brain." The antidepressants I'd been on after Rob's death hadn't helped either. Being off them at least made the idea of sex more appealing.

"Shit." She shook her head. "I would have gone insane." She shoved the bag holding the giant cucumber over to me. "You clearly need this more than I do."

"Don't be an ass. I'm not going to use that." Well, maybe to make a nice cucumber salad, but that would be it.

"Do you have something to use? A decent vibrator and some porn?"

I knew my face was bright red. Blushing at the drop of a hat was something I hated about myself. "I have something in the nightstand. I think."

Nikki grinned and leaned in close. "We should go to the sex shop. Even if you have something, this is all about new beginnings. You need to have new toys, ones that are just for you. And lube. And other stuff." She got to her feet and gathered everything up. "Come on."

"No."

"Now, Alyssa."

"No."

"Listen to your sister. You need this."

"I'm not going to—"

"Yes, you are." I was on my feet before I knew what was happening. Nikki pulled me along behind her, pausing only long enough to talk to a couple with a small child. "Need a table? We're all done here."

"I hate you." I didn't. In fact I was finally starting to feel as though I might have a handle on this. That with Nikki's help I'd be able to take my first step into my new life.

Apparently there would be lots of vibrators in my future.

But no cucumbers.

3

I would like to say that I'd handled myself admirably at the sex shop, but that would be a lie. My face had been flushed and I'd fumbled my way through looking at the packages on the shelves and in the bins.

Whenever we'd needed stuff in the past, it had been Rob who'd made the trip to the store. Alone. I'd always been too embarrassed to go in with him. Well, it was more than that. I was worried that I'd run into someone I knew there. How does a person explain to a coworker why they're looking at a butt plug? Or a strap-on? Not that we'd ever used either of those, but the potential for even having that conversation was enough to keep me away.

I no longer had the luxury of making someone else do the purchasing.

Nikki laughed at me the entire time and took perverse pleasure in shoving silicone cocks in my face. She'd always been more self-assured than me, even as a little kid. It was one of her more annoying qualities.

Nikki placed into my hands a giant cock so big that it

couldn't possibly fit into a human body. "I think I found what you need."

An older man turned the corner and walked into our aisle as I held the cock. We made eye contact for the briefest of moments before his gaze slipped down to what I held. Then he grinned.

I dropped the cock and turned to face the shelf in front of me. Vibrators. *Yeah, and this one looks good.* The package claimed attachments of some sort and *new multidirectional vibrating action.* Sure, fine. I turned and ran for the checkout. Nikki laughed as she trailed behind me. "You are the biggest chicken."

"Shut up."

"That might not even be a good one!"

The last thing I could handle right then was a dildo lesson from my sister. "It's fine." I didn't stop moving until I reached the checkout.

"Is that everything?" The clerk was a young girl who didn't look old enough to work here. Her brown hair was pulled back into a tight bun and her makeup was impeccably done. She smiled as she scanned the dildo, as though this wasn't the single most embarrassing purchase I'd ever made. "Do you have our frequent buyer card?"

"Yes and no." I wanted to die.

Nikki dumped a pile of things onto the counter. "She'll take these as well. Oh and this, too." A DVD was tossed on top of the pile. "That's a good movie."

The girl picked it up and her eyes widened. "Oh, I love this one. It's a bit low-budget, but you know the sex was great."

Nikki made the strangest noise, one that I could only classify as a purr. "The pirate. With the attachments where the hook should go."

"Yeah. He's fucking hot." The girl clicked her tongue. "You'll love this."

Yup, I'd actually died and this was hell. "Thanks." I glared at Nikki, who only smiled. "That's everything."

I only saw as far as the bottle of tingling lube before I handed over my credit card. I doubt I could return any of this stuff, so I prayed Nikki hadn't screwed me over. Proverbially speaking.

Now, having survived the trials of the sex shop, I was faced with the monumental task of opening yet another door, which proved to be challenging. Someday I'd relearn this basic skill. As I stood searching through my purse for my keys to the building, a bag filled with sex toys and various things tucked under my arm, I counted the minutes until I could lie on my bed and have a nap.

"Hey, can I get that for you?"

I jumped at the sound of the distinctly male voice behind me and my keys fell to the ground by my feet. Turning, I came face to face with Mr. Nice Ass. Unlike the brief glimpse I'd gotten of him the day before, I had nothing blocking my view of his physical perfection. Tall, built like a runner, with rich brown eyes and neatly cropped black hair. As he got closer, the scent of his aftershave and a hint of coffee washed over me. A pang of desire burned low in my belly, and my pussy took notice. He was easily one of the most attractive men I'd even gotten this close to in my life.

God, did that make me a bad wife? *Sorry, Rob.*

"I didn't mean to startle you." He reached down and picked up my keys. "I recognized you from the other day when I moved in and wanted to say hi. I haven't had a chance to meet many of my neighbors yet."

"No worries. I've just . . . it's been a weird day." I readjusted the bag beneath my arm and prayed he wouldn't notice the sex shop's logo. "I'm Alyssa Barrow."

"Harrison Kemp." He grinned. "My mom was a *Star Wars* fan."

"Nice." I turned and managed to find the proper key, sliding it home. It didn't help ease the tension building in my body. It was hard to take a deep breath and not be aware of my proximity to him. "How are you finding your place? Are you all settled in?"

The air was tremendously cooler than what it was outside and the T-shirt and lace bra I had on did little to cover my now hard nipples. Great, I could use the bag I had to cover up the perky evidence, but then I'd be showing off my purchase. Or I could do nothing and let the girls advertise their presence.

Aw, fuck it. I decided to borrow a lesson from Nikki and try not to care what Harrison might think, no matter how awkward it made me feel.

"I'm still surrounded by boxes. I learned long ago that I suck at unpacking. With luck I'll have everything where it should be right before my contract is up and I have to move again." He kept pace with me, his gaze dipping only briefly before returning to my eyes.

I straightened my shoulders and kept walking beside Harrison as we made our way toward the condos. "That would drive me nuts. My husband used to keep things in boxes just to get me worked up." I stopped walking and took a breath. "Rather, my late husband."

Harrison frowned. "I'm sorry for your loss."

"Thanks." There were many people I talked about Rob with, but it didn't seem right sharing anything with Harrison. "Well this is me. We usually have a condo association meeting once a month in the old cafeteria. It's coming up in a few days. I'll see you there if not sooner."

"I'll be in and out of my place a lot for the next little bit. I keep buying stuff. I'm sure I have it in a box somewhere, but you know. It was nice to meet you, Alyssa." He smiled, but didn't linger long at my door. "Have a great evening."

The air in my condo was still and filled with the scent of my air freshener. The urge to laugh was only slightly stronger than my urge to puke. Hot cute guy had chatted me up while I had sex toys in a bag and intended to go to bed and get myself off.

Or as I now called it in my house—Friday.

The one positive thing about running into Harrison was the added rush of adrenaline that now coursed through my veins. It would hopefully help ramp up my arousal so that I could garner some success with my Day One task. If I ever wanted to move on with my life, then I needed to get over my guilt. I had given myself permission to explore new things, feel fresh emotions. I had to conquer card number one.

Damn card number one.

I didn't bother to go into my bedroom this time, instead dumping the contents of my bag across the coffee table. Two bottles of lube—one heated, one regular—one silicone dildo, a DVD, a box containing a vibrating . . . egg? "Shit, Nikki." Beneath the other items was the one thing that I'd picked out for myself, albeit in a hurry, the package containing a blue metal vibrator.

I'd had a vibrator back when Rob and I had first gotten together, but it was nothing like this one. Long, thick, with a curve to the shaft that the clerk claimed would press directly against my G-spot. Guaranteed to make me scream and stars to appear before my eyes. I closed my eyes and emptied my mind of everything. It was hard to acknowledge the torrent of emotions spinning around inside me, but I did. Then I pushed them aside and prepared myself. I needed this. I owed it to myself.

Time to get this show on the road.

Setting the package on its edge, I stood and stripped off my T-shirt, shorts, and socks. My bra and panties were mismatched—not that I cared much about that these days—chosen for comfort rather than looks. Dropping my discarded clothing aside, I picked up the DVD and made my way to my entertainment center. I'd watched some porn in the past, but it wasn't a regular thing for me. I knew Rob had some videos on his computer, stuff he'd put on when he was horny and I was too tired or sore to do anything to help him out. Until today, it wasn't really something that I'd considered necessary in my sex life.

The case of the DVD proclaimed that this was some sort of

parody of a big blockbuster movie. Nikki assured me on the drive home that this was a female-friendly flick and that I'd enjoy it. I don't have a freaking clue about the difference between porn for men and women, so I was going to have to trust her on that one.

After slipping the disk into the player, I grabbed the package with the dildo and went and fetched a pair of scissors from the kitchen. It only took a few minutes to free it from its prison and clean it up for use. By the time I'd returned to the living room the movie was in full swing.

Pirates. There were sexy pirates on my screen. And they were getting naked.

Okay. I could work with this.

I set the vibrator beside me on the couch and turned my attention to the action on the screen. The man had dropped to his knees in front of the pirate queen and was kissing his way down her body. The appreciative noises coming from the woman were plentiful, soft moans punctuated by the occasional gasp. I braced my feet on the coffee table, letting my legs fall apart. While I was determined to enjoy myself, I suddenly didn't want to rush things. There was no pressure to hurry and finish. No one else I needed to take into account. There was only me, my body, and two sexy pirates. If I wanted to do nothing but watch the show, then that was fine. I could get myself off super-quick and get back to other business. I could be selfish and not worry about a thing.

Cool.

The entire first sex scene went by and I'd held off doing anything to my body. My nipples had grown hard beneath the fabric of my bra. My pussy dampened my panties as my excitement grew. There was an actual story to this porno and I felt myself getting pulled into the events. By the time the next scene came around and our hero was ready to seduce the heroine, I was ready for action.

The vibrator was a comforting weight in my hand as I picked

it up. I'd decided that I'd try to mimic the actions of the hero in the movie with the toy. Without taking my eyes from the screen, I ran the vibrator across my cheek and lips as he moved his hard cock across his pirate woman's face. When she opened her mouth and sucked and licked on the rigid shaft, I pressed the cool metal into my own mouth. I ran my tongue around the tip, shivering at the metallic taste. I sucked hard, licked the length of the shaft, and ran the tip across my lips again, all the while picturing the male pirate.

"I need to suck on your luscious tits." The line should have made me giggle, but instead my breath caught and my pussy pulsed. There was something in his voice, a note of control mixed with lust that resonated deep within me.

On the screen the hero pushed the heroine back against a rug in front of a raging fire. He pulled her shirt down, exposing her breasts and causing the woman to arch her back. I followed suit, pulling the front of my bra down without undoing the back clasp. My breasts were thrust upward, my nipples hard, sensitive. As the hero kissed his way down her neck to her chest, I moved the still-wet vibrator down as well, circling the first nipple before moving on to the second.

My body started to tremble and I knew I wouldn't be able to hold back much longer. It had been ages since I'd had any physical release that was related to sexual pleasure. Now that I'd finally set myself along this path, I couldn't hold back. Thankfully, the pirate didn't leave me waiting for long.

He stripped his lady-love of her clothing and likewise I removed my panties. They were already wet from my arousal, the heavy scent of my musk clinging to them. I let them drop to the floor and repositioned myself with my legs spread wide. I was anxious to simply push the vibrator into my pussy and turn it on, but I knew once I did that I wouldn't last long at all. Instead, I slowly dragged it down across my stomach and circled it around my mound before finally dragging the tip down across my clit.

Had the vibrator been turned on I would have come.

Instead I kept going until I could press the tip into my pussy and feel the pleasant stretch of my muscles after all this time. The pirate on the screen wasn't quite ready to fuck his lover, but I wasn't waiting for him. Reaching down with my free hand, I turned the end of the vibrator to activate it.

I gasped as the sensations brought me to life. I half-thought that I'd come right then, but my body held strong against the onslaught. It took a moment for me to adjust. I was finally able to relax into the pleasure, enjoying it without going too fast. I began to pump the vibrator in and out, teasing and circling my entrance every now and again. After a few moments, I turned the vibrator up another few notches, increasing the intensity.

My body loved it.

"Fuck me hard. Make me yours." The heroine was on all fours now, her ass on display and her breasts swinging free.

They were nice breasts. Big and full with nipples that were ready to suck on . . . and when the hell did I ever pay attention to breasts? *Who cares? Just enjoy.*

While I continued to fuck myself, I flicked my fingertip across my nipple. The sensation was swallowed up initially, overpowered by the strength of the vibrations in my pussy. But I continued, setting a rhythm that matched the thrusting metal and my breath came out in gasps. My breasts became more responsive as each flick of my fingers increased their sensitivity.

I was so close now. The muscles in my thighs twitched uncontrollably. Sweat pooled between my breasts and at the small of my back. Both the pirates were moaning loud as he fucked her doggy style, their skin flushed, too beautiful for words.

My orgasm was there, waiting for me to reach out and take it. I knew what I needed to do, but didn't want the pleasure to end. There would be more. Another time. Take it. Please.

I pulled the vibrator from my pussy and pressed the wet tip to my clit and pinched my nipple hard. One breath, two, and my eyes squeezed shut.

The pleasure, the release came from every cell in my body. An explosion that seemed to rip me apart from the inside out, blasting away the silence and loneliness, to replace it with light. I screamed and my back arched to the point that my ass came off the couch. First my hearing went, and then my vision faded as I collapsed down in a heap.

Passing out after sex wasn't something that I'd ever remembered doing. Don't get me wrong, Rob had given me some good ones over the years, but this was . . .

Christ, there aren't even words for how amazing that one was. I'd finally done it, pushed through everything and reclaimed something that was mine. Rob would be thrilled. Hell, I was ecstatic! I wanted to laugh, do a naked victory lap around the condo, watch more of the movie and see if I could do it again. That was, once I got my energy back, because damn I was sleepy.

As I sat there trying to gather my strength to move once more, I realized that someone was knocking on my door. Loudly.

Shit, someone was here. Wanted to talk to me *right the hell now!*

"Fuck." I grabbed my panties and T-shirt and pulled them on as I stumbled toward the DVD player and switched it off. "Just a second!"

Yanking up my shorts, I didn't bother to do up the button and instead looked out through the peephole. It was Harrison.

Ah fuck.

It was too late to pretend I wasn't home, and I didn't have time to check in the mirror to see if I still had a sex-face. My heart, which had previously been pounding due to my orgasm, continued to pound out of a sense of impending doom. Taking a deep breath, I ran my hands through my hair quickly before opening the door partway.

"Hi there." I smiled, cheeks twitching. *Please don't notice.* "What's up?"

Instead of the charming smile he'd had when we'd met up

outside, Harrison was now frowning, his entire body rigid. "Are you okay? I was heading out again when I heard a scream. I swore it came from your place."

I didn't need a mirror to know I was beet red. Yup, I was ready to die now. "Oh, yes. I'm fine. Thanks."

"I know you're here alone and I was worried that something had happened. That someone had gotten in . . ." He stared at me for a few heartbeats and I had no doubt what he saw. Flushed face, messy hair, half-dressed.

His eyes widened and his lips parted. *And the light comes on.* So now I would forever be known as the girl-who-came-so-loud-everyone-heard. Wonderful. *I wonder if it's too late to move?*

"Yeah, so I'm good." I pressed my hand to the side of my throat. My skin was still warm to the touch. "Umm, this is awkward."

"Sorry." He didn't look sorry. He actually looked curious. "Were you in the bedroom? I'd like to know because if the soundproofing is that bad in this place—"

"No!" God, I wanted to die. "No. The soundproofing is normally just fine. You won't need to worry."

I was never going to masturbate again.

"I've embarrassed you." He still didn't look sorry. No, I was fairly certain he was finding this amusing.

"No you haven't. Well, maybe a little." The floor could open up and swallow me whole now. Please. "It's . . . been a while for me. Dead husband and stuff. So, yeah. I'm fine. I think I'll go now. Okay, thanks for checking in."

Harrison didn't say anything else as I shut the door, but I swore I saw him start to grin just before it clicked shut.

My life so wasn't going the way I'd intended.

4

"This is the absolute worst idea ever." I stopped moving just past the coat check, crossed my arms, and glared at Nikki. "Seriously, I'm not going any farther."

I've let my sister talk me into a great number of *dumb things* over the years, but going to a nightclub filled mostly with university students was now at the top of that list. While I certainly don't consider myself old, it became painfully obvious to me in the first five minutes of our arrival that I was also no longer twenty. Even as I stood there glaring, a group of glammed-up girls walked past wearing outfits that—okay Goddamn they looked really hot—announced that they were here for a good time. I was at least ten years older than most of these people. How the hell did she expect me to find someone to have random sex with here? Just go up and be all *hey, want to fuck?*

Okay, that was a bit of a dumb question.

But still!

Nikki dismissed my concerns with a wave of her hand and a quick, "Trust me," before she pulled me onto the dance floor. I *knew* I shouldn't have let her read through Rob's cards. My sister on a mission was never a good thing.

She'd gotten this crazy idea that the best way to jump-start my reintroduction into the world of dating was to take a survey of the available options. I wasn't thrilled with her speed-dating choice, but in retrospect, it might have made more sense than this. Honest to God, I didn't even know what song was playing. And were they twerking?

No way in hell.

"Nikki—"

She covered my mouth with her hand. "Baby, just have fun. That's all this is about. Not about sex, or finding a life partner. We're just here to enjoy ourselves. Two girls out on the town having fun."

My sister is a dance freak and was quickly swallowed up by the throng of writhing bodies. Alone, I had two choices: dance or leave. Nikki was right about one thing, I hadn't let myself have much in the way of fun for a long time. So what if this wasn't my normal sort of evening out. The whole point was to get out there and do something different. A quick look around the club reassured me that I wasn't the only one here in my thirties. Everyone was having a good time. There was no reason why I couldn't go out there and have fun too.

I took a step toward the dance floor. When the world didn't end, I took another. As I moved closer, the bass from the music shook out my hesitation and the rhythm started to win me over. I got as far as the edge of the crowd, close enough to be a participant. I closed my eyes and tried to relax, to get into the flow of the beat. I let out a breath and began to move my hips in rhythm. The song didn't matter, the people around me didn't matter. I was here to enjoy myself.

For the first time in a long time, I had to give myself permission to be selfish.

So that's what I did.

Hands brushed against my body, bringing my attention back to the present. The occasional accidental bump gave way to something more intentional. Before I knew it, I wasn't on the edge of the crowd, but moving within it. The fear I'd been harboring gave way and I was able to let my guard down a tiny bit. A smile took root as I got more into the music and the energy of the crowd. Maybe Nikki was right about this. Maybe this really was exactly what I needed.

I remained an anonymous face in the crowd for a bit longer, until a dark-skinned guy who looked to be a bit older than the rest of the crowd slid up and fell into sync with me. It wasn't an accidental turn and *oops, look who I'm facing.* No, he was dancing *with* me. *Okay, so this is happening.* I gave him a smile, tucked my hair behind my ear, and just went with it.

This is just about having fun. You're not looking to pick him up. Within minutes I was laughing as I tried to not look like a thirtysomething white girl with no rhythm, dancing.

The song changed and my dance partner stepped closer. "I'm Marcus."

"Alyssa." I smiled a bit wider. Marcus was handsome, my height, and smelled amazing. His shirt was tight enough that I could make out his muscles even in the dim light. I didn't even get any weird creepy vibes off him. This was going better than I thought.

Without missing a beat, he put his hands on my hips and pulled me within an inch of him. "I haven't seen you here before."

I wasn't a great dancer to begin with, and having not done this with anyone besides Rob and a few friends, it was awkward being so close to a man I didn't know. I wasn't sure where to put my hands. Did I take his hips? Put them around his neck? I settled for reaching up and holding lightly onto his biceps. "No, it's my first time."

Marcus's grin sent a shiver through me, but I wasn't certain if I liked it or not. "Nice."

He dug his fingers in as he bucked his hips forward. The shift put his groin in direct contact with mine. I don't want to say I was shocked, but I totally was. I was grinding with a man I didn't know out on a dance floor in a club I'd never been in before. This wasn't the sort of thing I'd do, what I'd ever wanted to do, regardless of my relationship status.

I tried to take a step back, but Marcus held fast. His eyes were closed and he wore an expression of bliss as he danced. Shit, maybe I was overreacting to this. The guy clearly just wanted to have fun. I gave his biceps a squeeze and pulled back once more. Marcus opened his eyes and grinned before he pulled me fully against him.

"Come on, baby. Show me what you've got."

"I don't think—"

Someone bumped into me from behind, pushing me flat against Marcus. His eyes lit up and his grin could have melted the coldest of hearts. He wasn't a bad guy. I shouldn't be so squirrelly about a simple dance. I forced my body to relax and tried once more to get into the song. I let my eyes drift shut and went with the flow, letting myself melt against him.

That was when I realized that he had a hard-on.

My eyes flew open and I immediately stepped away. Marcus stumbled a bit from the sudden absence of my body. He gave his head a little shake. "What's wrong?"

"I . . . I need a drink."

Marcus grinned again. "I'll buy you a drink, baby."

"No!" I stepped back again. "I'll get my own."

"Hey now. We were having fun." He reached out for me but I avoided his grasp.

We'd moved toward the edge of the dance floor. The bar was clearly in sight—well, the throng of people in front of the bar was visible—as was the door. "I think I should go."

"Not having a good time?" His voice didn't hold even a little bit of a sarcastic note. He seemed more curious than anything.

"No, not really."

"That's too bad. A pretty girl like you should always have fun." The music changed again, this time to a slower beat. "We can talk. Or dance. Dancing is better."

Before I had a chance to answer him, another man stepped up beside us. He was taller than both me and Marcus, his brown eyes serious and his body tense. My brain took a moment to realize that the face those eyes belonged to was someone I knew.

I swallowed hard. "Harrison? What are you doing here?"

Marcus held up his hands. "Dude, I didn't think she was with anyone."

"I'm not." I reached out and put a hand on Marcus's shoulder. "He's a friend from my building."

Harrison still hadn't said anything, his gaze shifting between my face and where I was touching Marcus. I let my hand fall away. A sudden unexplained rush of guilt hit me hard. Stupid, considering I'd only talked to Harrison twice in my life. "I think I'm going to leave."

"All right, pretty lady. You take care." Marcus winked at me before stepping back into the crowd and disappearing.

That would have been nice—to disappear into the air. It would have saved me from what was about to come. For some reason, I was mildly annoyed with Harrison. He had no right to come here and scare away my dancing partner, even if I hadn't been comfortable and was considering leaving.

I crossed my arms and faced him. "Why did you do that?"

"Do what?" His voice easily reached me despite the bass-heavy song that played. "I didn't say a word."

"You didn't have to. Did you learn how to brood and growl in sales school?"

Harrison glanced over to a table behind him. "I'm here with a client. I was getting drinks at the bar when I saw you trying to get away from that creep. I was just making sure you were okay."

It was a chivalrous act. I shouldn't have been upset by this. And yet, my hackles immediately went up. "Marcus wasn't a creep. He was a nice guy who happened to like to grind while he danced. And for the record, I'm perfectly able to care for myself."

"Never claimed you couldn't."

"I've been looking after myself since I moved out from my parents' place."

"I'm sure you have."

"You don't know me. You don't know what I'm capable of. So next time you should wait to be asked"—I drove my finger into his chest—"before you poke your nose in to where it's not wanted."

Rather than retreat the way Marcus did, Harrison caught my hand in his and pressed it against his chest. His fingers were warm and his skin soft as he held me tight. Unlike with Marcus, my body responded immediately. Which totally wasn't fair.

He gave my hand a squeeze. "You're right. I don't know you. I shouldn't have interfered. But I won't apologize for stepping in when I think someone is in danger. I'd rather deal with your annoyance than see you get hurt."

When I thought *this is it,* he'd finally said his piece and was ready to let me go, Harrison surprised me once again. He lifted my hand to his mouth and pressed a gentle kiss to the back of it. "Have a good evening."

I'm sure I stood there, hand hovering in the air, staring at his retreating back for far longer than I should have. What the hell was that? Did I just get mad at a man who was only trying to do the right thing? Did he think that I was someone who needed rescuing?

Goddammit, I didn't know if my heart should be melting, or if I wanted to go over there and punch him. Both? Was it possible to want to do both?

"Hey, you coming back out to dance?" Nikki had bounded up beside me, oblivious to the drama that had just unfolded. "You can't leave yet. We've been here like ten minutes."

"It's been longer than that." I wasn't even looking at her, my attention was still locked on the retreating ass of my frustrating neighbor.

Harrison had sat back down at the table with a man and a woman. While he wasn't looking at me, I got the impression that he was very much aware of what I was doing. I didn't know him well enough to have much of an impression of who he was as a person, but I wasn't about to let anyone think that I was so easily swayed. It was going to take more than a misplaced act of kindness and an excellent pair of well-fitted pants to win me over.

Screw him.

I took Nikki by the hand and marched out into the middle of the dance floor. "Let's rock it!"

5

I'd managed to go a week and a half before I was forced to deal with Harrison again. Now, if I was being completely honest with myself, I would have realized that I'd possibly overreacted to the entire situation of our last meeting. Yes, I'd been thrown off by seeing him at the club. Yes, I had been trying to get away from Marcus. Harrison hadn't done much of anything that most rational humans would consider offensive.

Just because he'd stepped in when I'd been perfectly capable of saving myself, that didn't make him a bad person. It simply made him a nosy, if well-meaning, person. And sure, I might have been a bit freaked and totally not certain how to tell the handsome and dance-happy Marcus that I really wasn't ready for a one-on-one, but I needed practice at that aspect of getting out there as well. I had a whole new skill set that I had to pick up.

Not Harrison's fault.

So when he came sauntering into the cafeteria of our condo building for the monthly association meeting, there was no logical reason why I should be anything less than civil to my new neighbor. And yet there I was, glaring at him as he moved effortlessly through the group. I believe it was called working the room.

The Styrofoam cup in my hand cracked, sending hot coffee sloshing across my skin. "Shit."

My elderly upstairs neighbor, Mrs. Le Page, handed me a napkin. "Careful, dear. You can't squeeze those cups that way."

"Thanks."

"Oh, is that the new tenant you were staring at? He's on your floor, isn't he? That means he's one of those company men." Mrs. Le Page made a cooing noise that was slightly disturbing coming from the eighty-four-year-old woman. "Cute too."

"His name is Harrison." The last thing I needed was for Mrs. Le Page to get any ideas about going into matchmaking mode. I was having enough trouble dealing with Nikki and didn't need to add to that. "I doubt he'll be around long. He said something about being here on a contract. He's in sales."

"Sales. That means he's a smooth talker. Let's test that, shall we." Before I had a chance to take a breath, Mrs. Le Page sauntered over to Harrison.

"Damn." The hot coffee was getting unbearable. Ignoring the tittering laughter of my meddling neighbor, I made my way over to the refreshment table to replace my cup and snag another cookie.

It was strange, being able to feel the vibrations of Harrison's voice trip along my spine. I wasn't blind to his good looks—Christ, anyone could appreciate his strong jaw and be tempted to touch his rich black hair to see how soft it was—but he wasn't my type in the least. I'd never been attracted to alpha males. They tended to be too loud, too controlling, not inclined to curl up on the couch and watch a chick flick. He wasn't the sort of man I'd bother to speak to, even in a social situation like this.

So why was I straining to hear what he was talking to Mrs. Le Page about, a woman old enough to be his grandmother? Maybe I'd become possessed? Alien abduction or something.

Another burst of giggles from Mrs. Le Page blended with the low throaty chuckle from Harrison. I shouldn't be so tempted to turn and look, to see what they were laughing about, or what his expression might be. But I was. I really, really was.

"It's time to get started. If everyone could grab a seat." Pierce Wilton, the current president of our association, clapped his hands together and everyone shuffled to their usual spots. Pierce wasn't my favorite person in the building, mostly because of how curt he'd been with me since Rob passed, but he was efficient at making sure our building stayed in great shape, so I ignored the rest.

People continued to chat, albeit with softer voices as everyone got comfortable. These meetings tended to go longer than they needed to be, but it wasn't as though anyone could leave early without looking like a jerk in front of the rest of the tenants. Normally, Mr. and Mrs. Le Page would find their way to my row and would share the occasional eye roll with me as Pierce rambled on. It made the proceedings entertaining and gave us something to chat about over coffee afterward.

I really shouldn't have been surprised when Harrison took the chair directly beside me instead. My body tensed as the scent of his freshly applied aftershave reached me. This time I had on a padded bra to cover up my suddenly erect nipples, though my shorts were riding up quite high, putting pressure on my clit. The last thing I wanted was for Harrison to think he could make me squirm.

Even if he could.

Stupid libido.

"Thank you everyone for coming tonight." Pierce gave us one of his blink-and-you'll-miss-it smiles. "I want to welcome our newest resident, Harrison Kemp." Everyone gave polite applause. "I'll be reviewing some of the basic rules tonight for Mr. Kemp's benefit. Though I know we can all use the reminder. I won't bring up the gym incident again, even though no one has confessed to the off-hours use." He looked at us from over the top of his glasses. "Please pay attention, especially you, Mr. Kemp."

Harrison groaned softly. "Shit."

"Thanks, buddy," I muttered, my eyes locked forward. The last thing I wanted was to draw Pierce's wrath for not paying attention. "You can save me from this one if you want."

Harrison sighed. "You didn't seem a big fan of that last time."

"I wasn't."

Pierce stopped talking and looked directly at us. "Alyssa, I don't think Mr. Kemp will appreciate being fined for something because he wasn't able to listen to the presentation."

"Sorry." And now my face was burning. "I'll be quiet."

"There will be time for you to chat at the barbecue." He waited another moment before continuing.

I wanted to die. I'd never been someone to want the attention in a group. Even back when I was in school, I'd do whatever possible to avoid being called on in class. Ignoring Harrison, I scooted down in my seat and prayed Pierce wouldn't pick on me again.

Harrison was either still annoyed at me from the bar, or he had a bit of a childish streak in him. At first, I thought he bumped his knee against mine by mistake. But the second time was clearly an attempt to get my attention. The third time he was being annoying. On his fourth bump I reached over and pinched his thigh, glaring at him.

The bastard smirked at me.

How did I *ever* find this man-child attractive? Or chivalrous?

This clearly meant war. Ignoring Pierce, I made sure my timing was perfect and swung my knee away the next time he tried to connect with mine. He frowned. I grinned. He reached over and squeezed the top of my knee.

There was no way he could know that my knees are incredibly ticklish, so he wouldn't have expected my high-pitched squeal. Everyone turned to look at me and my stomach did a somersault. I wanted to die.

Harrison stomped his foot loudly on the floor. "There was a spider that startled her. I killed it."

"Sorry. Again."

"I hate spiders." Mrs. Le Page spoke, sounding way more amused than the topic would have allowed. "Pierce, we've noticed a lot more in our condo than normal. Perhaps this is something that we will need to address."

"I'll put it on the maintenance list." Whether or not he believed us, Pierce dutifully made a note in his book. "Are there any other issues to address?"

"No, let's eat." Mr. Le Page got up and held his hand out for his wife. "I'm starving and Bill is up there cooking burgers by himself."

Pierce scanned the room, shaking his head. We must drive the poor man nuts. "If there isn't any other business, then we'll adjourn. Our welcome barbecue for Mr. Kemp is on the rooftop garden."

I was able to hold my tongue long enough for the others to start talking before I turned to Harrison. "You're an asshole."

"No I'm not." His smirk wasn't very convincing. "I get bored easily."

"Pierce will give you a pass this time, but he's brutal when people aren't paying attention. He used to be the principal at this high school before they converted it to condos. They called him The Warden." I added air quotes, more out of habit than a necessity for emphasis.

"He wouldn't have liked me. A jock with a sense of entitlement that pissed even my parents off." Harrison stood, putting his groin dangerously close to my face. "Mind showing me the rooftop?"

"You can just follow the crowd."

"What, you're not coming up?" The bastard almost seemed disappointed. "I was accused of not knowing my neighbors. I was hoping for the opportunity to change that."

Why did he have to be so frigging logical? I couldn't accuse him of not knowing me and then walk away from a perfect opportunity to spend some time with him socially. Especially when I always went to the barbecues. My absence would be noticed and then comments would start. Followed by rumors. Shit, it would be worse than the time everyone thought I was pregnant.

Or when they all found out about Rob.

Ignoring his outstretched hand, I got to my feet. "Fine. But I'm still not sure that I like you. Come on."

Harrison was like a large, obedient dog trailing along behind me as I led him up the stairs to the rooftop garden. The scent of burgers being grilled mixed with the scratchy sound of music coming from the old radio that no one would claim. Laughter and light conversation wrapped around us as we joined the others. Far more people were here than had attended the meeting. The lucky married couples would tag-team attending the meeting, so that they both wouldn't have to suffer, and meet up at the barbecue after. Rob and I used to do that, though I'd preferred the rare times when we'd gone together. Those had been fun—like kidding around with Harrison had been.

I stopped moving so suddenly, Harrison walked directly past me. He stopped and looked back at me, frowning. "You okay?"

"Yeah. Sorry."

He came into my personal space much like he had back at the bar. "How about I get you a drink? It looks like someone brought beer."

"Sure." I wasn't a big drinker, but a bit of alcohol would do me some good given my current state. "Yeah, that sounds good."

I watched as Harrison made his way over to the bar, stopping frequently to talk to the other residents. At first I thought he was flirting, making the ladies blush as he chatted. But the more I watched him, the more I realized that wasn't what he was doing. Harrison was one of those guys who focused all of his attention on the person he was speaking to. Women or men, he would smile and nod as each person chatted with him. No wonder I was blushing like a preteen every time he looked my way. That level of intensity wasn't something I was used to.

"I think our new tenant has caught your eye."

Shit. "No, Mrs. Le Page. He's handsome, but not really my type."

The older woman linked her arm with mine and gave my hand a pat. It was the same hand Harrison had kissed. "There's only one type a woman should have. A man who'll treat them right. Just like your Rob did."

My chest tightened at the mention of his name. With Harrison's arrival in the building and my discovery of Rob's cards, I'd been thinking less about the man I'd lost and more about trying to move on. I wasn't certain that I liked that.

"A nice girl like you shouldn't be alone. While he might not end up being the one for you, it can't hurt to look." She made that cooing sound again. "You have to admit, he's very nice to look at."

"Yeah, he's not bad." Harrison had snagged two plastic cups of beer and was starting to make his way back over toward us. "Mrs. Le Page?"

"Yes?"

"How do I move on?" I swallowed past the sudden lump in my throat. "I never thought I'd have to look for someone else when I got married. I was never unhappy with what we had. How do I even start to look for something, for someone else?"

She turned to me with a soft hand to my cheek, giving me a smile. "One foot in front of the other. That's all any of us can do." She stayed by my side until Harrison retuned. "Mr. Kemp, how do you like your new place?"

He handed me the beer, his fingers brushing against mine as I took the sweating cup from him. "It's great for a rental. My company is putting me up while I work at this office for the next three months. I'm not unpacked, but I'll get there."

"Oh, that takes most of us awhile. I'm certain I still have boxes somewhere in our place. We've been here for ten years now." She turned to me and I could tell from the smile on her face I wouldn't like what was coming. "Alyssa here has been in the building for six years. I'm sure if you need any help getting situated she'd be more than happy to assist."

And with that she walked away.

Harrison tried to hide a smile behind his cup as he took a sip of his beer. "Are we being set up?"

"I think we might be." I shouldn't have sighed, but I couldn't stop myself.

"From your tone of voice, I gather that you're not too pleased." There was a sparkle in his brown eyes that told me he was enjoying the teasing.

"It's not that." I took a sip of beer, grimacing at the bitter taste. Blah, someone bought that hoppy stuff again. "She's tried things like this a few times since Rob died. Nothing too pushy, but not anything I'd wanted."

"That's right, you don't need saving. Even by little old ladies."

I should have taken his comment for the light teasing it clearly was, but I couldn't. I turned to fully face him. "What does that mean?"

If Harrison could sense the danger he was in, his expression didn't show it. "You're a woman who can take care of herself. Which is fantastic, though less fun for Mrs. Le Page."

"I'm sure she'll get over it."

Harrison moved a bit closer, and for a moment he was the only thing I could focus on. The size of his chest and arms. The spice of his aftershave. The way his nearness made my pussy tingle in a way it hadn't in years. I knew if I closed my eyes, it would be easy to imagine what his body would feel like pressed against mine, sweat-soaked. If I'd been thinking, I would have grabbed him back at the club and made him dance with me. How would it have felt to have had Harrison's hands on my hips rather than Marcus's?

"You really should be more careful when you're out on your

own though." He smiled, but the light in his eyes dimmed. "I didn't realize how rough that place got or else I'd never have brought my clients there. Thankfully, they're more flexible than others."

It's amazing how quickly a man can turn a woman off without even trying. "Pardon me?"

I'm not sure if he realized that he'd entered the Danger Zone with me, because he'd kept right on trucking. "It's important to do your research. I'm new to town. You're just getting yourself out there. It's easy to make mistakes."

"Mistakes?" My grip tightened on my cup. At least this time it wasn't coffee.

"If you don't want to be rescued, that is. You're a single woman, and I'd guess you don't have a lot of experience. You need to do your homework first—"

I never gave him the chance to dig himself back out of his hole. Like a scene from a movie, I threw my beer in his face. The amber liquid coated his skin and spread out across his no-longer-white dress shirt. He blinked the beer away as his mouth fell open.

"How dare you?" I tossed my cup to the floor, not caring that everyone on the rooftop was staring at us. "You don't know the first thing about what I'm capable of doing or not doing. I've had to bury my husband when I was thirty-three. I've had to figure out how to legally declare someone dead. Have had to convince people that no, my husband isn't avoiding your call. He really is gone."

Harrison reached for me. "Alyssa, I'm sorry—"

"No. You don't get to be sorry. You don't get to have any opinion at all. I'm leaving."

I marched past everyone, doing my best to ignore their pitying looks. This was the last thing I wanted or needed. It was hard enough putting myself out there, only to be subjected to the opinions of strangers who thought they knew what was best for me.

"Alyssa!" Harrison called for me.

I stopped before I reached the exit, but I didn't turn around. "What?"

"For the record, I know you're more than capable of looking after yourself. But there's nothing wrong with asking for help."

"Fuck you."

Fighting the urge to cry, I marched back to my condo.

6

I'd been standing in front of Harrison's front door for the better part of ten minutes, wondering how much of an ass he thought I was. God, I'd had my moments of being an idiot in the past, but this was the first time I'd embarrassed myself this badly. I had no choice but to apologize—he hadn't deserved me losing my shit on him like that, and at the very least I owed him a new shirt.

It was also a waste of good beer. Even if it was too hoppy.

I huffed and shuffled from foot to foot. There was no way this was going to get any easier. I needed to smarten up, apologize, and move on to the next step. If that was with Harrison, then great. But the only way I was going to find out was to talk to him. In order for that to happen I had to act.

Fine. Let's do this.

Holding my breath, I closed my eyes and knocked. My stomach churned and I couldn't stop my fingers from flexing around the index card I'd brought with me. I had no doubt that I was the last person Harrison wanted to see. But I usually tried to be honest with myself, if no one else. I knew deep down that my anger had nothing to do with what Harrison had said, and everything to do with how he made me feel.

I had a thing for him. Purely lust.

It pissed me off as much as it terrified me.

In the twenty minutes I'd paced around my condo, my mind had spun around, shifting from anger, to embarrassment, to the thought of what to do with Rob's cards. I'd stopped pacing, picked up the deck, and knew that if I was actually going to try this, Harrison was my best option.

Well, he was a safe option. Not to mention that he checked off a lot of my mental boxes when it came to finding someone to explore this with.

Close by. Hot. Not a complete creep. Hot. Will be gone in a few months.

Hot.

Was this cheating? It felt that way even though Rob was not only gone, but had more than given me his permission to do this very thing. So why did it feel like I was about to make the biggest mistake of my life in taking Rob's advice?

If nothing else, even if he turned me down, Harrison struck me as the sort of man who'd have some solid advice to offer on how to approach men. He was one, after all. Presumably, he knew what he liked from women. And his advice would be a hell of a lot more recent than what Mr. Le Page had to offer. Dinner and ballroom dancing lessons? Yeah no.

Really, I had nothing to lose.

Nope, nothing at all.

I got up the nerve to knock once more when Harrison didn't answer immediately. I was totally going to count to ten and then I was out of here. I could apologize the next time I saw him in the hall. Because clearly if he didn't show then this was the universe telling me that this was a bad idea.

One.

A really bad idea.

Two.

A really, *really* bad idea.

Three.

There was a thump somewhere beyond the door and I considered running away. Four. Maybe he hadn't heard the knock? I should probably knock again. Five. Right?

Sixseveneightnineten. *Oh well, guess he didn't hear me. Time to go.*

I turned and managed to get five steps away before I heard the door open behind me.

"Come to toss another drink in my face?"

Now, I suspect there would be many men who wouldn't greet me with such a teasing voice after having had a pint of warm beer sloshed over them, but lucky for me Harrison didn't appear to be one of them. As much as I would have preferred to continue my retreat to the safety of my condo, I couldn't leave things on bad terms with him. If nothing else, he was my neighbor and I needed to act like a good one. Without thinking too much about it, I lowered my head and shuffled my way back. I said nothing until I was standing directly in front of him.

"Alyssa?"

I looked up and did my best impression of a smile. Shit, he was still wearing his beer-soaked shirt. "Hi. Did I catch you at a bad time?"

Reaching up to bracket the doorframe with his hands, Harrison cocked his head to the side and grinned. "I was about to get changed. I had a bit of an accident."

My face was hot and if there'd been a way I could have hidden my blush I would have. "I'm so sorry about that."

"Don't be. I was being an ass." He let his hands drop but didn't move back. "You okay?"

"Besides feeling like a jerk for dumping a beer on you? Oh yeah, peachy." The index card was starting to curl from my sweaty palm. "I actually came because I was wondering if I could talk to you about something?"

"Sounds serious."

"Not really. Well maybe. I just . . . I need a fresh perspective on this. I don't really know you and weirdly enough that kind of works in your favor. I think. I don't know."

"Like I said, sounds serious." He hesitated for a moment before he stepped back and waved me in. "Mind if I get a clean shirt first?"

"Yeah, no problem."

It was weird crossing the threshold into his place. I'm not sure what I'd been expecting the inside of Harrison's condo to be like, but it wasn't this crazy mess. There were the standard framed pictures on the wall, the type someone would pick up at Walmart or Target. The furniture was all leather, the coffee table glass-topped with a curled iron underpinning. Even the carpet was lush. The entire place screamed corporate rental, especially when there were open boxes strewn about the place, packing papers lying in piles at their bases.

He'd been serious when he'd said that unpacking wasn't his strong suit. I was about to harass him about it when I realized that he'd pulled his shirt off and my ability to speak vanished.

Naked. Man.

Harrison turned to face me, his stained shirt in his hands. "Make yourself comfortable. I'll just be a second."

"Pardon?" Firm muscles. Tanned. Oh good, chest hair. I liked chest hair. I could totally run my fingers through it and tug, just enough to tease.

"Alyssa? Eyes up here, please." Dammit, he was teasing me. No, teasing would make me like him and that wasn't what I wanted.

My face heated again when I realized there was no way to make up for blatantly staring. "Sorry. I'm sorry."

"There are worse things for a guy's ego than to be ogled by a beautiful woman." He motioned to his left. "The kitchen is that way if you want a drink. I might even have beer in the fridge."

It was a comment on my mental state that I didn't even question his mentioning of the beer. I made a beeline for the fridge, found the aforementioned beverage, and was thankful that he had a magnetic bottle opener stuck to the side of the door. I closed my eyes and took three long drinks from the bottle before I stopped.

What the hell was I doing here? It wasn't as though I knew Harrison very well, certainly not long enough to proposition him. Not to mention the fact that I'd recently assaulted him in public with a beverage. Though I'd totally been provoked, it wasn't the sort of thing that won people over.

He might not be into sex with almost-strangers. Hell, he might not even like me that way. My stomach churned as the idea that I might actually get rejected crossed my mind for the first time. I'd have to play things cool.

"Oh my God, I'm an idiot." I took another long pull from the beer bottle.

"Good, you found it."

I jumped as he walked into the kitchen, still buttoning up his shirt. It was the same type of one he'd had on earlier, except navy blue. At least that one wouldn't show a stain as bad if we got into another serious discussion.

"Are you okay?" He stepped into my personal space and took the bottle from my hand. "You seemed off at the barbecue, too. Is there a problem that you need help—"

"I need to have sex with someone."

Both of us stopped talking and stared into each other's eyes. It took me a moment to realize that I'd actually said that with my outside voice. My first instinct was to cover it up, apologize, say something to ease the growing awkwardness that had manifested between us. But then I really looked into his eyes and was struck by the intensity of his gaze. He didn't appear to be offended or put off by my request.

No, he looked exactly the opposite.

"Hmm, yeah." I cleared my throat, knowing I needed to say this the right way to not come across as a lunatic. "Okay, so Rob, he's my late husband, but I think you knew that. Anyway, he was the only guy I've ever been with and he was worried that when I was ready to move on that I wouldn't do anything so he left me with these index cards to help me have sex with other men and I've been trying to start using them but the whole go to a bar and find some random guy didn't quite work out the way I hoped so I wanted to know if you would have sex with me? And if not that's fine, but then you said I should ask for help, so that's sort of what I'm doing."

Harrison reached up and bracketed my face with his hands. I held my breath when he leaned in and placed a gentle kiss in the middle of my forehead. "I'm going to get a drink and then I suggest we go to the living room so we can sit and talk. Preferably in multiple sentences. With pauses. And breathing."

My heart might as well have been a jackhammer in my chest it pounded so hard. "Okay. That sounds good."

He didn't let go of me, instead he reached down to capture my hand in his. It only took him a moment to get his own beer before he led me to the couch. I sat down with a huff and then realized that I'd been squeezing the index card in a death grip. As Harrison joined me, his thigh slid against mine, sending another shiver through me.

I knew that if I was serious about this, I'd have to show him what it was that I'd brought. I was putting myself out there, taking a chance that was turning out to be way harder than I'd anticipated. Looking down at the bent cardboard, I knew if I couldn't get this far with Harrison, I'd have zero chance of doing this with someone else.

"Is that the card?" He didn't reach for it, instead taking a sip of his beer.

"One of them. Rob left me thirty in total. I've done one of them . . . but the rest require that I'm with someone else."

"May I see it?" He still didn't reach for it, waiting for me to be the one to make the decision.

This was it. There was no reason why I had to follow the cards Rob made up for me. I certainly didn't need to show Harrison. I mean, I liked the guy and I was more than capable of starting something up if I wanted. I was tired of being alone, of not being touched, of not having someone beside me to tell jokes and laugh about the ridiculous things I'd found online. I didn't *need* to give him the card, but it was probably for the best if I did.

God, why was this so freaking hard?

I let out a soft huff, smiled, and held it out. "Sorry it's a bit damp."

"That's okay." His smile melted away my nervousness. "I need you to start from the top. What are these cards and why do you have them?"

I managed to get through the explanation once again, this time pausing long enough to breathe. The entire time I spoke, Harrison read over the card. It shouldn't have required that much attention considering how little was printed on that one, but he seemed fixated on the words. It was only after I'd finished that he put his now empty bottle on the coffee table and read the next step in Rob's plan for me.

"Touch a naked man." He set the card down on the table next to the bottle. "And you want the naked man to be me?"

I didn't bother to hide my embarrassment. "My sister was the one who took me to that bar to pick up a guy. Not that she said it in so many words, but that's what she was hoping I'd do. After you left I had one or two who seemed interested. It was nice. But the second I started to talk to them with any degree of seriousness in taking things to another level, I panicked." I groaned and leaned my head back against the couch. "I never had to do this before. I feel like a thirty-five-year-old virgin."

Harrison's thigh pressed a bit firmer against mine. "I guess your husband suspected that. Hence the cards?"

"Yeah."

"I have to be honest, some guys would be weirded out by this. Dead husband's sex list? Not normal."

My heart sank, along with my stomach. "I didn't even think about that."

Harrison chuckled. "I know you didn't. It's part of your charm."

I almost hated to ask, but we were beyond the point of no return here. "Are you? Weirded out, I mean? Because if you are, that's fine. I mean not fine, but I understand. And I can leave, like right now. If you want."

Instead of answering, he got to his feet and smiled down at me. In the blink of an eye, he started to unbutton the row he'd finished doing up only moments before. "I could have saved a step if I'd known earlier."

Oh. My. God. "I . . . honestly, I just . . . we're going to have sex?"

"No." The bastard smirked. He was actually enjoying this. "We're going to do what it says on the card. You're going to touch a naked man."

His shirt fell silently to the floor as he reached for his belt. I wanted to say something—encourage him, comment on his excellent abs, ask about the sex thing again—but my mouth seemed incapable of functioning. When his jeans hit the floor, my lips parted and an excited tremor passed through me.

Harrison was getting naked.

I was going to see an honest-to-God sexy naked guy. For real!

When he didn't strip off his boxer briefs, a mournful little cry escaped me. Harrison chuckled again as he braced his hands on his hips. "I think this is a good place to start."

"Huh?" I wanted to lick my lips, but didn't want to come across as desperate. Even though I was.

"Touching. No sex." He sat back down, this time keeping a small distance between us. "Let's start off with something easy and then you can see if you want to go any further with those cards of yours. I get the feeling you're not too sure of them yourself."

"But . . ." I might have been drooling, so I swallowed hard. "You're not naked."

"It's close enough for our first time." He leaned back, put his feet up on the coffee table, and closed his eyes. "Whenever you are ready, go for it. Or not. You can leave and I won't think anything bad about you. If anything, I admire the hell out of you even more now."

That wasn't what I'd expected to hear. I wasn't sure what to say, or even what he was expecting me to do after that. He admired me for what I was trying to do? Was trying to get laid even an admirable thing? I pushed that thought from my mind and tried to focus on the matter at hand. I had a nearly naked attractive man sitting beside me, waiting for me to reach out and touch him.

I turned on the couch and pulled my feet up so I was sitting cross-legged. It gave me a barrier, albeit one I could easily breach when I was ready. It made sense to look first. I mean, I hadn't seen a lot of naked men this close up who weren't related to me, and none of them were as fit as Harrison.

Dude had definition.

I cleared my throat, but didn't look away. He didn't have any fat to him at all, which was something I wasn't used to either. "I have to talk or else this is going to be too strange."

"I can talk. I do it for a living." That damn smirk of his again. I could see it getting annoying. "What do you want to talk about?"

His nipples were hard, though I didn't find the air all that cool. I wanted to run the tip of my finger across the hard nub to see the reaction I'd get. My hand was up and moving before I questioned what I was doing. At the last possible second, I chickened out and shifted my attention to his biceps. I touched my fingertip to his muscle, circling around the peaks and valleys of his arm.

"You must work out a lot."

Harrison swallowed hard. "I hit the gym every morning at five. I've been doing it for years. It helps to counteract all the sales lunches and cocktail hours I've been through."

Goose bumps rose on his skin as I continued exploring with my single point of contact. Shifting closer, I moved my finger up to his collarbone. The scent of his deodorant was strong, as though he'd reapplied it before putting on his clean shirt. Maybe he had. "Tell me about your typical day."

I changed from using one finger to three when I reached his chest. Careful to avoid his nipples, I raked my tips through his chest hair, sighing at the feel of its coarseness. Harrison had lots, something Rob's body couldn't produce. Shit, I didn't want to be thinking about him right now, even if it was understandable to draw comparisons.

"Gym, office, meetings, come home, make supper, work. I do some sightseeing if I'm staying in a city I'm not familiar with." He let out a groan. "Stay away from my sides. I'm ticklish. You've been warned."

"You can't wave that red flag in front of me and expect me not to charge." I rose up onto my knees and walked my fingers across his stomach—rock-hard abs, soft hair around his navel—down toward his side. "Is Mr. Kemp ticklish—"

"Don't do it. I'm warning you—"

"Right about—"

"Alyssa—"

"Here!"

I squealed and laughed as he roared, his hips bucking fully off the couch. I had a bit of a mean streak when it came to tickling and now that I knew he had a weakness, I couldn't stop. Harrison was laughing as he tried to squirm away from my touch. All I wanted was to continue to run and press and squeeze his sides, loving the way his face turned red as belly laughs rolled from him. What I wasn't expecting was for him to turn, grab me by the waist, and press me back against the couch cushions.

"Stop! Can't breathe." His eyes were squeezed shut and tears had beaded at the corners of his lids. "Evil woman."

I was laughing just as hard as he was, all my earlier tension finally gone. It didn't even matter that he had my wrists pinned by my head, or that the only thing preventing me from seeing his cock was a thin pair of black boxer briefs. As my laughter subsided, Harrison finally opened his eyes. He had a glow about him, as though he'd needed that moment of silliness as much as I had.

"How long has it been since you've had a girlfriend?"

Something changed in his expression. It was so subtle that had I not been lying directly beneath him I would have easily missed it. Harrison shifted his hands to the side, freeing my wrists.

"It's been awhile for me. Not a lot of time for that given the nature of my job. I don't stay long in one place." He cocked his head to the side. "Are you done exploring?"

I'd upset him, I could tell. If I was smart, I would have said yes, thanked him for indulging me, and left.

I never claimed to be smart.

"Not quite," I whispered.

Using both hands, I ran them up the length of his arms to his shoulders. The movement had me coming up, my face now several inches from his. But as tempted as I was to kiss him, to feel what it would be like to have a pair of lips pressed to mine that weren't Rob's, I didn't. Instead, I let my fingers slide over his shoulders to his back. The muscles were every bit as firm there as his chest and arms. I didn't need to touch his thighs and calves to know how rock-hard they would be. With the way Harrison was straddling me, I could feel nearly every inch of him.

Well, except for a few critical ones.

I shouldn't have looked, but as soon as the thought of his cock flicked through my mind my eyes shifted down to see. As charming as his briefs were, they did little to hide his erection. His *impressive* erection.

Wow.

He groaned. I lifted my gaze to see him staring down at me. There was no mistaking his arousal, even if the obvious evidence wasn't staring me in the face. Harrison's body shook as he cleared his throat. "This is harder than I thought it would be."

"Letting me touch you?"

"Not having sex with you."

My pussy was wet and I would have liked nothing better than to grind down on his thigh to get myself off. He was warm, smelled so good, and for the first time I could see myself with another man. The thought was as thrilling as it was terrifying. "You mean we can't?"

"Nope. It wasn't on the card."

Stupid friggin' cards. "I have more back at my place. I'm sure there are a few there that say we can have sex. More than one. Bunches of them."

"I'm sure they do. But according to this one, it's only day three. I think you need to do them in order. There's no sex on day three."

"I bet we'd be allowed to cheat and break that rule." I was willing to break many things if it meant I could have sex.

Harrison got to his feet and held out his hand. "I'll make you a deal. Bring the rest of the cards over tomorrow night. I'll make you supper and we can take a look at them. Discuss . . . rules."

My entire body was vibrating as I got to my feet. "Rules?"

He should have looked silly standing there naked with his hands on his hips, erection jutting out from behind his boxer briefs, but I wanted nothing more than to continue to touch every inch of him all over again. "Rules. That's the only way I can do this."

I'm sure I looked like a gaping fish. "But, you don't have to. I wasn't really going to do all the cards. Just some. And then have sex with someone random."

Harrison shook his head. "No. Tomorrow night. Supper. Cards. Talk."

I rolled my eyes. "Caveman speak. Woohoo."

"Alyssa."

"Okay, okay. I didn't have plans anyway. I'll come over."

"Good. Now I'm going to see you out so I can masturbate in peace."

"Oh God." I grabbed my sneakers as I jogged to the door. "Don't tell me those things."

"I'm not big on lies. Even white ones." I jerked open the door, stopping when he called my name. "Six o'clock work for you?"

"Yup." I grinned and nodded toward his cock. "Have fun."

I shut the door and scurried toward my condo before he responded. I jammed my key into the hole and yanked my door open, practically diving inside to safety. The second it closed I burst into giggles and slid to the floor. The wood was firm against my back and kept me from dissolving into a puddle of goo.

That just happened. I'd touched Harrison. We'd laughed. We'd almost had sex.

There were going to be *rules*.

My body felt alive, aroused, and ready to take on whatever he was going to throw at me. My nipples were hard and my clit was pressed firmly against my damp panties. It seemed that Harrison wasn't going to be the only one masturbating tonight. With a laugh I got to my feet and stumbled to my bedroom in search of my new vibrator.

Tonight turned out way better than I'd been expecting. I could only hope tomorrow would be just as good.

7

I'd called in to work sick, certain that there'd be no way I'd be able to concentrate long enough to open my documents, let alone add anything productive to them. While it would be fun to create screwed up process documents and see what the programmers did with them, it would only create more work for me in the long run. Instead, I'd tried to sleep in and not think about supper and what was to come after. That lasted for about twenty minutes past my alarm before I got up.

Apparently, I was excited. Or horny. Probably both.

I settled on watching the Food Network in the hopes of improving my culinary skills. After studiously watching a *Chopped* marathon, I got sucked in to a show that was featuring appetizers designed to seduce the palate. It made sense to bring something with me when I went over to Harrison's. Normally, I'd bring along a bottle of wine, but given my track record with beverages recently, food seemed like a more civilized option. I'd be less likely to dump it over his head at any rate. I grabbed a pen and started making notes.

The scent of roasting garlic and tomatoes filled my condo for the remainder of the afternoon. I so rarely did this sort of thing anymore the act of sautéing had a calming effect. I loved to cook, but it was hard to get up the energy when I was making a meal for only me. Maybe I made a bit more than what I planned to bring over tonight, but that was cool. Leftovers were my friend.

My mind wandered as I prepared the ingredients I'd picked up. It was fun to imagine Harrison's reaction as he bit into the skewers. I wondered if he'd lick the juice off his fingertips, if he'd suck them into his mouth to get every last taste. It was surprisingly difficult not to duck into my bedroom and get myself off. Who knew that my masturbation drought would end in such a spectacular way—porn and neighbor fantasies. *Woohoo!*

I'd been so busy banging around in my kitchen that I'd actually lost track of time. A loud knock sent a bolt of panic through me. Shit, it was five-thirty and I hadn't even showered yet. I grabbed my hand towel to work the garlic juice from my fingers as I jogged to the door.

"Harrison." This was still way too early. I peeked out the door to see if there was someone else around. "Everything okay?"

Now, I know I'm not very observant when it comes to the opposite sex. I've never been one to notice when a man or woman was checking me out. I used to assume that was because it rarely happened. However, I've been told time and again from a number of people that yes, I do get my ass checked out and yes, I'm oblivious. That said, even I could tell there was something heated in the way Harrison was staring at me. I'd thrown my hair into a bun and hadn't bothered to put on any makeup. My T-shirt and shorts were hidden beneath my linen apron, which was stained from years of use. Not my most attractive look.

"You're cooking."

There was something in the way he said the words that didn't seem right to me. "Yes. I thought I'd make an appetizer to bring over. I wasn't sure what you had in mind, but I couldn't come over empty-handed."

He licked his lips. "It smells wonderful."

"I'm a woman of many talents." And holy shit I was totally flirting.

Rather than retreat from it, I kicked my hip out to the side, flicked my hand towel across my shoulder, and braced my hands on my hips. If I was actually going to go down this road with him, then I had to own it.

"Are you still good for me to come over in thirty minutes, or do you need more time?"

His lips tightened and his gaze narrowed. As quickly as his body tensed, he let out a sigh and relaxed. "I had a meeting run late. As long as you don't mind watching me cook, come on over."

Rob had zero talent in the kitchen. Most of the men in my family barely knew where the kitchen was, let alone how to make anything beyond cereal or toast. How cool was it to be with a guy who could do more than pop something in the microwave. "Sounds like a plan. I'll be there as soon as the skewers are finished and I can get cleaned up."

"You look fantastic the way you are." He gave me a nod, his gaze briefly slipping down my body, before he marched down to his condo. "We can start our chat when you get here."

As tempting as it was to watch him go, I shut the door and dashed back inside to get ready. Ogling would have to wait.

There were *rules* to get ready for.

It took me a tad longer than thirty minutes to finish cooking and appear presentable. It would have taken far less if my goal was to continue with my sex-starved-dear-God-is-this-happening look, but I didn't want to come across as desperate. Or crazy.

Even though I *was* starting to question my sanity.

This time when I knocked on Harrison's door, he answered almost immediately. He'd clearly had a shower of his own, his hair still damp and his navy dress shirt sticking to his chest in places. I tightened my grip on the platter with the skewers and forced my attention to his face.

He was trying not to laugh at me.

"So hi." I held up the platter and smiled. "I have these."

"I have wine. Come on in."

Unlike last night, Harrison's place was decidedly neater. "You didn't have to clean for me." I followed him through to the kitchen, exchanging my platter for a glass of white.

"I didn't. I simply shoved a bunch of the boxes into the spare room." Picking up a skewer, he lifted it to his mouth and pulled off a cherry tomato with his teeth. "Tasty."

I whimpered.

"I'm roasting veggies to make my own sauce. I figured pasta would be a safe meal. Didn't know if you had any dislikes or allergies." He stuck his tongue out to lick the chicken cube before he pulled it free of the stick as well.

This is the part of the conversation where you respond. I cleared my throat. "I'll eat anything. I mean, I like it all. I don't have any allergies."

He laughed. Not a soft chuckle, or polite tittering. Nope, Harrison let out a belly-deep laugh. "How freaked out are you right now?"

"On a scale of one to ten? I'm swallowing a bottle of Ativan."

"This is going to take awhile longer. Why don't we go sit on the couch and talk?"

In a flash the image of his nearly naked body sitting back against the cushions flashed in my mind. "I'm good here. The wine's closer."

He filled up my glass. "Fair enough. Here it is."

Pulling up a stool, he perched on top of it and patted the seat beside him. A man that large shouldn't be subjected to such a tiny area, but there was no way I'd last ten minutes on the couch. I pulled the stool out to put more space between us. "Okay."

The pause was unexpected. How the hell was either of us supposed to move forward with this?

"I'm sorry." I sighed and rolled my glass between my hands. "I honestly have no idea what I'm doing, or why I'm considering enacting these cards. You were right when you said it's freaking weird. How screwed up am I to even consider doing this?"

"You don't strike me as screwed up. Lonely, yes. But not crazy."

"I guess that's something."

Harrison had propped his elbow on the counter and now bracketed the side of his face with his forefinger and thumb. It felt as though he was trying to get a read on me and still wasn't certain what he was seeing. This was the most awkward not-a-first-date I'd ever been a party to.

The first rule of being social was getting to know the other person. I could do that. "You're in sales? What's that like?"

His eyes sparkled as the corner of his mouth lifted. "I get to meet interesting people. Lots of verbal dancing."

"I'm a technical writer for a software firm. No dancing of any kind."

"I bet you're a champ."

"It's boring as hell, but it pays the bills." It wasn't really. I loved picking apart programs, outlining all the nooks and crannies so that some poor user wouldn't have to beat their head against it. I'd yet to find anyone outside of the business who enjoyed it, though, so I normally kept the work chat to a minimum.

"I've met all kinds in my line of work." Harrison leaned in and lowered his voice. "Do you know Charlie Brown?"

I blinked. "Pardon?"

"Charlie Brown. Bald-headed boy, cute beagle for a pet."

"Yeah, sure."

"Do you remember the bit where he'd line up to kick the football that Lucy was holding? Every time he gave it his all. He'd race down the line and give a huge-ass kick, only to have Lucy pull the ball away at the last second. He landed on his back. Every. Single. Time."

He moved closer again and I could smell the soap that still clung to his skin. I became aware of my body, how close it was to his, how large he was compared to me. I wasn't sure if I wanted to lean into him or run from his condo.

"I remember," I managed to squeak out.

"You remind me of Charlie Brown. Ready to race down that strip toward the football, ready to give it your all, knowing full well it might get yanked away at the last second. I wanted to let you know something." This time when he shifted in, our lips were only a hair's breadth apart. "I'm no Lucy."

The timer on the stove went off. In a blink, Harrison was up and around the counter, pulling the pan from the oven.

Fuck.

Fuck, damn, shit, lying bastard.

He *was* a freaking Lucy. Except it wasn't a ball that was getting yanked.

We chatted about inconsequential stuff while he finished preparing supper. I'm sure he intended to take the edge off, help me relax before the conversation took its inevitable turn toward sex, but it didn't work. As we sat down to eat, I couldn't help but admire his broad chest and the ease with which he moved. With every lift of his fork to his mouth, all I wanted to know was what it would be like to kiss him. Each time he reached for his glass, I wondered how hard he'd squeeze my breasts when having sex. When he'd reach for the rolls and I watched the muscles play along his exposed forearms, I fantasized about him pinning me to the mattress while he slammed into me.

"I have dessert. Chocolate cake."

He was trying to kill me. "Please tell me you didn't make this? I can't handle a man who can cook and bake."

"You're safe. Store-bought."

"Thank God."

I wanted to wait until he served the cake before I brought up the thing about *rules*. As pleasant as supper had been, I was getting tired of dancing around the reason I was here. The moment a microwave-heated chocolate lava cake was placed in front of me, I took a sip of wine, cleared my throat, and looked Harrison straight in the eye. "So."

"Yes?" He picked up his fork and pushed a large, gooey bit into his mouth.

"I . . ."

He licked the back of the fork, giving me a wink. "I take it you're ready to discuss your proposition?"

"Huh?" There was a smudge of chocolate on his bottom lip. I so wanted to lick that sucker clean. "Right. The cards."

"Did you bring them?"

The damn things had been burning a hole in my pocket since I'd put them there. "I know you said we should do them all in order, but that wasn't what I'd planned. I mean, they're just ideas, suggestions to get me back out there into the land of the dating."

I don't know why I was hesitating to show them to Harrison, but it was far harder than I'd anticipated sliding them across the table. My chest tightened, making it necessary for me to consciously force myself to breathe. "So yeah, this is them."

Harrison didn't take them immediately. He continued to devour his lava cake, his gaze shifting between me and the cards with each bite. Only once he'd finished did he place his fork on the plate, set it aside, and pick up the index cards.

Looking for a distraction, I ate my own dessert in three gulps.

He sorted through the cards until he reached what I could only suspect was Day One. He licked his bottom lip. "Now I know what you were doing that afternoon I thought you were getting murdered."

And there was my blush again. "I'm never going to live that down, am I?"

"Nope." He returned his attention back to the cards. "Your late husband had quite an active imagination. I'm assuming you haven't done a lot of these things."

"No. Rob wanted to expand my horizons." I'd spent some

time online doing a tiny bit of research on sex things to try. Yeah, that left me scarred for life. Seriously, the Internet is a scary place. "Honestly, some of those read more like his wish list than mine, but his intentions were good."

"I'd be happy to help you come up with new ideas." His smile made the skin around his eyes crinkle. "But as I mentioned, I think we need some ground rules first. Not just for you, but for me as well."

It made sense. We were both about to engage in a sexual relationship with a stranger we'd only known for a few weeks and met a few times. In the same regard, it didn't seem right to reduce our experiment to a list of *dos* and *don'ts*. Sex had never purely been about the pleasure for me. It had been my way to connect with Rob, to reassure myself that we were still okay as a couple. Half the time I didn't even orgasm. Not because Rob was unwilling to do something for me, but because I didn't feel the need for the release.

What I was about to undertake with Harrison was a completely different animal. I had no idea if this would change me, or make me see the world differently.

"Sure. Rules make sense." I laced my fingers together and leaned forward. "Do you want to start or should I?"

"How about we take turns. You go, then me."

"Okay." My mind was little more than a tornado whipping inside my skull. I let out a huff and said the first thing that came to mind. "We have to use condoms."

"Agreed. We each need to be tested for STDs before we start."

Whoa, I hadn't even considered that. "Agreed. I know Rob wrote these cards with the best of intentions, but I'm allowed to veto one if I'm not comfortable doing it. I think the same should stand for you."

"I didn't see anything too crazy on that list, but agreed." He paused for a moment, taking another sip of wine that had me squirming in my seat. "I need to be clear on one point. I'm here on a contract. The Toronto office only needs me for three months and then I'll be moving on. I like you and don't want to lead you on. If we do this, it will only be about sex. I don't do relationships. It's not you. It's just not my thing anymore."

It was strange when he put things that way. Having various people staying in this condo wasn't unusual. It was the reason we'd named it Tourism. Why I hadn't truly considered that Harrison's stay wasn't going to be long-term was weird. While I was attracted to Harrison, Rob was right that I shouldn't jump back into a serious relationship out of the gate. Knowing things between us would only be temporary made the relationship safer.

Setting my glass down, I rubbed my hands along the tops of my thighs. "Rob was the only man I'd ever slept with. I never dated anyone else. I think having a chance to have fun, learn some things about what I like and don't like will be good for me. I need it. Don't worry about me becoming attached. I'm not ready for a relationship. Not yet. This really will be all about sex."

I stuck out my hand, proud of myself that it wasn't shaking. Harrison looked at it, but didn't reach out to take it.

"One last thing." He leaned forward, forcing me to drop my hand. "We start back at the beginning of all this. Day One. We'll take each card in turn, talk about it if you want, but go through them all. If you want to veto something then fine, but that will end our exploration. I need you to trust me that I won't hurt you. I also have to trust you. My reputation, my standing with my company could be impacted if it gets out that I'm doing this. Several of my clients are ultraconservative and would run if they caught wind of this."

"I hadn't thought a lot about that. If this is going to cause you problems—"

"My sex life is none of their business." His gaze narrowed and I felt as though he was going to kiss me again. "As long as I keep things separate and quiet, it will be fine."

This time when I held my hand out, he took it. With one firm

shake we sealed the deal. How things were going to proceed
from here was beyond me.

"So." I tucked my hair behind my ear. "Now what?"

Harrison reclaimed his glass and took another deep sip. "We
start back on Day One."

"Well, I can do that tonight. Unless we count this morning."
I mumbled that last part, but the glint in his eyes told me he
heard it anyway.

"No." He set his glass down and stood. He took my glass
from my hand and set it on the table beside his. "We're in this together. That means I have to be a part of each day's task."

"You want me to masturbate? In front of you?" No. No way
could I do that.

"Is that a problem?"

"Yes." I'd never even done that in front of Rob. It was a pri-
vate thing, something that I'd always felt guilty about when I'd
been married. "I mean, I don't . . ."

He chuckled. "You can't tell me you don't know how. I heard
evidence to the contrary when I moved in."

"I was alone. And I had porn and a vibrator. I don't even
know where your bathroom is. How can you expect me to get
myself off here?"

"I didn't say you had to do it here. I just need to watch."

Rather than directing me to his bedroom or other likely location, Harrison disappeared into the hall, only to emerge a few
minutes later with a laptop. "I assume you are computer-
friendly?"

"Yeah, I'm fine."

"Have you ever used video chats before?"

"Sure. All the time at work." The realization hit me like a
sucker-punch. "You want me to get off on *camera?*"

"I have a Web site that I use for presentations. You can log in
and control all the settings, including blocking the ability for me
to record what you're projecting. It will be safe. I'll be able to see
you, talk to you, but I won't physically be in the same place."

My immediate reaction was to say no. There were so many reasons why this was a bad idea. So many potential issues, things that could backfire that only a raving fool would say yes. Instead of the refusal that should have come, I leaned in and took a look at the Web site. "The host doesn't record the session?"

"No. A friend of mine is the owner. He's given me some extra perks that normally aren't available. I promise that it's one hundred percent safe."

Well, if I was going to start on a sexual adventure, this was certainly a unique way to kick things off.

I reached out, letting my fingers brush along the side of Harrison's. "Day One?"

"With an audience. You can use your laptop, set it up wherever you want. You'll be in your own home, with your own things." He leaned in, his hot breath tickling the side of my throat. "I'll get to see what you like. What excites you. I'll know what to do to turn you on."

Only a fool would say yes. I turned my face and pressed a soft kiss to his cheek.

"Give me the login information."

8

The laptop wasn't even turned on and I could already feel its judgmental lens watching me. I'd set it on the opposite side coffee table from where I'd be . . . whatever the hell I'd end up doing. Since I'd come back home from Harrison's, I tried not to dwell too much on what I'd agreed to.

Seriously, masturbating on camera was either the most brilliant idea ever, or plain stupid beyond belief. I'd come to a decision as to which it was sooner or later. Most likely depending on if this backfired on me or not.

I kept trying to convince myself that this wasn't the sort of thing Rob had in mind when he'd set out to write his sex cards. Though as much as I wanted to believe that he would have a problem with what I was about to do, I knew he really wouldn't. If anything he'd cheer me on.

Well, if this was going to happen I had to turn the computer on and log in. I half-hoped for technical difficulties to give me an excuse to back out, but no, everything went smoothly. The login screen popped away and I was left with a welcome page. Within a minute a second user joined the room, *HanShotFirst*.

Lord, he really was a *Star Wars* geek.

The sound of a throat being cleared vibrated out from the laptop's speaker. Harrison didn't say anything else, but that one little noise sent my heart racing so hard and fast I'm sure if someone could see the inside of my ribs there'd be a mark from the pounding. Ignoring him would have been the ideal, but there was no way that would happen now.

"Can you see me okay?" I kept my face turned from the camera. I'm sure I was beet red. "I can shift the laptop around a bit if you need me to."

"You're coming in nice and clear."

When I'd logged in to the site, I'd turned off the option to be able to see him. I should have left it on because my mind was instead supplying all sorts of images that may or may not be reality. I could see Harrison sitting in the middle of his couch, leaning back against the leather cushion. His shirt would be unbuttoned and spread open. The memory of what his skin felt like, how soft and smooth the hair on his chest was, made my fingers itch to touch.

"Alyssa? Are you okay?"

Shit, I hope I'm not drooling. "Yeah, of course. I'm just going to finish getting a few things."

"You know you can still back out of—"

"Don't say it! If you give me an out I might take it and I really don't want to do that. Just . . . be quiet. Okay? Don't say a word."

"Yes, ma'am." Even through the computer I could tell the bastard was laughing at me.

I marched to my bedroom and gave myself a few minutes to chill out. This was weird and exciting all at once. My legs weakened as I sat down on the edge of the bed. My body was thrumming with arousal. This was new. It was the sort of thing I'd secretly always wanted to do. Thanks to Harrison's brilliant idea, I was safe in my own home and had the control of how much he got to see. There was nothing for me to worry about.

With shaking fingers, I took my hair out of the bun I'd shoved it into. Giving my blond locks a quick shake, I toed off my socks before standing once more to remove my shorts. With three quick moves, I took my bra off without removing my shirt. My nipples rubbed against the soft jersey material, which sent another tremor of arousal through me.

Masturbating on camera in front of a man who I barely knew. There were many things I'd imagined doing in my life, but that was a sentence that hadn't crossed my mind even once. It was daring, sexy, and something that I knew would change me. I just needed to be brave enough to go ahead with it.

"Let's do this." My words filled my empty bedroom.

Rather than settle on using my default vibrator, I reached into the bag from the sex store and removed one of the toys Nikki had tossed in. The silicone was soft, yet textured. I ran my finger up the length of the cock, my nail catching on the veins as I went. This sucker was *big* and would more than do the job of getting me off. I snagged a bottle of lube before I went back out to the living room.

"There you are." Harrison's voice sounded from the computer. "I thought for a second you'd changed your mind."

"Nope." But I did make one adjustment. I picked up the laptop and shifted its position. "Just needed to get my head in the game."

Rather than giving him a full view of my face—because as much as I wanted to trust him on the no-recording thing, I didn't know him that well—I placed the laptop so that he'd only be able to see my body. He didn't complain about the move. He didn't say anything at all. I took his silence as the start of our little project, picked up the remote, and pressed play.

There were my pirates!

It would have killed me to admit how much I actually enjoyed this movie. It was perfect fantasy material—being swept away by a pirate who wanted nothing more than to ravage you—where all partners involved were having a good time. I skipped ahead to my favorite scene—because yes, I'd watched it that much—and set my remote on the couch beside me.

Beside the laptop. Where Harrison was watching me.

I wriggled around in my seat, trying to get comfortable. Focus. I needed to focus on the movie and not on the sound of Harrison's breathing.

"Wench! Get over here with a flagon of ale." The pirate captain was shirtless, legs spread wide as he sat at a table. The actor was hot. Every muscle of his torso was well defined and he had strong-looking forearms. His face was unshaven, I assumed as their attempt to make him look dangerous, but it only highlighted his *GQ* looks.

A large-chested brunette sauntered over and slammed down a wooden mug. "There ye be, Captain. Is there anything else I can get for ye?"

Harrison snorted.

"Shut up." I picked up the silicone cock and waved it in front of the camera. "Don't distract me."

He groaned again before falling silent.

I realized I was smiling when I let the tip of the cock fall against my lips. My attention was split between watching the pirate captain tear open the wench's shirt to expose her breasts, and my desire to tease my invited voyeur. No, this wasn't about him. I had to remind myself to be selfish once again. I was the only one responsible for my pleasure. Not Harrison and not my pirate captain. I reached for the lube, and squirted a bunch on the tip before I shimmied out of my panties.

"I want my fill of your pussy." The pirate captain lifted the girl up and with a flourish "threw" her on the table. "I shall now lick your cream."

There was another snort from the computer, but this time I ignored him.

Mimicking what I saw on the screen, I matched the pirate's motions with the dildo. I ran the tip along my clit, teasing the flesh with soft almost-there caresses. My thumb hovered above the on switch, but I wanted to save that until I pressed it into my pussy. I circled my clit, taking time to press a little firmer on the top above the nerve bundle. A little gasp escaped me, and I had to clear my throat to help settle myself back down.

The wench moaned on-screen, bucking her hips as she held his head in place. I held my breath and watched. I loved this part, the moment where the pirate captain pulled back and the camera moved in for a close-up. His hair was long enough that it fell across his face, partially obstructing it. The focus went to his eyes and the devilish look he gave the woman he was about to fuck. The guy-liner was thick, and made his eyes stand out in a way that you couldn't help but stare at them.

Even though I'd seen this scene several times already, there was something different this time around. When the camera moved in, I realized for the first time that the pirate's eyes were the exact color of Harrison's. I gasped and the movement inadvertently pushed the cock harder against my pussy.

"I will fuck you until you scream." The pirate said the words low and they mixed with the sound of Harrison's heavy breathing coming from the computer.

Arousal can do strange things to a person's mind. In a blink the pirate on the screen morphed into Harrison and I was watching him seduce a willing partner. It was his black hair that kissed his stubble-covered cheek. It was his long, thick cock that sprung from the silken pants as they slipped to the ground.

I wanted to be that wench spread out on the table before him. I wanted to offer my breasts for him to suck on, to be the one impaled on his shaft until I came.

"Yes, I want to be yours." The wench pulled her skirt up all the way and spread her legs wide. Her pussy was wet from desire, glistening in the flickering firelight.

With hard-fought restraint, I positioned the cockhead against my opening and waited. Would Harrison be this patient with me? Would he continue to tease my opening this way, until I begged him to fuck me?

The pirate captain took her by the hips and pushed into her with one smooth stroke. My hand shook as I followed suit. The silicone stretched my pussy wide as I worked it deep into my body. I didn't wait for my body to adjust to the size of the dildo and began to pump into me with short strokes, matching what I saw on the screen.

The litany of moans from the couple was punctuated by the pirate grunting and the wench shouting, "Fuck!"

My lips had parted and the taste of salt and spice from dinner exploded on my tongue when it darted out to wet my skin. That small reminder pulled my gaze from the television screen toward where my computer camera watched. Looking at the darkened screen I could see the lust in my gaze and the flush on my skin reflected back to me.

Harrison was on the other end of that camera. While I couldn't see him, I could feel his presence in the room. It wasn't hard to imagine his gaze on my face, roaming across me as I fucked myself on the cock. Did he wish it was his? How would it feel to have his large hands grip my hips as he fucked me? Would he be as possessive as the pirate captain and take me over the table? Maybe he'd prefer to press me against a wall, using it as leverage and a means to keep me trapped against him? His cock would be thick and it would stretch me full until I could taste him.

I moaned a moment before the wench did on the screen. My eyes fluttered shut and my imagination no longer needed the visual stimulation to get me to my place of bliss. My mental picture of pirate Harrison was all it took. His firm chest clothed in the silken shirt. His tight buttocks clenching and releasing as he thrust into my wet pussy. I'd grab his ass, dig my nails into the firm muscles, and hold him there until I got what I wanted.

The porn movie played on. Their sounds filled my head as I madly fucked myself on the dildo. My orgasm was there . . . so . . . close. I panted, trying to get enough air into my lungs to keep from passing out. My eyes were screwed shut and I didn't relent.

Almost . . .

"Bloody hell, yes!" The pirate captain roared as he came. I could hear their sweaty bodies slap together as he fucked his way through orgasm. The pleasure-filled screams of the wench coming quickly followed.

I saw none of it. With a pace that should have been painful but wasn't, I met the thrust of the toy, pushing my hips down to connect on each motion. I sucked in a breath, mentally hovered on the precipice of release for a heartbeat before my body hurled itself over the edge.

I've often thought of orgasm as a burst of colors behind my lids; a bright light of pleasure that heats every cell in my body. Whether it was because of Harrison's involvement, or simply my body's sudden greediness for release, things were different this time. My orgasm was beyond an explosion or the light fluttering of colors in my head. My pussy squeezed the cock in a death grip, as pleasure obliterated my ability to sense or feel anything else. It was so intense it almost hurt as my muscles refused to give way to the pleasure. I cried out again as another wave hit me, but this time I managed to open my eyes and watch the pirate wipe come across the wench's stomach.

As quickly as my mind blanked out, my ability to think winked back into existence. Wow. Not just wow, but holy fucking shit wow. My toenails were tingling as a result of how hard I'd come. There was something different going on, and I knew it had everything to do with my new neighbor.

I dropped the dildo to the couch, my breath coming out in gasps as I fought to get myself back under control. I fumbled for the remote and turned off the DVD. My pirates deserved a rest after the outstanding job they'd done for me.

"Holy crap. That was intense." I laughed weakly and let my head fall back against the couch. It took me a moment to realize that there was a sound coming from the other end of the computer, one I didn't fully recognize. "Harrison? You still there?"

"I'm here for three months." His voice had taken on a raspy quality and it was punctuated by a rhythmic sound in the background. He'd been turned on by what he'd watched, that much was clear. "Three months for thirty days of sex."

My mouth opened to say something, but the words got caught in my throat when Harrison let out a moan.

Wait a second. "What are you doing?"

"I might have to go away, but you and I are going through those cards." The noises increased, a squeaking sound that reminded me of when we'd been fooling around on his couch. "I'm going to make you come, feel alive. Fuck!" His powerful moans caused my laptop speaker to distort the sounds.

Holy shit, he'd been jerking off. He'd just come!

My heart was racing once more and my body, which I thought had been drained of all sexual energy, threatened to spark to life once more.

"Did you hear me, Alyssa?" Unlike the fantasy pirate–Harrison, there was no teasing in reality-Harrison's voice. His words came out in short, clipped bites that underlined his seriousness.

"Yes." I swallowed down my desire as my lips trembled and my cheeks ached. "I heard."

"You and me. Thirty days of sex. We'll make each other feel good. Get what we need from this. Then we go our separate ways back to our normal lives. Agreed?"

Oh my God. He'd watched me while I'd masturbated and it turned him on so much he jerked off. This was dirty and awesome and completely unexpected in my life. Not only did Harrison not think I was a complete weirdo for wanting to do these cards, he was excited by the prospect. He was safe. There was no pressure for more than what was on the table.

I could have it all.

I swallowed hard and gave myself a breath before I turned and looked directly into the camera.

"Agreed." And then I slammed the laptop shut.

Part 2

Sex, Lies, and Revelations

9

I'd come to the realization that I required a sanity check in regard to Harrison and the whole sex thing. Unlike other people who would need to get a doctor's referral to see a psychologist, I had the blessing of being able to go talk to my sister.

Most people who met Nikki without knowing her profession would never guess that she was a psychologist. She was a bit crazy and couldn't hold down a relationship longer than a year. Not the typical person you'd want to give you relationship advice. But Nikki had a way of being able to see the heart of a problem and the uncanny ability to point a person in the direction they needed to go. She was my big sister and I loved her to pieces. If anyone could tell me what I needed to know, it would be her.

Over the years, I'd gotten used to drifting into her office toward the end of the day. I'd just come back from my STD test, which was all sorts of awkward, and found myself standing in Nikki's waiting room. I still found it difficult to reconcile the business attire–wearing woman I'd see step out of her office with a client and the girl who once dyed her hair green in high school just to piss off our mom. While she still would add the occasional streak of red in her light brown hair, for the most part she'd moved past her rebellious phase.

I caught her eye and offered a small wave before making my way toward the back of her waiting room. An old edition of *The New Yorker* magazine caught my eye and I immediately flipped to the book review section to see if there were any recommendations that I'd missed. Oh, that one sounded good.

"Alyssa?" Nikki stood with her hands clasped behind her back. Her previous client was still present, making an appointment with her receptionist, Linda, which meant she'd stay in *professional mode* until he was gone. "Want to join me in my office?"

"Sure. Thanks." I held the magazine in my fist and gave Linda a small smile as I passed by. "Did I catch you at a bad time?"

"Not at all. I just have some paperwork to finish up." Nikki closed the door and then caught me in a giant hug. "Hey, sweetie. What's up?"

"Oh you know, nothing. Do I need an excuse to come see you?"

"Normally, no. But you only come see me at the office when you want me to be serious and give you proper advice rather than encourage you to have sex with a cucumber." She beckoned for me to take a seat. "The doctor is in and all that stuff. Spill it."

I really did love my sister. Falling into the overly comfortable seat, I slipped my shoes off and tucked my feet under my ass. "It's about the cards."

Based on the amused expression on her face, I knew there was no need to clarify *which* cards. "I take it you've decided to do something about them."

We had the sort of relationship that allowed me to say just about anything to her. But sex, well, that had never been an easy topic for me. Rather than look her in the eye, I flipped open the magazine to a random page. "Umm, maybe."

"You're clearly looking for some advice on the topic. Otherwise you'd simply give me a call."

I had to fight the urge to squirm. "Did I mention that there's a new guy who moved into the condo down the hall from me?"

"No, you didn't." She sat on the edge of her desk, her hands braced on either side of her. "I take it Mr. New Guy is hot?"

"Do you remember the nightclub? The guy I was talking to just before you and I went out to start dancing?"

"Yeah. I mean I didn't really see that much of him and oh shit." Nikki licked her lips. "He's your neighbor? You've been holding out on me."

"Not your type." He was so her type. "Besides, I saw him first."

She rolled her eyes. "So, hot guy in your place. What's the problem? Has he not noticed you? I mean a few wardrobe malfunctions can take care of that in a hurry."

My face heated as she started to giggle. "Nikki, stop."

"No way." She leaned closer. "So he did notice you. Did he make a move? What did you do? I don't need specifics, but measurements wouldn't go amiss."

I might be close to her, but there was no way in frigging hell I was about to give her the details on our little video chat. "We had supper. He's here on a three-month contract and offered to help me out with my little sex problem."

When Nikki didn't immediately offer a smart-assed comeback, I looked up and was surprised to see her thoughtful expression. "What exactly did he offer to do?"

"Basically three months in which to have thirty days of sex. We do the cards in order after we've had STD tests and all that. I have full veto power. He leaves when we're done. He's not into relationships. Not anymore. Whatever *that* means."

"So no strings attached. Interesting."

I didn't like interesting. I wanted predictable, something safe. This was so far outside my comfort zone I might as well have put on a space suit. "I knew I was making a mistake."

"I didn't say that."

"You said *interesting*. Past experience has told me that means *bad idea*."

Nikki leaned forward, her hands still gripping the edge of her desk. "In this case it really does mean interesting. What did you say this guy did?"

"I didn't. And sales. He's here on a contract to fix an issue with a client. Then they send him somewhere else. To be honest I'm not even sure where he's from originally. But yeah, he's some sort of client guru."

"Ah. That makes sense."

"What does?"

"He's a fixer. He's used to being presented a problem and working through it. You and your sex cards are a problem and he's taking it on himself to help. He gets something out of it and has been clear about the no-relationship thing. I say go for it."

I blinked, needing a moment to let her words sink in. "You mean I'm not crazy for wanting to try something like this? He could be a stalker, or a crazy man or something."

"Do you really believe that?"

After all of the effort he'd taken to make sure that I was safe, that I'd been the one with the power with our one encounter, I knew there was no way Harrison would ever hurt me. "No."

"You need to trust your instincts with this. You're attracted to him. He's told you exactly what to expect from him. You can discover some interesting aspects to your sexuality without committing your heart. It's a win-win situation."

"Friends with benefits?"

"If it helps you to look at it that way, then sure. You need to get yourself out there. If this guy is the one to help you do that then I'll love him forever." Nikki wiped a tear that had somehow slipped from my eye. "Don't cry, sweetie."

"I'm not." I stood and madly wiped the remaining tears away. "Thanks. I just needed to make sure I was doing the right thing.

Those stupid cards of Rob's have made me sex crazy or something. I can't get them out of my mind."

Before I could get away, Nikki caught me in another hug. "You're not crazy. You'll always love Rob. You don't have to be alone. If you need permission to do this, then I'm more than happy to give it to you. Go live your life. Go have crazy-ass monkey sex with spatulas or whatever Rob wrote down on those things."

I had to swallow twice before I could get out a strangled, "Thanks."

Nikki pulled back, gave me a kiss on the cheek, and opened the door. "I'm always here for you. Look, why don't you come over to my place on Friday night and we can have pizza and beer and chat. You can tell me how things are going with your guy."

"Harrison. His name is Harrison."

She smiled. "Good name."

"He's a good guy."

"Then go have some fun. And keep me posted."

For the first time since closing the laptop on Harrison, a sense of relief washed over me. If Nikki was right and he was simply seeing me as a problem to fix, then I could safely follow Rob's cards and not have to worry about my heart getting involved. If Harrison was seeing me as simply another project, then I could do that as well.

I could do what Rob wanted of me and not feel as though I were cheating. Yeah, this might work out after all. The next order of business was pulling out the second card and doing what it instructed.

Harrison better be ready.

10

I don't know what I was expecting after finally coming to terms with the cards and Harrison's participation, but him leaving to go on a business trip two days later hadn't entered into my mental equation. Call me naïve, but I'd foolishly assumed that being in the same city was required to have sex.

When I got back from Nikki's and found the note under my front door from him telling me about an unexpected week-long business trip to Montreal, I pouted for a full five minutes before going in search of a tub of ice cream. Half a pint of rocky road later, I pulled myself together, got cleaned up, and went about my life. We had three months after all, and he'd made no promises on his time beyond that. The boy was in town to do a job and I had to buy more ice cream.

Plus, as much as I might want to ignore everything else and do nothing but stay home and think about sex, life did continue on. Tomorrow was Monday and I didn't fancy getting myself fired.

The office was busy when I'd gotten in the next morning. It was the odd week in summer when most people seemed to be in between vacation days. The resulting mad rush of meeting invitations filling my in-box left me with a sense of dread. Rarely was I actually needed to be present for update meetings. Things were bound to change with the product before it reached the documentation stage. Still, it was hard to say no when there was the promise of iced coffee and doughnuts merely for showing up.

It was a bribe I was fine with.

Gary Snelling stood in front of the room, a slide projected behind him that looked like a demented eye-test chart. The font decreased in size the lower it got, making it nearly impossible to read. I'd mentioned this to him in the past, though he clearly didn't get the whole we-can't-read-the-words part.

Gary was the project lead for Orion, our latest software update release. While he wasn't the most enthusiastic of speakers, he was excellent at documenting project changes. I normally only had to take his notes and repurpose them for my needs. Which meant that I didn't have to pay as close attention as I should when it came to these things. That gave my mind the opportunity to wander.

As we entered hour two of the update meeting, my phone vibrated where it rested on my thigh. I could have wept from joy for the distraction. Without being too obvious, I flipped the phone over so I could see my screen.

Hi.

The number wasn't familiar so I didn't respond. Still, I couldn't help but wonder who it was.

Hi?

The vibrations felt nice. A small means to shake away some of the boredom of the morning.

Alyssa? I hope I have the right number.

It took me a minute to realize that it was Harrison's number. I'd only seen it once, when he'd scribbled it down on some paper for me. The prospect of chatting with him improved my mood significantly. Making sure no one was paying any attention to me, I typed as stealthily as I could.

Harrison?

Yeah, it's me. I just checked into my hotel room. I wanted to touch base with you. Did you get my note?

I did. ☹

Sorry about that. Part of the job. I would have texted sooner, but my phone was dead. What are you doing?

Okay, normal enough conversation. It was strange having the whole sex thing hanging over our heads. I immediately wanted to start texting him dirty stuff rather than shoot the shit. But beggars couldn't be choosers.

My fingers hovered over the keys while I tried to come up with something to say that wouldn't make me sound like a dork. *I'm trying not to fall asleep at a project meeting.*

That sounds fun. What do you do again?

Technical writer for a software company.

Right. I remember. Like it?

I snorted, which momentarily drew Gary's gaze. "You're right, Alyssa. Only three days for testing the GUI isn't enough. Thanks for that."

"You're welcome." Someone would either thank or kill me after this meeting for that.

Once Gary continued on, I was able to return my attention back to Harrison. *The company is great. This meeting, not so much. Boooooring!!!*

LOL Is this a critical meeting? Should I let you go?

God no. I normally don't attend, but they had coffee and muffins.

That's how they get you. My work does the same.

I smiled and flipped my phone face down. Gary had moved on to the budget review and was calling on each of the department heads present to give an update. This was normally where I'd zone out and find my way to the coffeepot for a refill. Strangely, my body was humming with electricity and my skin was supersensitive, sending a shiver through me when my fingers accidentally brushed the inside of my forearm. This couldn't be because of Harrison—could it?

My phone buzzed again, but I had to wait to read it. The Educational Outreach manager who sat on my side of the table was giving her report, which meant most eyes were in our direction. After a few minutes the conversation shifted again, and I was free to flip the phone over and peek.

What are you wearing?

I stared at the words for far longer than necessary to form a response. Was this a friendly "Hey, I'm still trying to get to know you so tell me about yourself," or more along the lines of "Lie to me and tell me it's black lace."

No. He couldn't be asking that.

Could he?

I typed out the expected *Black skirt and sleeveless top* response, but didn't hit send. As much as the idea of sending sexy texts was exciting, I didn't know if this had anything to do with our arrangement. I deleted my answer and hoped no one chose that moment to look at me or else my blush would give away what I was up to. *It's Monday and this meeting has sucked my brain out of my ears, so I'm going to be blunt. Are we sexting?*

There was a pause. I could picture Harrison lying on his bed in the hotel laughing his head off. Of course we're not sexting! I'd just told him that I was in a meeting and I knew he'd just checked in to his hotel. It was a crazy idea. Clearly I needed to go to counseling or something because clearly I'm insane.

Have you not read your cards?

What a stupid question. Of course I'd read my cards! I'd spent hours poring over them, reviewing each suggestion that was written on them—

Oh.

Oh, Day Two *was* sexting.

Of course it was.

I immediately wanted to crawl under the conference table to

die. My neighbor-cum-lover was trying to engage me in a sexual encounter via my cellular device while I was sitting in a meeting and I was too stupid to notice.

Another buzz. *We can do this later.*

No!!!! I took a breath and pushed back from the table. "I'm so sorry, I need to step out for a moment."

Gary frowned. "Does anyone have any questions for Alyssa before she leaves?"

I smiled at the multitude of shaking heads. "Thank you. I'll catch up with the meeting minutes. Please feel free to e-mail me if anything comes up in the interim." And with that I bolted for the bathroom.

Nikki used to say that I was the worst liar in the world. It wasn't that I blushed or stammered. Apparently it was my eyes that gave it away. I kept my gaze averted and did my best to ignore the buzzing phone in my hand until I found my way to the ladies' room in the back of the building.

The stalls were all empty and I slipped into the farthest one from the door before I chanced another look at what Harrison was saying.

Alyssa? Are you there? Maybe this wasn't a good idea.

My fingers shook as I responded. I had to correct three typos before I managed to send my response. *Okay. I'm in the bathroom now.*

I'm going to stop.

Don't you dare! I left a meeting so we could do this. Now, what did you want to know?

There was a pause and I was scared I'd screwed things up before we'd even started. Harrison didn't strike me as an over-thinker. If anything, Nikki had hit it right on the head that he was a fixer of things. I had no doubt he was working out a plan on how to make this right.

I didn't need right. I needed to get through Day Two, and the only way that was going to happen was to engage in a little digital flirting. I sat down on the stall, pressed my elbows to my knees and leaned as I typed. *I'm wearing a black skirt and a sleeveless white shirt.*

There. A start at least.

Now to see where things were going to lead us.

Harrison's response came after a moment. I giggled without thinking.

How short is the skirt?

Short.

How short? Above your knees? Higher?

Right, like I'd ever wear anything like that to the office. This had nothing to do with reality and Harrison wouldn't care if I lied.

It stops three inches above my knees. You can see a generous amount of my thighs.

Are you wearing nylons?

No. It's too hot for them. I prefer bare legs anyway. I shaved this morning so my skin is nice and soft.

My imagination decided to join into the action. I closed my eyes and pictured Harrison in his hotel room, stretched out on the bed. His tie would be gone and the top three buttons of his dress shirt would be undone. I knew what his naked skin looked like, how much hair covered his chest, which only added to my mental image. The buzz of my phone had me staring at more words. A request.

I want you to place your hand on the inside of your knee.

It was arousing to have him tell me what to do without the pressure of him being here. I didn't have to comply, but it would prove far more interesting if I did. Holding my phone with my left hand, I awkwardly typed a response as I wrapped my cold fingers around the side of my knee.

Done.

Good. Rub your thumb over the skin. Nice and slow. I can imagine how it feels. How you smell.

Harrison's hands were far bigger than mine, but I did my best to picture it being him.

I've taken my shirt off. I have a hard-on thinking about what you're doing. You're such a bad girl, getting off at work.

Holy fuck. Seriously!

Spread your legs as far as your skirt will let you.

The cotton dug into my skin as I spread my legs. The skirt was in reality knee-length, giving me far less room to play than Harrison would assume. That will teach me to lie.

I want you to slide your hand along your inner thigh. Don't touch your pussy though. Drag your nails across your skin as you go.

I was hearing his voice in my head now. It was low, husky. He'd speak the words like he had after he'd come that night, an almost-growl that would vibrate deep in my chest.

My pussy was damp with need, and my nipples were hardening beneath my bra. I tickled my way along the sensitive skin, going oh-so close to my panties before sliding away. The tease was a seduction I hadn't experienced before. Not like this at any rate.

I want you to put your phone on your thigh. Touch your breast with your hand. Leave the nipple for now. Just squeeze the fleshy part like you know I would.

Biting my tongue to prevent myself from moaning, I somehow managed to do what he asked. This was so many kinds of wrong; I didn't know where to begin. I was teasing myself at work in the bathroom. Shit, there was a chance that I was going to come without him touching me. God, this was madness.

Slip your hand under your shirt. I want you to pinch your nipple now.

Oh, yes sir!

My brain stopped worrying about what was right and wrong and decided to go with the flow. Going from beneath, I pushed my hand under my bra and flicked my fingertip over the sensitive nub. I couldn't stop the sigh from coming this time. Nor did I keep my other hand from going too far beneath my skirt.

My nails grazed the wet cotton of my panties, sending a shiver through me.

That was when the bathroom door opened and the steady click of high heels filled the room.

Shit.

Why? Why now?

I want you to press your fingers against your pussy. Rub your clit.

Sorry, Harrison. That wasn't going to happen now. I grabbed my phone as I pulled my hand out from beneath my shirt. *Someone just came into the bathroom.* ☹

So.

So, I'm not doing anything else. They might hear. The woman in the other stall was now peeing. Wonderful. *We lost the moment.* ☹

You're calling a veto then?

Dude, she's peeing.

Yeah, that's a mood killer. Sorry.

Don't be. That was the most fun I've had in a while. I'll need the assistance of my vibrator when I get home. I needed to pick up a fresh set of batteries on my way. I'd worn the last set out already.

The real question is, do you consider this a successful Day Two?

Excellent question. Sure we'd sexted, but it didn't feel quite right. *Nobody came.*

That poses a problem.

Not really. While I might have a woman—doh, make that two women—in my space, he didn't. I grinned as I typed. *Do you still have your pants on?*

A pause. *Not anymore.*

The full extent of my experience with this sort of flirting had occurred in the past five minutes. Luckily for Harrison, I was a fast learner.☺

I want you to grab your cock through your underwear. Give it a good hard squeeze, but no stroking. He didn't respond, which I took as a good thing. *How hard are you?*

I could break concrete.

That must be uncomfortable.

You have no idea.

I think you should relieve some pressure then. Why don't you unbutton your shirt the rest of the way. Leave it on though.

Done.

Someone flushed the toilet, washed up, and left, but I still wasn't alone. This was turning out to be a serious lesson in self-control. *I want to see how fast you can come. Push your underwear down to your knees. Tell me when you're—*

Done.

—done. Fast. Okay, start stroking. Don't type, just read. The pressure was now on for me to make this good for him. Using my pirate porn as inspiration, I typed as quickly as I could manage.

I want you to picture me on my knees between your legs. I bet you didn't know that I love to give bjs, did you? I do. I love to lick up your shaft. I really love the taste of your arousal, that flavor that's only you. It's a bit bitter. Unique. I'd suck on your head a bit. Flick it with my tongue. Then I'd use my hands and tease your balls. I'd dig my nails into your thighs.

I bet you'd smell good. A bit sweaty from being in your suit all day traveling. I like that smell. Musky. You'd be close to coming. You put your hand on the back of my head. You want to control my actions, but I'm not letting you. I just keep sucking and licking. Your balls tighten in my hand. You're so close to coming. I pull back when I feel your body tighten. Your come splashes across my face, gets on my lips. I lick off what I can.

"Are you okay in there?" A woman's voice from outside my stall jerks me back to reality.

"Yeah, I'm fine."

"I heard panting. It sounded like you were going to be sick."

"No. No, I'm good. Thanks."

"Okay. If you're sure."

"Yup. Thanks again."

Dear God: I'd like to die now. Thanks. Sincerely, me.

I waited until the woman left and I was certain that I was alone once more before chancing another look down at my phone. Harrison hadn't responded to any of my texts. I tucked my hair behind my ear before typing. *Harrison?*

Still nothing. I stood on shaking legs, unlocked the stall door, and poked my head out. The coast was clear. I washed my hands and made it back to my cubicle before my phone buzzed.

Sorry. I had to take a shower after that. I got come in my hair thanks to you.

Sorry! I so wasn't sorry.

No you're not. But the sentiment is appreciated.

You're welcome. He'd come. It had actually worked. *I'm calling Day Two a success.*

Even if you didn't get to enjoy it?

Who says I didn't?? Twice now, I'd been able to make Harrison come without touching him. I was clearly already mastering this whole sex thing. Who needed cards! *Don't worry about me. I plan to have a repeat of Day One the minute I get home.*

I wish I could be there to witness it. Maybe when I get back.

Maybe. It will depend on what we need to do for Day Three. This was nice; easy banter with a man whom I liked. I'd missed the back and forth Rob and I used to have. The way we'd tease each other for hours before wrapping up in each other's arms.

The moment Rob flashed to mind, I lost some of the high I'd felt from the bathroom. This wasn't the same. Harrison had been clear from the start that his participation in these games was about the sex, about giving me a safe environment where I could explore. He wasn't interested in cuddling on the couch watching the evening news. *Do you watch the news?*

Random. No, I don't. I get what I need online.

Oh.

Alyssa, are you okay?

I'm good. I better get back to work.

I'll see you in a few days. I'm back in Toronto on Friday. Supper?

I typed *sure,* but quickly changed it. *I think I have plans. I'll let you know.*

Fair enough. Be well.

I didn't know how, but I was going to have to figure something out before he got back to town.

11

I needed a plan. Well, I always need a plan, regardless of what the situation was. That's been my thing ever since I was old enough to talk. I totally blame my mother. But if I was going to be successful with my thirty days sexventure, then I needed to approach this logically. I needed to make sure I had every angle considered to ensure we both got what we wanted. I took out a piece of paper and made a list.

Step one. Read all the cards.

Step two. Decide if there is something on said cards that I'm uncomfortable with.

Step three. ???

Step four. Have sex.

Well, it was a start.

Harrison had texted me a few times over the week, but we didn't have any repeat performances of Day Two. At first I'd been a little disappointed. Once I'd had time to think about what we'd done, I realized how much fun I'd actually had. Sexting at work might become a thing I do with a future boyfriend. If I ever got that far with someone. The longer we talked, the more I realized that he was giving me some breathing room. Which was great because I was putting more than enough pressure on myself.

Today he was coming home and I still hadn't figured out what my next step was. Instead of worrying about it, I got out my list and pushed my plan into high gear. The logical place was to start with step one. I placed each card on my kitchen table in neat rows, spreading them out so I could see the big picture.

That big picture was turning out to be a whole lot of interesting sex. Who knew Rob had such a creative imagination? As I reviewed the cards I made a list of any items I thought I might need to get through all thirty days. Lube (x4), box of condoms (x2??), a grapefruit (buy closer to the day), vibrator (use the purple one), latex gloves (he really took my suggestion that night seriously??), lingerie, a paddle (ask Nikki) . . .

Two sheets of paper later and I had my 30 Days survival kit list completed.

Yeah. So, this was going to prove interesting.

I tore through my closet in search of a gym bag that I'd be able to use to keep all of my implements of doom in one place. Some items I'd have to go shopping for, but there were a lot I could scrounge from my condo. All I had to do was find that old bag that I threw in here after signing up for the—

—there it was!

The bright neon logo from my rarely visited gym was buried beneath a giant garbage bag filled with old clothing. Both fell out when I pulled on the handle. I pushed the garbage bag to the side, determined to finally drop that puppy off at the donation bin down the street, and turned my attention toward my new sex survival kit.

I had a list and I had a bag. The only thing left to do was stock up and get prepped for Harrison's return.

By the time I heard the wheels of his suitcase roll past my door, I'd only managed to gather half of the items on my list. I'd intended to go out to the sex store to get a paddle and another two bottles of lube, but chickened out at the last minute. Still, I had enough from my shopping trip with Nikki to get us started. I did manage to walk into the pharmacy and pick up two packages of condoms. I apparently was having a blushing competition with the young boy behind the counter when he rang up my purchase. Thankfully, he'd mastered the art of not making eye contact and we both survived the encounter.

I waited until Harrison had passed my door before opening up to catch a glimpse of him. My breath caught at the sight of his disheveled appearance. His normally neat black hair looked as though he'd spent the better part of the day running his fingers through it. His dress shirt was still tucked in, but even from this distance I could see the deep wrinkles that had formed from sitting for long periods.

He looked like he needed a long hot shower and a good meal.

And possibly the opportunity to participate in Day Three.

Maybe.

"You're turning into a stalker." His voice echoed down the hallway. He looked over his shoulder at me and smiled.

"I didn't want to bug you. Just wanted to say hi." I stuck my hand out and gave him a little wave. "Hi."

"Hello." Without looking, he slipped the key into its lock and opened the door. "Did you have a good week?"

"I did." Feeling a little more confident, I shifted so I could lean against my doorjamb to look at him. "How were your meetings? Get your client sorted out?"

"Not completely, but I did avert a crisis." Using his foot he pushed his suitcase through the door before sauntering back toward me. "Nice to see you looking so happy."

"I'm in a good mood." As he got closer I was better able to see how tired he was. "You look wiped out."

"Yeah, it was a long week." He ran his hand along the back of his neck. "My only bright spots were talking to you."

Aww. My heart melted just a tiny bit. "Don't you want to know why I'm in a good mood?"

"Of course I do." He smiled, making the skin around his eyes crinkle. "Why?"

"I have a plan."

"Why don't I find that reassuring?"

"Because you're a smart man." Tucking my hair behind my ear, I took a chance, leaned in, and placed a kiss on his cheek. "Thanks for Day Two. It caught me off guard, but I've had a lot of fun replaying that in my mind."

Harrison reached up and braced his hand against the wall next to my head. His presence was as arousing as it was reassuring. "You were very good."

My heart pounded and I had to force myself to keep breathing at an even pace. "Thanks."

"I assume you've looked over the rest of the cards. That's where your plan came from?"

Even though he hadn't said it out loud, I knew he wanted to know if I was still good to move forward with our plan. I nodded once and tried to keep my lips from trembling when I smiled. "I've made a list."

He cocked an eyebrow. "Oh?"

"And a survival bag. Things that we'll need to complete the tasks laid out on the cards. I don't have everything yet, but we'll be good for the first little while."

"Good to know."

"I didn't know how busy you were going to be for the next little while. I didn't want to make any assumptions or anything, but I wanted to be ready to go just in case you had some time to fit me into your schedule in the next week or two—"

"Alyssa."

I swallowed hard. "Yes?"

"You're rambling."

"Sorry."

He tapped the end of my nose with his finger. "I'm in town for the next two weeks. Then I have to take another trip back to

Montreal. I'm sure we can fit a few of your cards into the schedule."

I shouldn't have been as excited as I was at the prospect of having sex with him, but I was. I might be a bit on the inexperienced side when it came to dating, but I did love having sex. Rob used to joke that it was our favorite hobby. Considering how often we ended up making love versus going out to the movies or doing anything else, it was totally believable.

"What just crossed through your mind?" Harrison was frowning and he'd pulled back slightly.

"Nothing. Just thinking about sex. I seem to do that a lot now."

"No, not sex. There was something else. Your expression changed."

Did it? I couldn't imaging thinking about Rob would be that obvious. Apparently I was wrong. "Rob."

"Ah." Harrison stepped back. "You let me know when you're ready to keep going. I'll be around. I need to have a shower and get cleaned up."

I should have said something to stop him from leaving, but the words were locked in my throat. It's not like Harrison didn't know about Rob. He'd been clear from the beginning that he didn't want anything but sex from this relationship. So why the hell was he acting this way?

And why did it bother me as much as it did?

12

When I'm trying to work out a problem, I tend to pace. It's my thing. After Harrison disappeared into his condo, I took to walking up and down the length of my hallway. I'd upset him by thinking about Rob. Not that I'd done it intentionally, but it didn't excuse the fact.

If I was going to move forward with Harrison and my 30 Days experiment, then as difficult as it might be, I was going to have to push all thoughts of Rob aside.

Easier said than done, but in the end, it was the only way I'd truly be able to move forward.

With my mind made up, I grabbed my sexvival kit and marched over to Harrison's condo. I knocked twice and waited for the inevitable thud of his approaching footfall. I didn't wait for him to invite me in, instead pushing my way into his place with a smile and an "I get it."

"Hello, Alyssa. Sure, come on in. Make yourself at home."

I kicked off my shoes and headed straight for his living room. "Really, dude? You still haven't unpacked."

"Been busy."

"I can help if you need it."

"No thanks. What's up?"

I set the gym bag on his coffee table. "I told you. I get it."

Harrison crossed his arms and stood with his legs hip width apart. "Get what?"

"Why I upset you earlier."

"I wasn't upset." He looked down at the floor and gave his head a shake. "I had a long week and I'm tired."

"Fine, you weren't *upset*. Miffed. Do men get miffed? Ticked? Annoyed? Whatever. Listen, I think we need to get this out into the open if we're going to continue."

Harrison smiled, but it was tight, practiced, the sort of one I imaged he showed his clients. "Get what out?"

The little speech that I'd hastily planned in my brain on the thirty-second walk over here evaporated. Guess I'd have to wing it. "I'm a thirty-five-year-old widow."

He jolted, but said nothing.

"Rob was my one and only. Or I'd assumed he was. I'm sorry if it makes you uncomfortable if I think about him every now and again. I don't mean to. I'm not comparing you or anything. It's just . . . he's my frame of reference. Before you, he was the only other man I'd ever touched. Been intimate with. My brain will go there whether I want it to or not."

I couldn't imagine what he was feeling. What we were doing was at the top of the list for weird. That said, he knew the score when we'd started.

"You're right." He nodded, though it appeared to be more in response to his own thoughts than anything I'd said. "Neither of us are in this for a relationship. It has nothing to do with me who you're thinking about. Like I said, it was a long week."

"Thanks." I fingered the handle on the gym bag. "How about we end it on a better note?"

"What do you have in mind?"

Reaching into the bag, I pulled out the pile of cards. I shifted the first two to the bottom of the pile, leaving Day Three on top. I tossed it on the table and on impulse added the Day Four card as well. Then I crossed my arms and mirrored Harrison's stance.

He cocked an eyebrow. "What?"

I nodded toward the cards. "That."

"You have two cards there."

I shot him a smirk. "What's the matter, can't handle it?"

Leaning forward, he peered at them. "We've done one of these."

"You said we had to do them in order. Touch a naked man is Day Three."

"Dry hump your partner is Day Four." Despite him trying to remain disinterested, I could tell by the front of his dress pants that I had his attention. "These seem counterintuitive."

"Well, you can get naked, and I'll stay in my underwear. That way we won't be tempted to cheat."

He seemed to consider that. "What else is in the bag?"

"I told you, things we might need for the other days. I just wanted to show you that I'd been—hey, leave that in there!"

"Got enough lube?" He chuckled as he sorted through the various containers. "I have condoms. You didn't need to buy them."

"I didn't want to assume. Plus it hardly seems fair to make you pay for anything. You're the one doing me the favor here, so thanks for that."

"Don't thank me." When his gaze met mine I took a step back. There was a hunger in his eyes that I'd never seen directed my way before. "I'm getting something out of this too."

Harrison dropped the package of condoms back into the bag and without breaking his gaze, started to unbutton his dress shirt. "I haven't showered."

"I don't care." The words came out in a rush. "I want to smell you."

His lips twitched into a smile. "Be careful what you wish for. This isn't the movies. I stink." The cotton fell to the floor with a soft *whoosh.* "You gonna just stand there?"

"Yup. I want to watch." He didn't need to know that I needed a minute to catch my breath and clear my mind. The last thing I wanted was any stray thoughts to ruin the moment.

Plus, it wasn't a chore to watch Harrison get naked.

With sure motions, he removed everything but his briefs. Back to where we'd started a few weeks ago, I waited in anticipation. It was strange how comfortable I'd gotten with the idea of another man's body. I already recognized the various dips and curves of his chest. The ripple of his abs and how the treasure trail of hair led down to the cock that I hoped I'd be able to see soon.

Harrison hooked his thumbs beneath the band of his briefs, caught my gaze one more time, and he pulled it down to his ankles. Once he straightened up, I gave myself a moment before I allowed my gaze to travel down the length of his body to the last piece that had remained hidden from me.

Wow.

That was . . . yes, that was in fact a nearly perfect cock.

"Alyssa, your mouth is open." He was totally laughing at me.

"This is only the second real-life penis I've seen. I'm savoring the moment."

He braced his hands on his hips, bracketing the object of my attention. "I'm getting the short end of the stick here."

"Huh? Was that a dick joke? Cause buddy, your stick isn't short."

"Day Four. Remember?"

Right! I had to dry hump this vision of male perfection. Oh, such a task. Guess I'll take one for the team.

Somewhere in the back of my brain I must have planned out how this moment was going to happen, because I thankfully hadn't put on a shirt with buttons. My hands were shaking madly and there would have been no way I'd have managed them. I grabbed the hem of my shirt and pulled it off, tossing it on top of his shirt. My shorts wanted to bring my panties with them, so a slight adjustment was necessary before I was able to fully face Harrison.

I wasn't sure if the look of desire he had on his face was a reflection of my own, but it certainly matched the lust that ran through me. This was going to happen.

"Sit on the couch." My voice had regained a little of my earlier confidence. "In the middle. Hands on the back so they're spread out. I don't want any barriers getting in my way."

The smile hadn't left his face. If anything, it seemed to brighten the sparkle in his eyes. "Yes, ma'am."

His cock stood at full attention as he settled into position. The head brushed against his thick hair that covered the lower part of his belly, leaving a bead of precome caught on a strand. He was easily bigger than . . . any other man I'd seen. Not porn-star huge, but still impressive. It helped that we'd actually done this before. That I'd run my hands across his skin, felt his muscles beneath my fingertips. My breasts ached and I wished he was already touching me. It would be easy to straddle his lap and let his cock slide inside me. He was clearly as aroused as I was, it would be fast and hard and dirty.

No, things needed to be done right.

I made my way over and stood between his legs. Harrison gripped the back of the couch, the force of his hold making the cords of muscles stand out on his forearms. Why that was turning me on was a bit of a mystery. His restraint, maybe? I sucked my bottom lip into my mouth and teased the flesh with the tip of my tongue. Blow jobs weren't on either card. Too bad.

"So?" He tilted his head to the side.

So indeed. I dropped to my knees and cupped his calves with my hands. "This time I'm going to start from the bottom and work my way up."

"Thanks for the warning." I was pleased that some of his cockiness had fled. "Avoid my sides or else you'll have a repeat of the other night."

"You said you work out, right?" I ran my hands down to his feet, massaging the muscles as I went. He had strong arches and hairy toes. I approved. It made him less perfect and more human. "You're a runner?"

"Yes." He forced the word out through gritted teeth as I rubbed my thumbs into his arches. "That tickles."

"As bad as your sides?" I would need to make a list at this rate. *Here there be tickles.* "Don't kick me."

"Don't linger."

Not willing to tempt fate, I changed directions and began back up across his calves to his thighs. I paid more attention to the firmness of his muscles as I went. I hadn't realized how much of a turn-on a nice pair of legs could be on a man; strength, a solid foundation, someone who worked hard.

The closer I got to his cock, the faster the blood pulsed beneath his skin. Oh, yes. He wasn't immune to my touch, to the way I would lean in and let my breath tease his skin while I alternated hard and soft caresses.

"Not yet," I whispered. "I want to take advantage of our time. I need to learn you."

Harrison growled, but didn't move.

Unlike before, I knew enough to avoid his sides. While that had been fun, tonight was about mutual orgasms. Instead, I focused my attention on his chest. His nipples were hard nubs peeking up through the thicket of hair. Rob hated when I went anywhere near his. Maybe Harrison wouldn't mind so much. I stuck out my tongue, giving him as much warning as I could as I lowered my mouth. Rather than pull away, he sucked in a mighty breath, and bucked his hips up against me.

"Fuck!"

"Want me to stop?" I kept licking.

"No."

"Good." I gently bit down. "You're fun."

"I'm a better ride than exhibit." He bucked his hips again.

I continued biting and licking my way across his chest and up to his neck. "No riding tonight. Lots more touching though."

"I was promised dry humping."

"Don't rush me. I might not get another chance at Day Three."

Harrison shifted and for a moment I thought he was going to throw me back onto the cushions the way he had before. Moving far faster than I would have ever given myself credit, I straddled his thighs and pushed his hands back down against the top of the couch. "Don't. Move."

Our mouths were now inches apart. It would have been easy to bend down and kiss him, long and slow the way I normally liked. But nothing about what we were doing had to do with normal seduction. This was about fucking; raw, pure sex and the mutual enjoyment that came from it. I didn't have to fall in love to enjoy Harrison's body. No, I was going to relish each of these experiences for exactly what they were.

I grabbed his face between my hands, letting my fingers rub hard against his stubble. His sweat mixed with his deodorant and the remnants of aftershave. I breathed it in deeply, doing my best to memorize it, burn it into my brain for later recall. His lips parted, revealing a flash of white hidden beneath. Yes, that was what I wanted. I kept my eyes open as long as I could, only closing them when I got close enough to suck hard on his bottom lip.

A rush of air tickled my cheek as he sucked in a breath. I didn't want him to speak. Not when I finally got my head to the place I wanted it to be. I bit down on his lip, eliciting a flinch from him. His hands found their way to my hips, but rather than pull me off, he encouraged me to move.

It took me a second to get the hang of grinding down on him while holding his face, but I managed to set a pace that had us both panting in no time. His cock might as well have been stone it was so hard against my pussy. The wet cotton stuck to my skin, increasing the friction and pressure on my clit. I moaned into his mouth before breathing in his breath.

"That's it." He squeezed my hips harder. "Fuck me. Rub off

until you come." There was no sweetness and light in his words, only raw desire.

Who was I to deny the man his request?

Placing my hands on his shoulders for leverage, I increased the pressure on his cock. I must have done something right because the next thing I knew his eyes rolled up and his lids squeezed shut.

"You like that," I whispered as I licked his ear.

"Yeah." His breath was hot against my neck.

"You gonna come?"

"Not yet. You first."

It wasn't going to take much prompting. This was the first time I'd been with a man since Rob, and while my pirates and vibrator certainly did the trick, they couldn't replace the mind-blowing need that being held by a man could induce. I gave up with seductions and teasing and instead pressed my face into the side of Harrison's neck and focused my attention on coming.

Sweat covered us, mixed together between our bodies as I rode him. My cotton panties were soaked with my desire and effort to get off. The fabric pulled tighter than before, creating the perfect pressure on my clit. I lifted my body up enough to force the side of his shaft against my clit. There it was! That sensation of bliss, and the promise of oblivion. I dug my nails into Harrison's shoulders as I ground down. Heat rose within me as my chest tightened and the muscles in my legs began to quiver. Almost there, reaching for the precipice . . .

"Shit!" I cried out against his skin as pleasure rolled through me. My breath came back in a gasp as I rode through the release, greedily wanting to squeeze out every ounce of bliss that I could.

It was only after my hearing came back to me that I heard Harrison chanting softly. "Yes, yes, yeah baby. Yes."

I didn't stop moving. My clit was oversensitive from my orgasm, but I didn't care. The small fissure of discomfort was worth the way his body came alive between my thighs. His hips bucked harder and his cock pressed farther up against my belly.

I pulled back just far enough so I could watch the red head poke up between us. The stark contrast of flushed skin against white cotton was the single most erotic thing I'd ever seen.

Harrison shifted his hands so they bracketed my ribcage. "Gonna come."

I was torn between watching his face and watching his cock. I chose the latter and held my breath as come shot from its head in long ribbons between us. The hot spunk smeared across our skin as we continued to rub together, binding us in a primal way. Finally, once I was certain there wasn't anything left in him, I stopped moving and collapsed against his chest.

For a long time there was nothing but our mutual breathing, coming out in a syncopated rhythm. I jumped slightly at the brush of his fingers along my skin, but relaxed into the feeling as he continued to stroke me.

"Day Four." He said the words with reverence.

"Don't forget Day Three. It was an important repeat performance."

"Yes, it was."

We fell silent again. It was strange how comfortable we'd grown together in such a short period of time. Maybe it was the sex. It had to be. It's not like I knew much about him, where he grew up, his favorite shows or music. Could people have a relationship borne simply from sex? Could it last?

Not that either of us wanted a relationship. Stupid sex-addled brain. But still.

"What's your favorite color?" I rolled my head so my chin pressed against his chest and I could see his eyes.

He glanced down at me, but the awkward angle had him look away. "Why?"

"Just curious. I don't really know much about you."

"Alyssa—"

"Don't worry, I'm not trying to trick you into dating me or something. Call me old-fashioned, but I want to know a bit about the man who I'm sleeping with."

"I'm not worried." He pressed a kiss to the top of my head. "Brown."

"Really?" Rob's favorite had been blue. "Why?"

"Does it matter?" There it was again, that odd note in his voice whenever things got personal.

I didn't want to ruin what we had going on, not when I'd just gotten my head in the game. I wanted to go through Rob's cards, learn more about myself and what I might enjoy when it came to sex. While I didn't need Harrison to do this, it was a lot less intimidating to have him with me.

"Sorry. No, it doesn't matter. Ignore me. My brain is misfiring from the amazing sex." When I pulled back, he didn't stop me. "That was awesome."

"It was."

"You still okay with helping me with this? I mean, we still have lots of cards to get through. I know you're pretty busy with work."

Harrison chuckled. "I'm sure I'll be able to fit you in."

"Good." Whatever cloud had descended upon us had blown over. "I better get dressed and go have a shower."

"I need one too." He patted his chest just above where the come had dried. "Good thing I hadn't showered earlier. You know, you could always stay and join me. Might be fun to get cleaned up together."

"I better not. I really should get back and get ready for bed." I pulled my shirt and shorts on while he watched. "Besides, we can't have a shower together."

"Why not?"

I poked the end of his nose with my finger. "Shower sex isn't until Day Sixteen."

This time when I left, the sound of his laughter followed me home.

13

Every condo in the building had a small plot of the roof garden set aside for our use. Most of the tenants took advantage of the space and planted what they could. Some loved flowers and would tend and grow the most beautiful perennials you could ever want. Mrs. Le Page focused her attention on vegetables, mostly tomatoes, and at the end of the summer would distribute the fruits of her labors to anyone who asked for some.

Me? I tried to grow flowers, but never quite remembered to water them. The garden had been another one of those chores that Rob and I had always tackled together. Neither of us excelled at it, but together we managed not to kill the few plants we had. When he died, I let things go for a while. It wasn't until Pierce actually threatened to revoke my privileges if I didn't make a better effort to mind my plants, that I forced myself to refocus my efforts. I wasn't going to lose my spot, one of my memory places, so here I was. I'd decided on a new approach and after taking Mrs. Le Page's advice, I planted vegetables.

As I knelt down in front of my plot, a long zucchini in my hands, I wondered if it was firm enough yet to use it as a dildo.

Yes, this is what my life had come to. I officially had sex on the brain.

Rob would be pleased. So would Nikki.

My current ponderings were the result of a Harrison drought. After our session Friday night, I hadn't seen much of him. I heard him come back from the gym Saturday morning when I finally rolled out of bed in search of coffee. I didn't hover near the front door in the hopes of seeing if he'd slow down. Or knock. *Fresh brewed coffee. Come on in!* I wasn't even disappointed when I heard his front door echo shut. He was MIA for the rest of the weekend and I eventually had to push my curiosity aside.

It was actually fine. I needed a few days to remember that I had a life that required my attention. Bills had to be paid, parents had to be called and reassured, matinees to attend alone. Zucchini to be fondled.

Naw, this one was way too big to be useful.

Maybe I should reconsider my moratorium on cucumbers.

The roof door squeaked open and new voices joined the gentle buzz of the city below. I might not be much of a gardener, but I did enjoy the sense of calm that being up here brought. I said hello to the new arrivals and went back to rescuing the fruits of my labor from their weedy prison.

I let out a squeal when a bag was unexpectedly dropped beside me. "The hell!"

Harrison stood a foot away, arms crossed and grinning. "You left this at my place."

The neon gym logo was the only reminder I needed as to the contents. "Shit."

"I wanted to get it back to you. Just in case you need it." He cocked an eyebrow. "You can never be too prepared."

I got to my knees and lifted the bag out of the way of my zucchini patch. "This is way heavier than I remember."

"I took the liberty of adding a few more items from your list."

Lord, help me. "This feels like more than a few."

He shrugged. "I needed to get out of the condo and wanted to explore Toronto a bit. The adventure did me good."

"Glad I could help." The zucchini was heavy in my hand. Instead of dropping it, I held it up. "Here."

"I didn't know you were a gardener." He took it and ran his hands along the verdant skin. "Nice specimen."

Dirty mind, dirty mind, dirty mind. "Thanks. I normally kill things, but this year I was more focused and this was the result."

Harrison came closer and dropped into a squat next to me. "You know you can pick the flowers, too. They're tasty in salads."

"Wait a second. You garden?"

"My dad does. He can grow just about anything. I picked a few things up over the years." Without me asking him to, Harrison reached down and began to weed.

This was . . . different.

We'd both been crystal clear about not wanting to get involved in a relationship. This was supposed to simply be about sex. And also apparently now zucchini. There wasn't anything else to do except go back to harvesting and weeding, so that's what I did. It was nice, working side-by-side with him, no expectations of anything else. I caught a hint of his aftershave, stronger than it had been the other night, but not so overpowering to make my eyes water.

"Aww, Mr. Kemp. How kind of you to lend Ms. Barrow a hand. That's very sweet."

I congratulated myself on not groaning at the sound of Mrs. Le Page's amused voice. I looked up to see her standing there, her arm linked with her husband's. They were so cute together it should be illegal. "He's giving me some pointers."

"Nothing better than a man with a green thumb. I find they're handier in more than one way." She patted her husband's hand. "Isn't that right, dear?"

"If you say so, love." He winked at me.

I turned around to face my plants. I didn't need mental pictures of what those two got up to behind closed doors. I had no doubt it was dirty.

"She's not a natural, but I bet she can be taught." Harrison nudged me with his shoulder. "I don't mind showing her a few things. At least when I leave I'll know the zucchini will survive."

"You're not staying?" The couple looked between each other before Mrs. Le Page continued. "But you just moved in."

"I'm only here on a short-term contract."

"You're not moving *now*, though." She looked at me with a frown. "Our poor Alyssa."

No. Not poor Alyssa. Please don't go there.

Harrison bumped his shoulder against mine. "No, ma'am. I'm here for three months."

"So lots of time to enjoy yourself. That's a good thing." Mr. Le Page gently toed the gym bag. "Gardening tools?"

I stood and shoved three of the largest zucchini I had into Mr. Le Page's chest. "Here, have some. I have more than I'll ever be able to eat and I'd totally take some baked goods in return."

Harrison chuckled. "Sounds like a good trade."

"Yes it does." Mrs. Le Page rescued the produce from her husband's precarious hold. "Thank you, dear. I haven't had a nice big one like this in years."

Fuck me. I bit the inside of my cheek to keep from laughing. "Happy to help."

Harrison had returned to weeding during this exchange. I saw him trying, and failing, to hold back a grin. He managed to keep his laughter in check until the elderly couple wandered away, their prize in hand.

"She knew exactly what she was saying, didn't she?" He pinched the bridge of his nose, his shoulders shaking with laughter. "What a pair."

"A few months ago someone used the gym for what Pierce is convinced was a weird sex game. I'm fairly certain it was the two of them. They've been far too smug ever since. They also giggle like kids whenever Pierce mentions it in one of the meetings." I reached for another bunch and carefully plucked the flowers from the vines. "I can only hope I'm that happy with someone when I'm that age. And still having sex."

"So you want to get married again someday?" He turned slightly away from me as he reached for one of the plants near the far side. "Won't that be hard?"

"Well, I hadn't really thought that far ahead. I mean . . . I don't know. I can't picture being with someone other than Rob, but I can't see myself alone either." The ache in my knees was getting to be too much. Ignoring the dirt, I sat down on the stones. "I know that doesn't make sense."

"No, it does. My dad was the same when my mom passed." He then got to his feet. "You have a lot of vegetables here. Are you going to eat all this?"

"Your mom died?" Okay, rude, but he'd caught me off guard. "I'm sorry."

"It was a long time ago." He bent down and captured two zucchini. "Mind if I take some?"

"Go ahead." Why did it feel as though we'd crossed some sort of line? Something threatened to change between us and I wasn't sure I liked it. "We should have sex."

"Mr. Kemp, I see you're trying to help Ms. Barrow. The condo association thanks you." Pierce came up the path, clipboard in hand. "I'm glad to see you're taking your garden seriously this year. Mr. Kemp, if you want to use the plot associated with your condo, I ask that you keep in mind not all of the occupants care for greenery. Make sure it's something easily maintainable."

A litany of curses flew through my mind. "Hi, Pierce. Zucchini?"

"Can't stand them. If you have more than you want, please remember not to let them rot. Place them in a basket on the communal table for others to have." He nodded and strolled away.

"I swear this building is Melrose Place," I muttered.

"Yeah." Harrison reached down and picked up the gym bag. My heart rate jumped up a notch as I watched him sling it over his shoulder. "Day Five, eh?"

I couldn't even remember what it was. My entire focus was on Harrison and the way his T-shirt stretched across his chest. My mind had been spinning for ages, trying to figure out where my life was headed. When I was with him, the only thing I needed to worry about was how long it would be until I would come.

Yeah, this was better. Nothing about family history, death, or produce. Just sex, pure and simple. I smiled, stood, and brushed the dirt off of my hands. "Your place or mine?"

14

It took until we reached my front door for me to make a decision as to where we would have our little rendezvous. If I kept walking, Harrison wouldn't even hesitate to open the front door and let me in. At some point I was going to have to invite him into my inner sanctum, in a manner of speaking. Day Five seemed as good a time as any.

I dug into my pocket and took out my key. "I don't remember if I actually cleaned my kitchen before I went upstairs."

He cocked his eyebrow. "I haven't unpacked in three moves."

"Good point."

My nerves began to chew at my insides as I opened the door and stepped through. "Well, here it is." I kicked my abandoned shoes closer to the closet. "Careful not to trip."

The thud of the gym bag landing on the floor sent a shiver of anticipation through me. "This place is exactly how I pictured it."

Looking around, I tried to see it through Harrison's eyes. Organized chaos was probably the best description. My laptop was on the coffee table beside an empty chip bag and my e-reader.

The pillows were still on the floor where I'd kicked them off, piled like a soft form of the game Jenga.

I ignored the mess and turned to face him. Harrison rested his hands on his hips as he looked the place over. The half smile that I was now associating with his amusement was fixed in place.

Clearing my throat, I shrugged when his gaze snapped to mine. "I'd apologize, but this is me."

"You're fine. And never apologize for who you are. If people don't like it, then you don't need them around."

The gym bag was on the floor between us. The cards were somewhere inside and on one of them, the plan for how we were about to spend the next several hours. At least I hoped it would be hours, because now that I had sex on the brain, I really wanted to take my time scratching that itch.

"I don't remember what Day Five is." There. That was out there now. "But unless it's something really strange, there won't be a veto on my part."

"There's still no penetration." He cocked an eyebrow as he nodded his chin toward the bag. "You won't want to add a second card."

"No?" That sounded like a dare. "Maybe I will. Maybe I'll throw in two cards just to test our limits."

"Day Five is for us to masturbate each other."

Oh.

Well.

I cleared my throat. "One card will do."

Harrison walked past the bag to stand in my living room. "Your call. We can get a blanket, stretch out on the floor. Or if you're comfortable, we can take things to the bedroom."

"The floor." The words were a reflex, something I didn't want to question. I was fine for him to be in my place, but I wasn't ready for Harrison to be in my bed. Not yet.

"Fine by me." He threw the pillows on the couch and gently lifted the coffee table and all of its contents to the side. "We can do a little prep work and then take our time. Might want to check the kit for anything we might need."

The task made it easier to get my mind back onto the path I wanted it to be on—sexy fun times with my hot neighbor. While Harrison rearranged my furniture, I dug through the additions he'd gathered. Water bottles, towels, a few porn DVDs . . . "Holy crap, more lube?"

"You didn't have any of the good stuff. And I picked up a good waterproof brand. For later."

"Day Sixteen," I muttered. "Any requests?"

"Use your imagination."

"You asked for it."

Lube (boring). Water (necessary). Silk scarf (interesting). Nipple clamps (hell no). Oooh, latex gloves—

"Those are for Day Seven."

Dammit.

In the end I decided to keep things simple: lube, water, and the towel. Having Harrison's hands on my body would most likely be all the stimulation I would need to have this whole mutual masturbation thing work.

By the time I'd brought my items over to him, Harrison had spread the blanket from the couch on the floor and arranged the pillows in a somewhat comfortable-looking fashion. "I have provisions."

"We should add a zucchini to that pile." He winked at me. "In case we get hungry."

I burst out laughing. "Thanks. Now I'm picturing the Le Pages upstairs molesting my produce."

"I suggest we leave them to their shenanigans." He plucked the towel from my hands and spread it out on top of the blanket. "And we get up to our own."

It didn't matter that this was technically Day Five, I got nervous when he reached out to touch me. Harrison was still my fantasy man. The make-believe prince who would swoop into my dreams to make love to me after I'd eradicated hunger and gained world peace. It didn't seem real to have him here in my living room, his fingers carding through my hair as he stepped in close to kiss my temple.

"I want to undress you." He spoke the words against the spot he'd just kissed. "I want to feel your skin against mine. Your breasts on my chest. I want to push my fingers into your pussy until they're wet from your come."

Christ!

He ran his fingers down the length of my spine, massaging the skin beneath my shirt. I could hear his heart thudding in his chest, or maybe that was mine. I couldn't tell for certain.

"Tell me that's what you want." He cupped my ass, squeezing as he pulled me closer. "That you want me to make you scream."

"Yes." I grabbed his biceps to hold myself upright. "I want that."

I didn't have to ask twice.

Harrison picked me up and carried me the short distance to the blanket. With a strength I didn't realize he had, he leaned forward and laid me gently on my back with my head resting on the closest pillow. He knew now that I liked watching him undress and moved with slow, deliberate motions as he took off his shirt and opened the fly on his jeans. He was already hard, his cock straining to escape its cotton prison.

Not content to be a passive observer, I reached down and made quick work of my own jeans and shoes. Next time it would be fun to get undressed at the same time, stripping off the same articles of clothing. I'd have to remember to add that to one of the cards. Or make up some ones of my own.

Sitting up, I held his gaze as I reached back and undid the clasp of my bra. I held the fabric in place for a moment before letting the cups slip free from my skin, the weight pulling it down my arms.

"Fucking beautiful." He stared at me, his gaze jumping from point to point across my body. His hands flexed at his sides, as though he wanted to reach out and touch me, hold me. I loved that he didn't. There was something strangely magical about the moment; the two of us here, mostly naked, staring at each other. I'd always felt the need to jump into action when faced with the prospect of sex. It was a reflex with Rob, to get right to it. Sex was that wonderful thing we did to pause the craziness of our lives. There was no reason to delay because we both had other things to do after.

The luxury of simply looking . . . if I'd only known how much of a turn-on that was, I would have taken more time to look at Rob before he'd gone.

"Alyssa," Harrison whispered.

I blinked, forced my gaze from the jut of his hipbone to his eyes. "Yeah?"

"Touch your breast."

I swallowed, my eyelids sliding closed for a lazy moment before I reached up and lifted the weight of my breast with my hand. If this was part of the mutual masturbation, then I was all for it. It was also an opportunity for me to show him exactly what I liked. Harrison might have more experience with various partners, but I wasn't a blushing virgin who didn't know what turned her on. If I wanted him to know my body, to know me, then it was up to me to act as his guide.

With the weight of my breast still in the palm of my hand, I shifted so I could tug my nipple with my forefinger and thumb. It was already hard and sensitive and it took little effort for that invisible road through my body to open up. That direct line of pleasure from my breasts to my clit pulsed with every flick of my fingers and caused my breath to quicken.

"Does that make you wet?" He reached down and squeezed his cock through his briefs. "I wish I had my hands on you right now."

"Nothing stopping you." I mirrored my actions with my

other hand on my free breast. "This is all about coming, after all."

"Not yet. I love watching you. Your expressions." He gave his cock a few strokes before letting his hand fall away. "I'm going to have to be careful."

"That's right. I get to be the one to pull the trigger." I pinched both my nipples hard. "I really like that."

"Have you been spanked before? Tied up? Anything kinky?"

"No. We talked about it sometimes, but Rob always seemed to like the idea more than putting it into practice."

"What about you? Do you like the idea or want to try?"

Picturing being on my hands and knees, Harrison behind me, his hand coming down hard on my ass, turned me on. "I want to try."

"Good. I look forward to introducing you to a few things." He moaned before dropping to his knees beside me and reaching for my panties. "I'm taking these off. I want to see how wet you are."

I let go of my breasts and helped him. When I was finally stripped free, I waved my hand around his groin. "Those too. I want to be able to play." He was a magician. Poof, they were gone. "Thanks."

"Anything for you, m'lady."

"Cute." I looked around and tried to figure out how best to complete the task at hand. "Side by side?"

"Yeah. Stretch out."

It took a moment to get into position. I shifted one of the pillows so I wouldn't get a cramp in my neck. It was wide enough that he was able to steal a corner as well, putting our faces inches apart. We didn't breach the invisible line that kept our bodies apart, though I knew it was only a matter of minutes before we would. Harrison was flushed and for the first time since we'd met, he looked unsettled. Patience was never my strong suit, the urge to slide my hands across his chest a temptation I didn't want to deny myself for long.

"One at a time?" I don't know why I'd whispered, but it suddenly felt necessary.

"Together." His breath tickled my nose and sent a shiver through me.

Harrison reached past me, allowing his forearm to brush against the top of my shoulder, and grabbed the bottle of lube. I held out my hand and waited for the cool, slick gel to fill my palm. It was clear and appeared to magnify my skin beneath. I should have waited for him, but I wanted to get my hands on his cock, wanted to feel its weight in my palm. Wrapping my fingers around his shaft drew another moan from him. He paused his own actions as I made a few tentative strokes.

"You have a very nice cock. Thick and veiny."

"You're the first person to say they like the veins."

"I'm a bit weird." I gave my hand a bit of a twist around his head before continuing down once more.

"I like weird." He chuckled and filled his own palm with lube. "Can you lie on your back a bit more?"

I did, though it made it awkward to stroke him. I might have protested, except he took his hand and covered my breasts with the lube. Now that was a sensation I wasn't expecting. His fingers slid across my skin, causing goose bumps to rise.

"Wow." I closed my eyes and enjoyed the uniqueness of the feeling.

He pinched my nipple, sending a surprised gasp from me. "You really do like that."

"I do. Maybe I'm a closet pain fiend."

"I'll be more than happy to help you figure that out."

"Good. Later." I spread my legs, letting my foot slip between his calves. "Touch me."

This time, he squeezed the lube directly onto my pussy. The gel was cool against my heated skin and clung to my pubic hair. The stark contrast of his warm fingers against the cool lube confused my body for a moment, not knowing what to think of the different sensations. He shifted so that he was now more on his side. The new position made it easier for me to stroke him.

"Yeah, exactly like that. You were doing it perfectly." Harrison nipped at my earlobe as he flicked my clit with his fingers. "I want to come on you. On your belly."

Hot spunk. Cold lube. Soft blanket. My mind spun trying to take in all the details. I was reduced to nothing but sensations, desires, and the need to orgasm. As much as I simply wanted to be passive and enjoy the moment, I had a task of my own to complete. The lube I'd been using had grown a bit tacky, and I wanted more to increase the feeling. Fumbling for the bottle, I squeezed way more than I should have onto his cock and balls.

Harrison opened his mouth, probably to make some sort of wisecrack, but I didn't want to hear it. I leaned in and captured his mouth in a kiss.

Despite all we'd done to this point, we hadn't really kissed yet. Sure there'd been the brushing of lips, little pecks to the cheek and temple, the sucking on lips, but not this. His mouth was hot, greedy once we'd begun. So was I, wanting to memorize the taste of him to go with the other sensations.

Once the kissing started, the touching began in earnest.

I stroked his cock with a steady, even rhythm. He matched my moves by slipping one finger into my pussy while using another to rub against my clit. The dual motion quickly amped up my desire to the point where I knew it wouldn't take long for me to come. I squeezed his cock and sucked on his lip at the same time, hoping I could telepathically make the images in my head appear in his. I wanted to swallow him down all the way until I could taste his come. I let my hand slide down lower so I could cup his balls, and scratched my nails across their sensitive skin.

"Can you add your other hand?" He spoke against my mouth. "I like having my balls played with. I'll come harder."

It was not the easiest thing to do, not with his hands between my legs. "You'll have to stop."

"It can wait then."

"No." I pushed him back, not even sorry for the loss of his touch. "You first."

I wasn't normally one to take what I wanted, but that was about to change. With Harrison now at my mercy, I gripped his cock in one hand and his balls in the other. I felt powerful and the most feminine of my life to have this confident, sexy man under my control. Determined to make him come as hard as I could, I fisted his cock as I played with his balls. The more he moaned, the bolder I grew. Reaching between his legs, I pressed my fingers to the bridge of skin behind his balls. Harrison bucked up hard into my hand as he squeezed the blanket in his fists.

"Fuck, yes!"

Before I realized what was happening, come shot from his cock and covered my hand, his pubic hair, and the lower part of his belly. Harrison's cries continued on until the last of the come fled his body and he collapsed back onto the floor. He didn't move for a long time and I couldn't help but wonder if I'd possibly broken him.

He licked his lips and finally peeked out at me from behind one lid. "I didn't get to come on you."

Laughing, I rubbed the come from my hands across my breasts to mix with the still-wet lube. "How's that?"

"It will do for now." Without asking, he pushed me back and slid his hand between my thighs. "Next."

"Next." I smiled and closed my eyes. "It's not going to take long."

He ran his fingers through the come-lube, pushing the mess across my nipples. He tried to pinch the skin, but the surface was now slick and he didn't get the same traction. He continued to try as he used his other hand on my pussy.

"You're so tight. I love your hair. I've been with women who'd shaved or waxed. I'd forgotten how nice it is to have hair there. It holds your smell. I want to lick your cunt, taste you, nip at your skin until you're begging me to fuck you."

I blindly grabbed at him, cementing my grip on his shoulder. "Do that. Do that now."

"No."

"Harrison."

"No. Not now. Another day."

Stupid. Fucking. Cards.

"I'll take my cock and push hard inside you." He took his finger and mimicked the action. "I'll start off nice and slow, just so I can hear all those delicious noises that you make. I'll want to take my time, but you're too fucking wild under me. I won't be able to hold back and I'll fuck you harder. Faster."

His thumb was pressed to my clit as he pumped his finger in and out of me. This was better than any dildo, better than any fantasy man from a movie. This was pure, raw desire. Hot sex between consenting adults, purely for pleasure.

"Yeah, that's it, baby," he cooed. "You're close now. I can feel your muscles trying to pull my fingers inside you. Come for me."

He pinched my nipple as he increased the pressure on my clit. "No. No, no, no." I didn't want things to end. Not yet. Not when I finally felt as though I was on the verge of coming back to life.

"Yes. Come for me, Lyssa."

The shock of hearing my nickname pushed me into orgasm. My eyes screwed shut as I came apart from the force of pleasure. I screamed, my body bowed off the floor as my muscles contracted. I wanted to stop it, enjoy it, soften it so I could be back in control of things. I couldn't. All I could manage was to ride the waves of pleasure until they finally, blessedly subsided and I slipped into unconsciousness.

* * *

Passing out after a powerful orgasm wasn't normally a thing I had to worry about. Rob had been a good and attentive lover, and I'd always been satisfied, but he'd never blown my socks off quite the way Harrison had. If I could describe it as anything, the best I could come up with was gobsmacked.

Harrison had gobsmacked me with sex.

When I realized I was alone on the floor, Harrison's shirt draped over me, I smiled. Taking a moment to breathe in the smell of his body, I closed my eyes and listened to see where he might have gone. I thought maybe he'd jumped into the shower, but I couldn't hear the hiss of water. Weird, but then again there was nothing exactly normal about our relationship. He could have easily walked half naked to his home and it would have made as much sense as getting cleaned up here.

The mental image of him scurrying naked down the hall had me smiling again. I could totally see him doing that and I couldn't help but love him a bit at the thought.

Whoa. No, not love. Where the hell did that come from?

Though I wasn't being honest with myself if I couldn't admit that I was starting to have *feelings* for him. It was only natural after all, considering the sex. But love? No. This was just sex. End of story.

Eventually, I got enough energy to push myself to a sitting position. I slipped my head through the hole and my arms into his sleeves, adjusting the hem until I was mostly covered. It wasn't until I stopped moving that I noticed Harrison sitting on a chair a few feet away.

"Hi." I smiled and brushed my hair from my eyes. "Why are you over there?"

"I was watching you sleep."

"Oh. That's sweet."

He nodded. "What do you want? From life?"

A normal person would have responded fairly quickly, but I

had to give my head a shake to make his words connect. "What do you mean?"

"You're a thirty-five-year-old widow who works as a technical writer. You're having sex with your neighbor so you can become more experienced and yet you seem terrified of moving forward. So I'm curious. What is it that you want?"

I immediately thought of that test they made you fill out in grade nine, to help you figure out what you wanted to be when you grew up. There was that weird sort of pressure that if you answered their questions the wrong way, you'd end up making a huge mistake and ruin your life. Harrison had the same look that my guidance counselor had when he slid the Scantron sheet in front of me.

You get one shot at this, Alyssa. Don't screw it up.

"I don't know." I got to my knees and tugged on his shirt to make sure I was mostly covered. "I haven't really thought about it."

"Fair enough." But it didn't seem to be the answer he was hoping for. "I better get home and cleaned up. I didn't want to leave until I knew you were awake and okay."

"Your shirt—"

"Keep it." He walked over and kissed the top of my head. "Though you might want to wash it now that it's covered in lube."

"I will. Harrison?"

He stopped moving and looked back at me.

"I know you're not looking for a relationship. I'm not either. But this has been good. You've been good for me."

The spark that had been missing from his eyes suddenly flared back to life. He gave me a smile and a nod before he left. I wrapped my arms around myself, holding his shirt closer and breathing in his scent. This was totally about sex. Yup. No way I was going to let myself fall for the first guy I hook up with after Rob, because that had *bad idea* written all over it.

Really bad.

Super bad.

Jumping to my feet, I made a mad dash for my phone and hit the speed dial for Nikki.

"Hey, hon. What's up?"

"Sister, we have a problem."

15

I'd already had a coffee and was working on my second one when Nikki finally blew into the shop. The telltale rush of caffeine pulsed through my body and made me think I totally had to pee. Which was weird, because normally I didn't react this way.

Nikki frowned before she even sat down. "You look like you're going to explode."

"I'm wired for sound." I stilled my hands even as I continued to bounce my leg. "Thanks for coming."

"You said there was a problem, so I'm here." She plopped into the chair, locking her fingers together on the table, and gave me her best professional smile. "What's up?"

So many things. "I took your advice."

Nikki straightened. "Crazy monkey-sex with hot neighbor?"

"Oh yeah."

"Excellent." She leaned in close. "Was it awesome?"

"I'm not going to give you details."

"Yes you are."

I leaned in, mirroring her. "We got naked and masturbated each other with copious amounts of lube."

"Messy," she said with a grin. "I approve."

"Of course you would."

"So what's the problem? It sounds like things are going well."

How the hell to tell her that was actually the issue? "I like him."

"I would hope so. Considering the monkey-sex."

"No. I mean . . . I mean I *like* him."

Nikki grinned. "Dear God, it's grade eight all over again. You *like* like a boy. My little sister is growing up."

"Don't be a bitch." I gave her hand a slap for good measure. "I'm not supposed to like him."

"Why not? Is that one of the rules?"

"It is, actually. Well, neither of us wants to have a relationship. He's been very clear about that and when he's leaving." Nikki lifted my hand and proceeded to examine it. "What are you doing?"

"Checking to see if you're a robot."

"Why?"

"Oh good, you're not." She let my hand fall to the table with a soft slap.

I rolled my eyes. "There's a point here. I can feel it."

"You just told me you were having great sex with a man who sounds charming and generous. You also told me you might have feelings for him, which I would consider normal. I just wanted to make sure you were still you. Because any normal person in your situation would form some sort of attachment. You can like him, even *like* like him, without it meaning you need to get married."

"I know." I downed the last half of my coffee, enjoying the slight burn as it went. "I do."

"Ah." Nikki sat back and tapped her fingers against the table. "You actually want this to lead somewhere."

"No I don't!" I put the empty cup down onto the table hard, the noise rising up to join the rumble of voices in the place. "Why would you say that?"

"Baby, you're on the rebound. An extended rebound years in the making, but a rebound nonetheless. You need to just enjoy this as a fling. Don't let your head get too wrapped up in things. That's it."

"I'm well aware, Nikki." The caffeine jitters were getting really bad now. I needed to get up and get moving or else I would wear a hole in the floor. "Can we walk?"

"No, I think we need to talk this out without distractions."

If only she knew. "Fine. I'm allowed to like Harrison, but not get involved beyond sex. Keep my emotions as far away from him as possible. I get that."

"Do you?" Nikki did that little half-frown thing of hers that told me she wasn't buying what I was selling. "How many boyfriends have you had again?"

"One." I knew where this was going. It was the same talk we'd had back when Rob had first proposed to me. "I am an adult. I do understand how relationships work even if my own experience is limited." The barista brushed past me on his way from the back room. I looked up in time to catch his wink as he went by. *The hell?*

"You know the intimate workings of one relationship. You and Rob. This thing with Harrison is good for you. But you owe it to both of you not to go too far too fast. Rob was right when he said you shouldn't hook up with the first guy you meet. The expiration date on this is a bonus. He'll be less likely to become attached. So will you."

It might be many things, but knowing Harrison was going to be gone in less than three months didn't feel like a bonus. "Maybe."

"It is. You can have fun and then move on. Once you're ready I can help get you set up on an online dating site. Or we can do some speed dating! I know you don't like the idea but it could be a lot of fun. Maybe even double-date a bit. There are lots of possibilities."

When I looked into my sister's eyes, I saw for the first time a strange mix of excitement and desperation. Our whole lives she'd never been able to settle down long-term with a partner. She'd gone from a string of boyfriends in high school to a string of husbands after graduating from York. In all that time I'd been with Rob. I knew she'd never wished anything bad to happen to him, but this was the first time that I realized she and I now had something in common—we were both single and looking.

Clearly, she was more excited about the prospect than I was.

"Yeah, lots of things we can do." I didn't want to troll for guys, which was the appeal of being with Harrison now. He was right there, sexy, single, and not afraid to hang out with me. But it was temporary, which meant I'd soon be joining my sister in the dating abyss.

"That's right we can." She leaned in closer once more. "And because I know you are clueless about these things, I wanted to tell you that the hot guy behind the counter has totally been checking you out this whole time." She squeezed my hand hard before I could turn around to look. "Don't do that."

"You just said—"

"You have so much to learn, young one."

A rush of energy made it impossible to sit still any longer. "I have to go."

"You are acting a bit more hyper than normal."

"I'd say someone spiked my coffee, but I haven't left it alone."

"Hey," the cute barista—Len, my regular guy—called out to me.

"Hi there." I smiled and my fingers shook as I tucked my hair behind my ear.

"Did you like your coffee?" There was eagerness in his eyes as he practically bounced from foot to foot.

"Yeah, it was good. Packed a punch."

"Awesome. I put an extra shot of espresso in both of them with a new flavor shot. I'm going to name it The Rocket."

I blinked. He was trying to OD me on caffeine. "The Rocket.

Yeah. That's accurate." I needed to go run a marathon. "I'll be sure to ask for it by name."

"I'm Len." He stuck out his hand, leaving me little choice but to shake it. "You've been coming in a lot recently."

"Yeah, I have. Nice to meet you, Len."

"Her name's Alyssa," Nikki provided from behind me. *I'm going to kill her.*

"Alyssa. A beautiful name for a beautiful lady." He winked again and let me go. "I'll see you tomorrow."

"Maybe." I turned and grabbed my purse in one speedy spin. I needed to get out of here. "Thanks, Nikki."

"Just trying to help."

I ignored her grin and took the long way home.

16

I should have earned a medal. After the super-lube rubdown on my floor with Harrison and my not-really-helpful chat with Nikki, I went a whole week without thinking about sex. Well, not thinking about my sex cards. Of course I thought about sex. I mean, pff, come on. Sex.

For the first time since this crazy ride began, I felt as though I was ready. I didn't have to let Harrison know that I was starting to have feelings for him. Nikki was right in that it was a perfectly natural reaction to become attached to the man I was screwing. He was only my second lover and was helping get me through a rough time in my life. I wouldn't have to do anything about it, as our relationship had a natural expiration date. One day we'd shake hands, maybe a kiss on the cheek and he'd be gone.

Poof.

So I'd come to the point in my mind where I would be able to enjoy things for what they were. And if I had a little cry when he eventually moved on, then there was speed dating and hot baristas once I got my emotions sorted. Which was good, because I really wanted to have sex.

Like, right the hell now.

Instead I went for a run.

I'm not an athlete by any stretch of the imagination, but I do enjoy the exhausted high that comes after I've been out on the roads for a good five miles or so. I'd started running when Rob got sick as a way to deal with stress. It also got me through the first six months after his death, a way to burn out my anger before it flared too bright. Finally, it became that thing I did whenever I found myself with too much energy. Halfway through my route, I realized that it was a distinct possibility that I'd substituted running for sex.

If someone had told me that was going to happen a few years ago, I would have laughed and laughed. And laughed.

It's actually quite entertaining to run in Toronto. I like to take the subway down to the lake and run along the shore. There are lots of people coming and going, especially in summer, making it a fun people watching adventure as well. When I didn't have time to head all the way down there, I'd simply run through my neighborhood, dodging the other pedestrians and their myriad of purses, backpacks, and purchases.

One of the more challenging routes took me past the gym. I really hadn't thought much about the place recently, not until I'd started using the free bag they'd given me for my sex kit. In fact, there was a chance that my membership might actually still be valid. I slowed down to a walk, taking in my sweaty appearance reflected in the window. Inside, the floor was filled with the after-work crowd. I recognized a few of the regulars from when I'd been going consistently, but most of the faces were strangers. I turned to go when I caught a glimpse of Harrison doing chin-ups on the bar near the front desk.

He worked out daily. This was the closest gym to our building. It made sense.

In the next moment I walked through the front doors into the air-conditioned room greeted by the scent of sweat, antiseptic, and metal. A young man who barely looked to be in his twenties was behind the desk. His biceps bulged out from the fitted cuffs of the crew shirt he wore.

"Hi there, welcome. Are you a member?"

"Hi"—I leaned in to read his name tag—"Brandon. Umm, I had a membership awhile ago, but I don't actually remember when it expired. Is there a way you can check?"

"Sure can. If you don't have your gym card, just give me your details and I'll look you up."

I was only half-paying attention to him and his questions. I took the time to catch glimpses of Harrison from the corner of my eye. It didn't take me long to realize that I wasn't the only woman who was fascinated with his routine. He'd switched from doing chin-ups to push-ups, the muscles in his back and shoulders visible through his sweat-soaked shirt.

"Here you are. Alyssa Barrow. Yup, you actually have a month and a half left on your current contract. Want me to get you another membership card?"

Harrison got up when a young brunette came over, smiled, and indicated that she wanted to use the chin-up bar. I watched as she made an attempt, falling to the ground without managing a single one. She then shyly smiled at him, giving a little shrug. *Subtle as a sledgehammer, lady.* I anxiously waited for him to give her the brush-off, to see her disappointment as she wandered back to the yoga room, or wherever she'd come from.

Instead, I was treated to Harrison motioning for her to try again, him taking her around the waist and lifting her up as she did five chin-ups.

"Ms. Barrow?" Brandon looked more than a little terrified when I glanced back his way. "Is everything okay?"

"Oh yeah, it's fine. Just saw an old friend. He's too busy to talk though."

I must have spoken far louder than I'd realized because as Harrison helped the woman down, he looked my way. His expression of shock would have been amusing if it weren't for the brunette taking that moment to place a kiss to his cheek.

"You jerk." More than a few people, including the woman, looked my way.

"Alyssa?" Leaving the woman without a backward glance, he closed the distance between us with only a few strides. "What are you doing here?"

"I was running by and wanted to check on my membership status. I wasn't following you, if that's what you think." I didn't give him a chance to answer, snatched my card from Brandon's hand. "Thank you. I'll have to see about renewing at a later time." Then I bolted.

Why the hell had I stopped my run? I might not have any claims on his time or affections, but I didn't need to have his flirtations thrown in my face either.

"Alyssa, wait!"

I should have known he would be able to catch up to me with my run. Damn long legs and athletic body. "What do you want?"

"Stop so we can talk."

"Nothing to talk about." He kept pace with me long enough that I knew he wasn't going to leave me alone. I growled, making my displeasure clear as I slowed to a walk. "Happy?"

"No."

It was then that I realized that his workout attire was even sexier close up and covered in sweat than it had any business being. Thankfully, I was too annoyed at myself to give in to any unsightly temptations, like licking the sweat off his neck.

For his part, he seemed just as fascinated with my outfit as I was with his. "I wasn't expecting to see you."

"I gathered. And like I said, I wasn't following you. I've had a membership at that place for three years now." It didn't matter that I never went. I'd paid!

"I never thought you were." He braced his hands on his hips as he stepped into my personal space. "I wasn't leading that woman on."

"No, you were just helping her with her chin-ups. Because

that happens every single day at the gym. Random guy. Cute girl. Chin-ups."

"Lyssa."

I cringed. "Don't call me that. My name is Alyssa. I'm worth the extra syllable."

"You're right."

Then we just stood there in the middle of the sidewalk staring at each other as the crowd moved around us. It was clear that Harrison didn't know what to say, which I imagined was a new experience for him. Strangely, I didn't have the same issue.

Enjoying the slight widening of his gaze, I stepped in so my breasts were flat against his chest. "Damn straight I'm right. I'm worth more than just your passing fancy. We had an agreement, and while I don't have any claims on you romantically, I don't want to be sharing you with every gym bunny out there. Otherwise, those blood tests we did were pointless."

"I haven't been with anyone else."

I held up my finger, silencing him. "Fine, but if we're going to continue this, then I'm the one calling the shots. I'm adding to our list of rules. Addendum number one is no other women. If you want to walk away, then fine. Go. I can find someone else to help me." I made a shooing motion.

That brought a smile to his face. "Why would I want to go anywhere? We have cards to complete. I accept your addendum."

"Good." I stepped back and crossed my arms in the hopes of hiding my now erect nipples.

"Any other changes?" He'd stepped closer as a group moved past him.

"Not yet." I looked away, embarrassed and excited by my reactions. "I want you to come to my place tonight."

"I can do that." Bastard was starting to sound more than a little smug. I wasn't sure I liked that.

"And bring a sports drink or something because I plan to get my fill of you. I want to do two, maybe three cards. More if I'm in the mood." I risked showing a nipple to poke my finger into his chest. "Got it?"

"Yes ma'am." He leaned in and nipped my earlobe. "I won't let you down."

"You better not." Before I made a complete ass of myself, I took off running at a pace that didn't look as though I was running away from him. Simply running.

The moment I turned the corner and made sure that he wasn't following, I burst into laughter. I didn't really understand what I'd just done, but I was going with it. Harrison was coming to my place for sex. I was in the driver's seat and for once wasn't freaked about the prospect.

I was in such a good mood, I kept on running.

17

It is a terrible thing to feel every muscle in one's ass. My body needed to remind me that I wasn't a marathon runner, or even all that in shape, so the next time I felt the need to run like the wind I wouldn't be such a dork.

Idiot.

I'd taken an extra-long shower after limping my way up the stairs of the building to my condo. The hallways were empty, which meant I didn't have to share my lack of athletic prowess with anyone else. Shit, Harrison was supposed to be coming over sometime tonight for a round of marathon sex. Because I had to be all *I'm the woman and you'll fuck me when I want* instead of a rational human being.

Double idiot.

Once I'd emerged from the steam like some strange angelic drowned rat, I pulled on a sundress, leaving my bra and panties off. Sure, it wasn't exactly date clothing, but then again this wasn't a date. It was a booty call. He was my fuck buddy. A hookup. Friends with benefits. If we actually considered each other friends.

It would have been nice if we really were—friends, that is. I missed having a guy pal of my own. It wasn't as though my married buddies were going to ditch their wives to come hang with me or go to an action movie. I could always go with some of the girls, but it was different. I was allowed to be different around men, something I hadn't realized before now. I was more relaxed, could be a bit more of a dork and not worry about what others thought. Guys were more what-you-see-is-what-you-get than women. At least the women I tended to hang out with. I missed that.

When the knock came thirty minutes later, I realized I'd been standing in front of my DVD collection fingering my Jason Statham collection. I wondered if I could substitute one of those movies for my pirate porn. *Worth a shot.*

"Just a second!" I touched my breasts and hoped that the dress didn't reveal my nipples too much. I mean there was such a thing as being too anxious. "Harrison, I'm glad you were able to make—" I opened my door and stopped when I realized who was standing there. "Pierce. I'm sorry, I wasn't expecting you."

Thankfully, he kept his gaze locked onto my eyes. Shit, I was never going braless ever, ever again. Ever!

"Ms. Barrow." He shoved a flyer at me. "Here's the home-owner newsletter for August. The board has a review of our updated bylaws that you'll need to take a look at."

"Thanks." I pressed the sheet to my chest. "Bylaws."

"I know you're not one of our more active members, but do please try to read them over. It will save you on fines."

"Yeah, I'll do that."

He made a humming noise. "I'll leave you to get ready for your date."

"It's not a date." I snapped my mouth shut, not entirely certain why I felt the need to correct him.

"Oh?" He raised his eyebrow and gave me a once over. "If you say so."

"Well, yes. I do." I couldn't keep staring at him. "I mean, yeah, I guess it could be a date depending on what definition you were using. But it's not anything that serious though. It's just like . . . you know . . ."

"Sex?" His lips threatened to twist into a smile. "I am aware of what sex is, Ms. Barrow. I've even been known to have it on occasion."

God, I wanted to die. "I didn't think you didn't."

"It's good for you to get out. Rob wouldn't want you to be alone." He nodded and walked away.

Did Pierce just give me permission to have sex? That was . . . strange? Yes, *strange* was the right word. Probably best if I didn't dwell on that. I peeked out my door to see if there was any sign of Harrison. Pierce's footsteps echoed down the hall as he went on his way to visit the other tenants. That was currently the only sign of life.

The moment I shut the door my phone buzzed. I ran over to the counter and started to laugh when I saw the message. *Is he gone?*

Oh, Harrison. *Chicken.*

No.

Yes.

He makes me feel like I'm a teenager in trouble.

That's giving yourself a lot of credit.

Don't start.

Just get over here.

Yes, ma'am.

Hot damn, he was coming. I made sure my front door was unlocked before racing over to the couch. I leaned against the cushions, draping my hand along the back. That felt awkward, so I shifted so my legs were stretched out on the couch and I braced my chin against my hand. No, that was too casual. I sat up straight and crossed my legs, which pulled my skirt up past my knees. Too eager.

The second I heard my door open, I got to my feet, no longer able to sit. Harrison came in, a smile on his face and a bottle of wine in his hand. "Hey."

He also looked freshly showered—good thing shower sex wasn't on the agenda—his black hair still damp and slicked back. He'd put on jeans and a button-up shirt. Either he wasn't big on T-shirts, or he wanted to treat our encounters as something special. I wasn't going to argue. I liked the look on him.

"Hey. Let me get some glasses." I wasn't stalling at all. He'd brought wine and I was only being a good hostess.

"Consider this apology wine. For the chin-up girl."

I shouldn't have been happy that he didn't know her name, but I was. "I'm sorry too. I totally overreacted."

"Maybe a little bit, but you were right. It wasn't fair to anyone. We have an agreement." He came over, set the wine bottle down, and took my hand in his. "I made you a deal and I have every intention of sticking to it. No other women."

My skin came alive as he began to stroke the inside of my wrist with his thumb. It was one of my erogenous zones, one that never failed to get me going. It was hypnotic to see his thumb moving across the pale skin, slowly back and forth. The scent of his shampoo and the warmth rolling off his body relaxed me as much as it aroused.

"So." His voice was a low rumble that seemed to penetrate every cell in me. "What did you have in mind?"

For once, I'd had the foresight to prepare for things ahead of time. "On the table. I'll pour us some wine."

It was a pretty ambitious list of things I'd hoped to accomplish in one night. But given how things had changed between us today, I wasn't about to back down. This might have started out as Rob's sex list for me, but I'd claimed it as my own. Now it was time to prove to myself once and for all that I was ready to move beyond Rob to someone or something new.

"This is quite the list." Harrison had picked up the cards and was reviewing them. "I'm glad I brought wine."

"It will work well with that first one."

"Give a massage with masks." He frowned. "Why masks?"

"Rob had a thing for them. Said it gave me a chance to pretend he was someone else. Fuel for my fantasies."

He made a face at the objects in question on the table. "Is that a Zorro mask?"

"It's all I could find at the sex store. Well, unless you wanted full-on bondage headgear, which, yeah no, not ready for that."

"I'd rather be Zorro, thanks. What's yours?"

The green sparkly mask had been one I'd picked up when Rob and I had spent a week in New Orleans. The time was more than a little fuzzy, but I do remember lots of food and booze and something about getting a lot of beads. Rob wouldn't let me wear a bra for almost a week when we'd gotten back. "Mardi Gras 2006. Good times." I filled our wineglasses and joined him.

He held my mask as he took the wineglass from me. "You've done a lot of planning."

"I have." Well, I'd had a lot of fantasies starring him over the past few weeks. That constituted planning, didn't it?

"So you know where you want our little encounter to take place?"

Unlike some people, I knew Harrison wasn't angling for a particular outcome. There was no doubt that I was in control of how things were going down. If I'd said *yeah baby, I rented a hotel room* then he'd be good for that. It was one of the things I appreciated about him.

My little condo held a lot of memories for me. It was my haven, my little world that had only ever been inhabited by me and Rob. I knew there would come a time when I'd have to have another man here if I was going to truly move forward.

Ignoring my pounding heart, I took a sip of wine and counted to three in my head before looking up at Harrison. "Well, my bed is a lot more comfortable than the living room floor. I even have fresh sheets on it right now."

"Fresh sheets." He hummed. "That's a temptation for sure." I held still as he set down his glass. "Then we better get ready."

The mask was cold as he pressed it to my face. I held it still as he tied it in place, my body responding to his nearness. The eyeholes weren't very big, making it difficult to see all of him. Which was the point if I stopped to think about it. A safe form of mystery and all that.

"Let's take this someplace more comfortable." Abandoning my glass, I took him by the hand and led him to the bedroom.

It wasn't as difficult as I had assumed it would be, bringing another man into my inner sanctum. I didn't even hesitate as we crossed the threshold. Though I did pause before leading him to the side of my bed to see it through his eyes. I hoped he liked it. "Here we are."

Rather than immediately jump me, Harrison stood still, looking around. I don't know what he was looking for; it was a pretty typical room. I had several black-and-white nature pictures that I'd picked up over the years, framed and strategically placed on the walls. They nicely balanced against the moss green walls and cream trim. It was quite large for a master bedroom. The far wall was lined with bookshelves, each one filled with some of my favorite books and lined with knickknacks.

"Funny, this is how I pictured it." It wasn't surprise in his voice as much as awe. "Not too frilly. Classic."

He thought of me as classic? I was happy to have the mask on, because I knew I was blushing. "Thanks."

"No, thank you. I know this is a big deal." He placed a kiss on the inside of my wrist.

If he was trying to win me over, then he was doing an excellent job. "If it had to be anyone, I'm glad it was you."

"Now then, I think I need to get ready." He let go of my hand and lifted the silk mask to his face. "We have a lot to do tonight."

Looking down to the items resting on the foot of my bed, I smiled.

"Time to get going."

18

In my mind, here's how I'd imagined things going: I'd give him a lap dance, he'd give me a massage, he'd spank my ass a bit, and I'd finish things off by jerking him off with a latex glove. Not a typical Tuesday evening, but certainly one for the memory banks. The masks had been intended only for the massage, but now that they were on there seemed little point in removing them. We knew who each other was, after all; it was more for the game than any air of mystery.

Those were all good things. It was a good plan! The one itty-bitty tiny detail I hadn't taken into account during all of my spontaneous planning was the one thing I should have.

Harrison.

Damn man had a mind of his own.

"I think you need to sit down here." He guided me so I was on the edge of the bed. "And lie back."

"But the cards—"

"I'm following the cards."

I'd learned by now not to question Harrison's intentions. If there was one thing that was clear, it was that the man knew and enjoyed sex. I could trust him to make things good for both of us. I'd been wearing my slip-on shoes, which made it easy for him to pull them off, dropping them to the floor. His hands were warm and once again I marveled at how large they were against my body.

He cupped my ankles with his palms, gently massaging my feet and between my toes. It tickled for a moment, but the longer he continued on, the more I relaxed.

"That's nice." I sounded slightly drunk. "You're going to spoil me."

"Just doing what I've been told." Then he winked as he slid his hands up my legs to my calves. "This would be better with massage oil."

"There's some in the bathroom. It's in the medicine cabinet."

"Don't move." He set my foot down on the bed, leaving my knee bent. The angle had my dress slip down, exposing my bare pussy to him.

"Fuck," he muttered, pointing at me. "Soon."

I giggled as he strode to the en suite. "On the top shelf. It's vanilla, I think."

"Found it."

His grin deepened the crinkles at the corners of his eyes. I liked that look on him. It gave his face character, depth. Harrison squirted a generous amount of the oil into his palm and I was immediately graced with the scent of vanilla. He rubbed his hands together, coating every digit before picking my foot up once more and returning to the task of giving me a massage.

The oil allowed his fingers to dig into the knots of my muscles, easing his way as he moved up my legs. He seduced me with gentle strokes, careful touches that felt as though he were trying to learn my soul through my skin. Tingles moved up my inner thighs until my pussy was hyperaware of his every caress. My body tried to fight against the temptation to relax, wanting instead to dive headfirst into the pool of pleasure until I was begging for release.

Harrison was having none of it. He moved with slow,

deliberate motions until he reached my thighs. Careful to avoid my pussy, he continued to knead my skin. I was a mewling mess, two parts horny, one part relaxed.

"I think you should roll over." He was already guiding me before I could protest. "Let me get the back of your legs."

The act of turning pulled my dress even higher. The air from the room kissed the bottom of my ass. As I squirmed, my thighs put added pressure on my pussy.

"No coming." He spanked my ass with an open palm.

I yelped. "The fuck?"

"It was on the list."

I looked up at him over my shoulder. "Fine, but a little warning next time."

He shrugged. "Lie down or I might have to spank you again, sooner than later."

This was so not how I'd imagined tonight going.

Harrison returned to my feet and began the process of rubbing up my legs once more. This time he took the time to spread my legs, leaving my ass and pussy visible. The next smack on my ass wasn't as hard as the first time. The skin stung for a moment before it melted into a pleasant burn. More oil on my skin, the massage continuing along the outside of my thighs.

I twitched when he hit a sore spot. "I ran way too long."

"I can tell. Your knots have knots."

Then he spanked me again.

"You're a bastard." I wanted to cover my ass with my hands to stop any further attacks, but couldn't bring myself to move when he returned to the massage. "Ruining a perfectly good massage with all that smacking and stuff."

He squeezed my ass cheeks with his hands. "I'm simply doing what I'm told."

"I know you are. Let's cross that one off the list then."

"Vetoed?"

"Apparently I'm not into spanking."

Harrison dipped his hand between my thighs and ran his finger up the length of my pussy collecting the moisture. "Could've fooled me." He circled my clit before rolling his knuckles against it. "I bet we could get you to like it. Start you off slow, some light spanks." He moved his hand again, demonstrated what he meant by lightly tapping my skin. "Then I could go a bit harder, faster." *Slap.* "I could have you on all fours so I could reach through and pinch your nipples."

I pressed my face to the mattress and groaned.

"Yeah, I can tell you're not into this at all." Another spank, this time sharper, more biting. The stinging aftermath faded away quickly, leaving a deep heat in place of the pain. It began to spread down to my pussy, heating me from the inside out.

I was going to freaking come. "Harrison . . ."

"Soon." He went back to massaging my ass.

No, I was just starting to enjoy that!

Stupid man.

I began to lose track of time, lost on a sea of sensations as he continued to touch me. God, I still had my dress on and hadn't come yet and I was probably the most sexually satisfied I'd ever been in my life. When he rolled me over once more onto my back, my mask was knocked askew. I adjusted it, only to see that he'd stepped away.

"Where are you going?"

"Nowhere."

Then the craziest thing happened. He started to sway his hips.

I was staring openmouthed at him as he reached up and began to unbutton his shirt, one by one. I'd actually chosen a few songs that I'd intended to use when I gave him his lap dance, and had them cued up on my MP3 player. Watching Harrison gently buck and roll to a silent beat, his gaze locked onto mine, was far sexier than any music I could have played. More intimate and erotic than any seduction I could have manufactured.

Pushing myself onto my forearms, I kept my legs splayed open as he continued to strip for me. Inch by inch his chest was revealed, until he let the cotton slip down his arms to catch at his hands. The shirt hugged his hips, framing his stomach and groin briefly before it fell to the floor.

"I thought this was supposed to be a lap dance." I'd intended to say it teasingly, but it came out more of a desperate plea.

"I'm warming up." As if to prove his point, he stepped closer so his knees bracketed one of mine. "I'm a novice at this."

"You're killing it." He was killing *me* with the way he'd roll his hips, thrusting his obvious erection toward me.

It should have been ridiculous, me on the bed with him doing this weird, twitchy-swaying thing to no music. It wasn't. I loved it. It made my heart melt, made it wander dangerously close to the space between *like* liking him and possibly falling in love.

I held my breath when he braced his hands on the bed and lowered his groin to my thigh. In a move that I could only imagine he'd witnessed at a strip club, he rubbed his cloth-covered cock against my leg. My pussy fully appreciated the move, pulsing with the need to touch and be touched.

"That's hot," I whispered. "More."

Clearly showing off how much time he spent at the gym, Harrison held the squat while he reached up and opened up his belt and pulled down the fly of his pants. The black briefs were in full sight, as was the press of his erection. He ground down again on my thigh, pressing his shaft against me.

"We might not get to that other card." Feeling bold, I reached up and lightly held his waist. "We can always forget it and move on to sex."

"What we've been doing is sex." He took my hands and pulled them up along his chest as he straightened his legs.

"It's mostly sex. I want this"—I grabbed his cock through his briefs—"inside me."

Harrison groaned. "Not until Day Eleven."

I'd never been so anxious for a day in my life. "That means I need to jerk you off with the gloves."

There was a happy haze that filled his gaze. "No reason I can't do the same for you."

Oh, now that was a very excellent idea. "Deal."

"You first." He gently pushed me back against the bed. The glove that I'd laid out on the mattress had fallen to the floor. Harrison picked it up and slid it onto his large hand as best he could. I'd picked up a box of gloves from the pharmacy. They were similar to the ones found in the doctor's office, soft. "It's not a great fit."

"I don't think I'll mind." I spread my legs and hiked my dress up the rest of the way. "Shall we?"

He grinned before climbing onto the bed beside me. "Just relax and enjoy. This might feel a bit strange."

What it felt like was cold. The fingertips were textured and skipped across my moist skin. There wasn't a lot of warmth in his touch, despite the intimacy of where he was caressing. It was weird yet thrilling, this stranger's touch. The novelty alone would have pushed me to orgasm.

Harrison took things one step further. He squirted a generous amount of lube across the latex, before he pushed a covered finger into my pussy as he bent his face to my breast and began to lick at my nipple through the fabric. My hips bowed off the bed as I met the thrust of his fingers and tried to escape the wickedness of his mouth. I felt more than heard him laugh as I began to buck my hips in time with his fingers. He sucked on my nipple, the wet fabric bunching up and sticking to the skin. His saliva cooled everything, making my nipple peak even harder than normal.

For once, it didn't seem as though he was trying to drag things out. He set a firm and steady rhythm that had my pussy clenching around his finger in no time.

"That's it." He sucked on my breast. "I want you to scream. Come for me, baby."

My eyes squeezed shut so hard I saw red. I went rigid as I

cried out, my orgasm slamming into me where it was almost too much to handle. Wave after wave rippled through me until it finally dissipated, leaving me behind in a quivering mess.

Harrison kissed his way up my body until he was looking down into my eyes. *Smug bastard.*

"You look happy." He pushed my hair from my cheek.

"Mmm. Can't imagine why." I placed my open palm against his chest. "This wasn't how I'd planned things."

"They turned out okay."

"You haven't come yet."

He cocked an eyebrow. "Yet."

I shoved him until he fell flat on his back. "Give me that glove."

The glove was damp on the inside from his sweat and the outside from my come. I knew it wouldn't be enough to make things pleasant for him. I grabbed the bottle of massage oil and poured enough onto the glove to ensure it would be slick enough to do the job. Putting on a bit of a show, I ignored Harrison and began to talk to his cock. As one does.

"Well now, what do we have here?" With my glove-free hand, I pulled down the front of his briefs. "That looks a lot like a very nice cock."

"If I could assist, I can get rid of these extra bits of clothing."

"Hurry please. You're interrupting our quality time."

"Our?" He raised his hips and pulled off his pants and briefs with one smooth motion.

"Me and your penis."

"You're crazy." But he still laughed. "Sorry for the delay."

"Thank you. Now, where was I. Oh yes, right about here."

With a sure grip, I took his cock in my hand and squeezed. I couldn't feel his skin through the latex, but I knew the sensations that were running through him as I began to stroke. The oil on the glove made weird squeaking noises as I began to pump him. Harrison threw one arm across his eyes while his other hand fisted my quilt. "That's . . . interesting."

"I know, right?" I picked up the pace. "I wish I'd grabbed the second one. I could play with your balls with it. I guess I'll have to settle for this."

With my free hand, I tugged on his sack, tickling the skin with my nails. The dual assault drew a thrusting of his hips in response. That was exactly what I'd been hoping for. There was one final thing I wanted to do, something that I'd been dreaming about since we'd started our games.

As carefully as I could so I wouldn't alert him of what I was about to do, I shifted forward and took his cock in my mouth.

"Fuck!" He thrust up hard and I barely pulled back fast enough to stop from choking on him. "Sorry."

I assaulted the tip of his cock with my tongue. It tasted of oil, lube, precome, and latex. It should have been disgusting. Instead I swallowed him down lower and matched my jerking motion with my mouth. The smells and sounds were primal, grounded, and arousing. Drool added to the mix, reminding me just how messy and wonderful sex was. There was one more thing to add, which would make everything perfect.

It didn't take long for me to feel the telltale tensing of his body beneath me. It had been a long time since I'd given a blow job, and I was going to enjoy it. He groaned and touched the back of my head in warning of his impending release. I didn't care, staying put, wanting to taste his come in my mouth.

Micro-tremors racked his body until I felt the first gush of come across my tongue. It was only then that he cried out, thrusting deep into my mouth. Come hit the back of my throat, bitter and thick. I know a lot of women don't like the taste of it, but I for one do. There's nothing else like it on Earth, no taste that can compare, and I greedily swallowed every ounce he gave me.

Discomfort in my legs and back finally drove me to release him and stretch out long beside him on the bed. As he lay there panting, I pulled the glove from my hand with a snap and tossed it to the floor.

"That was fun." I turned my face to look at him, but he still hadn't opened his eyes. "You okay there?"

With his arm still draped over his eyes, Harrison licked his lips. "We should go out to supper."

I blinked several times. "Pardon?"

"Dinner." He turned his face so he was able to peek at me from beneath. "You and me."

"I . . ." Frowning, I gave my head a shake. "I thought you weren't interested in a relationship."

He rolled his eyes. "Dinner, not marriage."

"You're a jerk. Why would I want to go out with you?" I didn't want to appear anxious for his answer, because as much as I tried to hide it, eating out with him was an idea far more tempting than it should have been.

He finally dropped his arm and rolled onto his side to better look at me. "Despite knowing that I'm leaving in a few months, despite having other women express interest in starting something up with me, despite knowing neither of us is ready for anything beyond this, I can't help but want to take as much as I can from our time together. In other words, I like you and want to get to know you better."

Oh. I blinked past the sudden rush of unshed tears. I shouldn't feel excited about the prospect. I shouldn't feel guilty either, but somehow I was both. "Well fine then. Since you put it that way. I'll happily go out to dinner. But you're still a jerk."

He smiled. Not a smirk, or a grin, or anything else. A genuine smile that lit up his eyes and ignited a warm glow in my chest. Maybe, despite everything that was working against us, things would be okay.

Ignoring the whispering doubt in the back of my mind, I snuggled in close to him and let my mind drift. After all, we were going out to eat. How bad could things be?

19

The next few days became a series of text-flirting, researching restaurants that were nice but didn't scream *we are having a date,* and masturbating. I had to work as well, which totally put a kink in the whole fantasizing about meeting up with Harrison. He had several client meetings through the week, which made it challenging to spend time with him.

No wonder he was single. Dude was a total workaholic.

The amount of time working had been the one thing Rob and I had argued about. He was a teacher, which gave him lots of time off, but in specific time frames. He'd poke at me when I wasn't willing to use up some of my precious four weeks off to go to a matinee, or take a long weekend just to fool around. But even I worked less than Harrison.

It meant some careful planning when it came to arranging our dinner. After looking at schedules, we settled on Thursday night at seven.

I was a distracted mess at work the entire day. I managed to blunder through a revision-note meeting on the newest security hardware manual, which went right up until five. Then I quickly said my good-byes and bolted for the subway.

It took me an unreasonably long time to get ready once I got home. It wasn't as though Harrison was going to think any less of me if I wasn't all decked out. Hell, I still wasn't exactly sure if this was a *date* date, or if we were just two sort-of friends who'd had sort-of sex going out for dinner. Because dressing for one of those was *way* different from dressing for the other.

As I stood looking at my closet, I saw a blue-and-green sundress that I'd bought quite a number of years ago. I took it out carefully, remembering the last time I'd worn it. Rob and I had been able to go out on a date before he went into the hospital for the final time. He'd told me that he loved the color on me and the way it hugged my waist and hips perfectly.

My chest tightened as I slipped it from the hanger and pulled it on. I'd lost weight since the last time I'd had it on. Stress always did that to me. Looking in the mirror, it struck me how much I'd changed since my first and only wearing. There was nothing wrong with it; if anything it looked better on me now than it had then.

But it didn't *fit* right, like it belonged to another person in another life. Emotionally, I'd been battered and was only now coming out the other side. Harrison had been a big help in getting me into the light once more. While this dress would forever be linked with Rob's final illness in my mind, the garment deserved as much of a second chance as I did.

And yet, I couldn't help but feel this wasn't being fair. Not to anyone.

No, I needed to do this. I found some of my newer costume jewelry to dress it up and give it a fresh look. I also took a few extra minutes to straighten my hair, letting it fall down around my shoulders for a change. It would be different enough from last time.

I know I was.

The knock on my door came at five after seven. I peeked through the peephole, not wanting to mistakenly hug Pierce, and saw it was Harrison. Strange, he looked a little off. Nervous even. Maybe he'd simply had a bad day and needed a bit of a break. I slipped into my sandals and opened the door with a smile.

"Hey, you."

I was greeted with a small bouquet of flowers. "For you." Rather than his normal cheeriness, Harrison sounded tired.

"Thanks. I'll quickly put these in water before I go." Harrison was checking his phone when I got back to the door a minute later. "Problem?"

"No. Had something I thought was resolved rear its head again today. Shouldn't impact our plans." With a smile he tucked his phone into his pocket and held out his arm. "Shall we?"

"I know you said dinner was up to me. So I was thinking we could go to The Peartree. Casual, but they have a great wine list. I made us reservations for seven-thirty."

"Perfect." His phone buzzed, but he ignored it.

The drive over was pleasant and we chatted mostly about the building tenants. Harrison rolled his head to the side and looked at me from the corner of his eye. "I think Pierce threatened me."

"He what? No way."

"What did you tell him about us?"

"Not a thing! When he stopped by the other night with the newsletter he saw me dressed up and commented. Said it was good for me to get out and date again. I never said who I was meeting." *I didn't . . . did I?*

"Well, he figured it out. I ran into him last night on my way in. He said if I hurt you that I'd have to answer to the homeowners' association."

I pressed my hands to my heated cheeks. "I'm sorry. He shouldn't have said that to you."

"It's fine. It's good that you guys look out for one another. You don't see that every day. Especially in a big city."

"He's never done anything like that before. God, I didn't

even think he liked me." I was more annoyed than flattered. Given all the times he'd harassed me for not following the rules, he had no business sticking his nose into my fledgling love life.

"Clearly he does. Here we go." And he pulled into the parking garage.

The Peartree was packed by the time we arrived. Even with reservations we had to wait ten minutes for our table to be cleared. Instead of the easy back-and-forth conversations we'd had in the past, I couldn't get myself to relax. There wasn't any reason to be nervous. Harrison was as charming and funny as always. So why the hell was I so tense?

"You look like you need a drink." He handed me the wine list. "Tonight's my treat. Get whatever you'd like."

Yes, alcohol was always a great idea. When the waiter came, I smiled and gave my order. The moment he'd slipped out of earshot once more, Harrison leaned in and took my hands in his. "Why are you nervous?"

I couldn't help but laugh. "I've been asking myself the same thing. It's not as though this is a first date or anything." Except that it totally was.

"We both wanted a chance to get to know each other, so here we are. Good food, good wine, and excellent company." He placed a kiss on the back of my hand. "Let's play a game."

"I saw that movie, it didn't end well." I hated horror movies. Yet, I'd watched all of the *Saw* movies regardless because they were awesome.

"I promise no body parts will be removed. I was thinking more along the lines of twenty questions."

We paused when the waiter brought us our bottle of wine and a breadbasket. I took a generous sip of wine—and dear God that was good—before focusing my attention back on Harrison's proposal. "I think that's a good idea. You go first."

I wanted to lick his lips, especially when he smirked like that. He nodded and lowered his voice. "Okay. Are there any rules you want me to adhere to?"

"We can only plead the Fifth for two questions." I was proud of myself for taking such a liberal approach.

"We're Canadian. We don't have *the Fifth* to plead."

"Don't be a smartass." I giggled. "Other than that, I say anything's fair game. Ask away."

"Fine." Harrison swirled his wine around his glass, his gaze locked on mine. "How old were you the first time you had sex?"

And there was my blush. "Umm. Wow, you like to start off strong. I was seventeen and it was with Rob. We'd been officially dating for six months, but we'd known each other forever."

He took a sip, never breaking eye contact. Despite having spent as much time with Harrison as I had, I still hadn't gotten used to that crazy intense way he'd look at me. It was as though I were the most important person in the world, but he still hadn't figured out how I worked.

I cleared my throat. "Okay, my turn. How old were you when you first had sex? And who was it with?"

"That's two questions."

"I'll take the hit."

The expression on his face changed, for a brief flash he looked fond. Not the sort of thing I'd come to associate with him. "I was sixteen and her name was Amelia. She was my best friend's older sister."

I leaned in and lowered my voice to a whisper. "How much older?"

"That's another question." He winked. "Want to use your third already?"

I leaned back and pouted. "Bastard. No. You're next." His phone chose that moment to buzz. "Do you need to answer that?"

The fond expression was vaporized the moment he looked at the screen. "No. It can wait."

"Are you sure?" I couldn't have said why exactly, but I knew whoever he'd been talking to didn't have anything to do with his job.

"I am. What was the one thing on your sex cards that freaked you out the most?"

"Having a threesome. I suspect that's why Rob put it at the bottom. That was always his fantasy more than mine." That was enough to lighten the mood and get us back into the swing of conversation.

We did this back-and-forth thing for the twenty minutes it took for our appetizers to be replaced by our meals. I'd finally relaxed enough to be more than a little silly. Harrison started to go along with things, but every so often his phone would buzz. A quick glance at the screen, a frown, and then a question to me.

By the time our entrees had arrived, I was starting to realize that this maybe-sort-of date wasn't going so well. "How was your steak?"

"A bit overcooked." He scowled at the phone.

"My fish is awesome. I love tuna and they cooked it just enough."

He was still scowling at the phone. "Are you up for dessert?"

"Maybe." I squirmed in my seat and not for the good reason. "Harrison?"

"Yes."

"How many questions do I have left to ask?"

"Not including that one? Two."

"Okay." At this point in the night, I really didn't have much to lose. "Who is calling you?"

He closed his eyes briefly. "I plead the Fifth."

Ah.

There was only one reason he'd not want to answer that particular question. "It's your girlfriend, isn't it?"

The easygoing man who'd willingly offered up his body to allow me to experiment with my sex cards was gone in a flash. There was a hard edge to his face, though I wasn't sure if it was because of my question or the fact that I'd just caught him out in the biggest lie ever.

My chest tightened and it became difficult to breathe. It was as though my heart was being squeezed by my lungs.

"Well, thank you very much for the meal. I think I'll be skipping dessert." I neatly folded my napkin and stood.

"Lyssa, it's not—"

"I told you, my name is Alyssa. A. Lyss. A. Three syllables. You haven't earned the right to drop any of them."

"Fine. Alyssa. It's not what you think."

"It doesn't matter what I think. You lied to me. There are many things I can forgive, but lying about another woman isn't one of them."

I pulled my shoulders back, grabbed my purse, and marched out to the nearest taxi.

20

Never again was I going to go on a date. Correction, never again would I date on a Thursday night. Because if things went down the shitter like they had with Harrison, I'd have to face people at work the next day. That meant I needed to pretend to be happy, when really I was just an angry, bitter sourpuss.

I needed wine, chocolate, and a chick flick. Or maybe some porn. I hadn't decided yet.

When I finally pulled my sorry ass back home, armed with my provisions, I cringed at the thought that I might run into Harrison. I should have considered our proximity to each other when I'd started down this whole bonking-your-neighbor thing. I steeled myself before marching up the stairs and making my way to my condo.

As fate would have it, Harrison was nowhere in sight. I scampered as quickly as I could to my condo. I once again fumbled trying to pull my keys free. It was as I stood there, searching for them through the abyss that is my purse, that I heard the dreaded creaking of a door opening.

"Alyssa?"

I didn't look Harrison's way, more focused than ever on getting into my home.

"Alyssa, we need to talk."

His approaching footsteps increased the pace of my frenzied search. *Ah ah!* The metal was cool against my hand as I palmed them and pulled them free. I shoved them into the lock, jerked open my door, and slammed it shut. For good measure I snapped the deadbolt locked before pressing my head to the door.

Harrison's footsteps stopped, and while I couldn't make out the words, I could hear him muttering. I shouldn't care that he was frustrated by me obviously avoiding him. I was justified in my actions. He'd lied to me. He hadn't even bothered denying the fact that he had. Just because things hadn't gone well with him didn't mean that my plans to go through Rob's cards were thwarted. Harrison was a tool. A means to an end. It wasn't as though I'd started to fall in love with him or something. No relationships, our one hard and fast rule.

There were plenty of fish and all that crap. Nikki would know how to set me up with a guy who'd be willing to play out some of my fantasies. I might even let her set me up for one of those speed-dating things she desperately wanted me to try.

The knock on the door vibrated through my forehead, which was still pressed to the wood. I staggered back, nearly dropping my shopping bag and losing the precious contents within.

"Alyssa?"

Fucking Harrison. "Go away."

"Please. Let me talk to you."

"No." I made sure to stomp extra loudly to the kitchen. I slammed the cutlery drawer shut once I liberated a spoon for the ice cream.

Another knock.

"Go away, Harrison!" I then marched to the living room, popped in my DVD, and proceeded to half-watch my movie while pouting.

Stupid men.

Fifteen minutes of silence had me convinced that he'd given up and gone back to his place. I would never admit to being disappointed that he hadn't tried harder, even though I was. The ice cream in the tub had softened and had started to form rivers of cream around the mini peanut butter cups embedded within. I didn't bother to pause the movie while I returned the tub to the freezer.

There was another knock, but this time it was softer than before. It didn't sound like Harrison. Though apparently I didn't know him as well as I thought. He could be trying to trick me or something.

When I looked out the peephole, I was greeted by the smiling face of Mrs. Le Page. It looked as though she had something in her hands, but the glass distorted what it was enough that I couldn't see it.

Carefully, I opened my door and peeked around the corner. "Hi."

"Hello, sweetie. Did I catch you at a bad time?"

"No, I was just watching a movie. It's fine. What can I do for you?"

I should have realized something was up when she smiled up at me with that sparkle in her gaze. "I was wondering if you could help me with a little problem I have."

"What's that?"

I opened the door further and realized that Harrison was leaning against the wall. "Hi."

I glared at her. "Traitor."

Mrs. Le Page patted Harrison's arm. "This charming young man has been standing out here in the hall waiting for you to open up so he can apologize to you. It would help me tremendously if you could hear him out. If you don't like what he has to say you have my permission to slap him."

"Hey!" He pushed away from the wall. "That wasn't part of our agreement."

"You did something dumb. Not surprising because you are a man and you are genetically predisposed to upsetting women. It's nature." The slip of a woman moved Harrison so he now stood fully in the door directly in front of me. "Now, you two have your talk." Before she moved away she pressed a hand to her chest.

"Are you okay?" Meddling or not, I didn't want to see her sick.

"Just a bit of indigestion that's been with me all day. I'll be fine once I lie down."

"Do you need help?" Harrison placed his hand on the small of her back, helping to steady her. "I can see you upstairs."

"And have you lose out on your chance to apologize?" Mrs. Le Page snorted. "Start groveling, young man." Then she abandoned me to deal with Harrison.

I squeezed the door edge, hoping it would ground me somehow. "You have one minute."

"It was my ex-wife who'd been calling."

You know when you read in books about a character having a realization so powerful that they felt it like a blow to the face? That totally happened. One second I thought I knew everything there was to know about him, and the next, BAM!

My mouth fell open. "Your . . . you were married?"

His face was devoid of emotion. "For five years. It ended badly."

I probably should have invited him in, cracked open the wine, and talked about this in a civilized manner. Instead I tightened my grip on the door and hoped I'd be able to make sense of what he was saying. "You might have mentioned that."

"It wasn't important. Things were over."

"Then why was her calling you so upsetting? How long have you been divorced?"

"It was finalized six months ago." He looked away, the muscle in his jaw working madly. "She's under the delusion that there's a chance we can get back together."

Something twisted in my stomach, until I felt the bile rising in my throat. Harrison had been honest when he said he wasn't ready for a relationship, said that it wasn't even on the table. It was weird, but I hadn't even thought of him and his life much beyond our arrangement. Sure, I knew he had a family, friends, and a busy job, but an ex-wife? That made Harrison more real somehow. A person with his own challenges who might enjoy having the company of a friend. Someone he could talk his problems over with. Someone to cuddle on the couch or to run interference for him.

I caught myself leaning closer to him. My gaze traveled up to his and stayed there. God, he looked tired and lonely. Maybe as much as I was.

Maybe . . .

No. He'd been clear with me from the start. He wasn't looking for something. His ex was clearly still having difficulty coming to terms with their divorce and he was busy dealing with that. I'd let myself believe that there might be something that could grow between us, putting more pressure on him than he needed. That wasn't his fault, it was mine. Just like I'd needed time and space after Rob's passing, I'm sure Harrison needed the same.

But I also knew myself well enough that I couldn't be around him, to continue doing what we were without my emotions becoming entangled. Having a recent ex-wife in the mix wasn't something I could handle. He deserved someone who could be there for him in all the ways he needed. Right now, I wasn't that person.

Best to break things off while we both still could.

"It sounds like you have a lot on your plate." I straightened up, my gaze slipping to the floor. "I want you to know that I really appreciate everything you've done for me over the past few weeks. I've learned a lot. Both about sex and myself. But I do think it's best if we just end things here. Part as friends. I just don't think . . . yeah." I stuck out my hand. "Okay?"

"I don't want to." He hesitated before taking my offering. "Fine."

We let go nearly as quickly as the shake had begun. I stepped farther into my condo and began to close the door, when he stopped me. "I am sorry. I never meant to hurt you."

The tightening of my throat made it difficult to lie. "What makes you think I'm hurt? See you around."

The clicking of the door and the shuffling of his steps moving away from me increased the sick feeling in my stomach. Ignoring the movie and my glass, I picked up my bottle of wine and headed straight for the bedroom.

21

The downside to being a grumpy bitch was that even I was getting tired of dealing with me. I tried talking to Nikki, but that devolved into a bickering match that would have been impressive if we were still in high school, but was simply sad given our approaching middle-age status. I could have called Mom, but she'd be all sympathy and kind words, when what I really wanted was someone to fight with. The last thing I wanted to do was pick on her.

I should have gone for a run, but that didn't work out so well last time.

Instead I decided to treat myself to a movie. It had been ages since I'd gone and it was out of the norm for me. There was one of those loud summer blockbuster things playing—it didn't actually matter what it was about—and I took myself there to lose myself in the noise.

I didn't realize until too late that Harrison Ford was in it.

Of course he was.

Toronto's streets were busy and the air humid as I made my way home. It wasn't chaotic, but it certainly wasn't the calming influence I'd hoped for. Our street is off the main avenues, and normally doesn't have a high volume of traffic. So when I turned onto it, I was shocked to see a fire truck at the end and a small group of people milling around.

Wait a minute. They're in front of my building.

Oh no.

I picked up the pace until I was running full tilt. The crowd was being held back by a police officer. I pushed my way to the front and reached out to tug on his arm. "This is my building. What's going on?"

The young man kept his face expressionless. "I'm sorry, ma'am, you'll have to wait for the all clear before we can let you back in."

"What happened?" My heart was in my throat. These weren't strangers, they were my friends. Even the ones I didn't know as well as I might have liked, they were all a part of my comings and goings. My life.

"There was a kitchen fire in one of the units." The muscle in the officer's jaw jumped. "That's all I can say."

Shit, that was beyond useless.

There were a number of people from the building milling around, but no one seemed to know any more than I did. It wasn't until Pierce came out onto the front steps of the building that everyone perked up.

"What's going on?" someone called out.

"When can we get back in?" another joined in.

Pierce came down, ignoring the looks the officer was shooting him. "Everyone, please. Let's let these people do their jobs. Go out for a coffee, or to the mall. You'll be able to get back in in about an hour. Maybe two."

That sent several people wandering away. Others set up camp on the sidewalks a short distance away. I did neither, choosing to stand there until Pierce came closer. I'd been too shocked to move when I realized that he'd been crying.

Pierce, stone-cold former high school principal who'd terrorized more students with the threat of detention and homeowners with the threat of the association's ill will, had been crying.

"Pierce?" My voice shook and I had to clear it. He paused long enough for me to squeeze his arm. "Are you okay?"

His smile was feeble at best. "I'll survive."

"Is there anything I can do to help?"

"No, my dear." Then the strangest thing happened. He turned and hugged me. "Just pray."

"What?"

The paramedics chose that moment to emerge from the building, a stretcher between them. My mind didn't want to accept what I was seeing. My body stiffened beneath Pierce's grasp. "No."

"I'm sorry," he said as he pulled back.

Mrs. Le Page looked so tiny cocooned in the stark white hospital blankets. Her pallor was gray and her lids looked sunken. This couldn't be the woman, so full of life and teasing, who just the other day tried to intervene in my relationship troubles. This woman was old, frail looking, deathly.

And yet there was her husband, crying and fighting to stay by her side as they loaded her into the back of the ambulance. They helped him up, banged the doors closed, and took off, lights flashing but the siren silent.

My world bottomed out on me. "God."

"They couldn't tell me anything." Pierce clacked his teeth together. "Foolish privacy laws. But I overheard them mention a heart attack. She must have taken a spill when she was cooking, which started the fire."

"She'll be okay." I don't know who I was trying to convince with my statement. "She's tough."

"My dear." His voice cracked and he had to clear it. "My dear. They . . . I . . . she didn't make it."

No. No, no, no, I couldn't lose someone else. I wasn't ready. This wasn't fair! They were the perfect sweet couple that was still so very much in love. They were everyone's surrogate grandparents, teasing us all and making sure we didn't take ourselves too seriously.

She was my friend and I was going to miss her.

Pierce pulled away, giving me one final squeeze before he stepped back. "I'm going to head to the hospital to see if there is anything I can do to help Mr. Le Page. I believe they have a son he can stay with. He'll need to be contacted. The insurance company as well. Excuse me."

The crowd around Pierce parted as he marched off toward the parking spots. He might be a stickler for the rules, but he really did care about us and our homes. If there was anything to be done, Pierce would see to it.

As I stood staring up at the building, I tried to calm my breathing and keep my tears from falling. I wished Rob were here. He'd be just as stunned, but the feel of warm arms around me, a solid chest that I could lean against, to cry on, was what I needed more than anything. He would have given me that.

But Rob wasn't here.

I was alone.

"Alyssa?"

I turned and saw Harrison standing there looking dumbstruck. Sliding past the others he came up to me and pulled me into a hug. The moment his arms wrapped around me, the dam inside me broke and I began to cry.

"It's okay." He ran his fingers through my hair. "I'm here."

Harrison led me away to his car, helping me slide into the passenger's seat. He shut the door and I was surrounded by wonderful silence. Without a word, he got behind the wheel and started the car.

"Where are we going?" I sounded like I'd been crying for a year.

"I don't know. Just not here."

"You don't even know what happened?"

He placed his hand on my thigh, giving it a soft squeeze. "I don't need to know to see that you're upset." He looked over, his frown marring his good looks. "Would you rather stay?"

"God no. Anywhere is good."

Fighting through Toronto traffic, he pulled into the Westin parking lot and led me down to the lakeshore. It felt good to get out and breathe the air. There was a breeze coming off the water, cooling the sun's rays as it hit my skin. Harrison didn't say anything, he didn't fill the silence the way Rob would have. Instead he hooked his finger with mine and strolled beside me.

We stopped by a bench and sat. The lake was beautiful. The sky was full blue with barely a cloud anywhere in sight. I took a deep breath, picked a point far out on the horizon, and finally said the words: "Mrs. Le Page had a heart attack. She didn't make it."

I should have told him immediately what had happened. While he hadn't known Mrs. Le Page as well, he'd clearly formed a fast friendship with her. He stiffened, his grip tightening. "That's . . . fuck. The poor thing."

"Mr. Le Page went to the hospital with her in the ambulance. I . . . I know how hard that will be for him." While Rob hadn't gone to the hospital in an ambulance, that final car ride had been nothing but tears and heartache.

"Is he alone?"

"Pierce went to be with him. They have a son, too. I think Pierce was going to call him or something."

"That's good." He pulled my hand closer to his thigh. "Are you okay?"

"Not really. It brings back a lot of bad memories." The breeze tickled my face and sent my hair blowing. "It also reminded me of something."

"What?"

I turned, took his face in my hands, and kissed him. "That life is far too short."

He looked at me for several long moments before taking me

in his arms and pressing my back to the park bench. His lips were soft as he deepened the kiss. His body was a hard mass of muscles, blood, and bone. His heart pounded in his chest and beat against my hand that I'd pressed to the skin above it. It somehow seemed wrong, taking pleasure when I felt nothing but pain. But I took it. And I'd keep taking it because life *was* too short. I didn't need love from him. Hell, I wasn't certain I needed honesty at this point.

What I wanted, what I needed was someone who saw me and gave a damn. I needed to feel alive and to chase the specter of death away.

When the kiss broke and he looked down at me, I knew despite his faults, Harrison was the one I wanted. I licked my lips, knowing that what I was about to say would change things between us once more. "We're only on Day Ten."

"I thought you were done with me." He placed a kiss on the end of my nose.

"I was." I gently pushed him up until we were both sitting once more. "I'd mistakenly gotten it in my head that we had a chance to have a relationship."

"I told you—"

"I know." I chuckled. "You were my rebound fling and I got carried away. I had this whole plan developing in my head. How our relationship would develop no matter how we both said it wouldn't. So when I found out about your ex, I overreacted."

"I should have told you." Harrison hung his head. "I'm sorry."

"I know. I do like you, like spending time with you. I want nothing more than to continue our fun. I think we could both use a bit more fun in our lives."

"Agreed."

He held out his hand and I took it. Unlike before, this time when our hands entwined, I felt grounded. As though this was the beginning of something fresh and exciting. It encouraged me in a way I wasn't expecting.

"One thing." I sucked on my bottom lip for a moment as I tried to figure out how to word things properly. "I think we need to be a bit more flexible in regard to the cards."

"What do you mean?"

"Rather than do them in order, let's just see where things take us."

The sadness in Harrison's gaze was tempered with a spark of something else. It might not make things better, it might not chase away the pain of losing a dear friend, but it was a start. If nothing else we'd have each other in the short term. Beyond that, well, I'd figure things out when I got there.

Harrison nodded. "I'm still leaving in a month and a half."

"I know. But for now, I'll take what I can get."

Hopefully, it would be enough.

Part 3

The Realities of Self

22

_____

"I swear to God you're becoming the sous chef of sex." Nikki sat on my desk chair watching as I reorganized my sex survival bag.

"There's nothing wrong with being prepared." Shit, I really did have a lot of lube here. _Maybe I should take a few out? Naw._

"Of course not. As long as you finally get to screw him."

I stopped my rummaging to frown at her. "What are you talking about? We've had sex."

"No, you and hot-pants have gotten each other off, but there's been no actual penetration to this point. Penis must go into vagina." She held up her hands to demonstrate.

"You're an ass."

"And you're apparently doing it wrong. I need to hear about some actual fucking."

"Really, Nikki?"

"Don't _Nikki_ me. I'm right and you know it."

Unfortunately, she was. Harrison and I had done a lot, but we hadn't partaken in the one thing I was anxious about. Now that we'd talked things out and were both clear on how far things were going to go between us, all I had to do was get through

Mrs. Le Page's funeral and then Harrison and I were going to have a long weekend of marathon sex.

Three whole days to take my mind off the realities of life.

"So where are you going?" Nikki fingered the handle of the gym bag. "Some place nice I hope."

"He wouldn't tell me. Said it would ruin the surprise." I wasn't going to get my hopes up for a five-star hotel or anything, but I wouldn't be upset if that's what he had in mind.

"A funeral and then a getaway." Nikki flopped back on my bed with a sigh. "You do seem to have all the luck. Good and bad."

Mrs. Le Page would have appreciated and even approved of the fact I was bringing my sex survival bag to her funeral. It would be safely tucked away in the trunk of Harrison's car, ready for action once we got to the hotel, or wherever he was planning to take me. I'm sure she was smiling down somewhere on us, happy that something good had come from her passing.

Even if that good was only temporary.

The service was held on Saturday morning at the Le Pages' Anglican church. It had been years since I'd been to a mass of any sort and was pleasantly surprised when I didn't burst into flames the moment I'd crossed the threshold. Not really sure of where to go and what to do, I sat down in a seat toward the back of the church.

Harrison refused to come in when I'd met up with him before things began. "I didn't really know her."

"But you *did* know her." I shrugged and nodded toward the people going in. "No one would mind."

"I don't do death very well." He wouldn't meet my gaze and instead focused on the passing traffic.

"No one does. It will give you a chance to say good-bye."

When he finally looked at me, I could see the unshed tears in his eyes. "The last funeral I went to was my mom's. I was fifteen and everything about it . . . scared the shit out of me. I've tried to go to others since then, but I'm ashamed to say I usually leave with a panic attack. Not very manly, I know. I have my own way of saying good-bye instead." He gave me a small smile. "Okay?"

"Yeah, of course." Strange as it was, I tended to forget that I wasn't the only one who'd dealt with death before. Losing his mom at such a young age . . . God, I couldn't imagine how hard that must have been. "I'm sorry."

"So am I. I'll come back in an hour."

So instead of having him by my side, I sat alone and listened to the hymns. I was doing fine. Really I was. I learned that her first name was Charlotte, not Mrs. Her favorite thing to do was to travel, the warmer the climate the better. And that she'd worked as a florist for thirty years before retiring.

I managed to get through the eulogy by her son, someone I'd only ever heard about, but I could see the resemblance between him and his father. I even held back the tears when her three grandchildren got up and sang "Ave Maria."

The moment Mr. Le Page got to the pulpit and looked out over the gathering, the tears broke and rolled down my cheeks in steady drips.

"Thank you for coming." His voice was surprisingly steady. "My Charlotte was the best woman I knew. She was my confidante. My lover. My best friend. I'm going to miss you, sweetling."

I bit my cheek to stop from sobbing outright.

I left as soon as the service was over, deciding to avoid talking to anyone I knew. I wouldn't be able to manage anything beyond sobs and sniffles at this point. Harrison was leaning against the trunk of his car just down the street from the church. I walked right up to him and into his waiting arms. God, I really didn't want to cry anymore.

He gave me a good five minutes before tipping my chin up. "Want to go?"

I sniffed. "Yeah. Where are we headed?"

"It's a surprise."

I started to relax when I realized he was taking us out of Toronto. It had been a long time since I'd been out of the city and this was perfect timing. It wasn't until we were off the 401 that Harrison looked my way. "Three days and two nights to get through as many of your cards as we can."

"I like the sound of that." The idea of a whole lot of raunchy sex with him was the perfect cure for my current ills.

"Excellent. We are going to cross one off of your list in about an hour, so sit back and relax."

We chatted about inconsequential stuff and bickered about what songs to play next on the satellite radio. We even shared a bag of chips that he'd brought along, which made it one of my better road trips in recent memory. The gloom from the funeral was blowing away as we sped up the highway toward our destination, to be replaced with the thrill of expectation and hope.

That was until we pulled into the gravel parking lot of what must have been the cheapest dive of a motel north of Toronto.

"Dude." I didn't even undo my seatbelt. "No way."

He grinned so widely I thought his cheeks might split. "Day Eleven." He then hopped out of the car, whistling.

A five—no, I'd cut him some slack—four-star hotel with a spa. That's what I'd been hoping for. Or an upscale B&B at the very least. But no, he was being oh so diligent with my sex list, making sure to tick each box off.

Rob would approve.

I have no doubt that the two of them would have gotten along famously. They would have laughed about the look on my face upon my arrival. Rob would have wanted to take a picture for posterity. Thankfully, Harrison didn't have that particularly annoying habit.

Clearly, this was where things were going to go down this weekend. I could either suck it up and play along like the adult I supposedly was, or I could stay in the car and pout. My bottom lip crept out for a moment until Harrison slammed the trunk closed. Along with my overnight bag, he had my sex bag slung over his shoulder.

I was out of the car in a flash. "You better make Day Eleven worth it."

He laughed as he draped his arm across my shoulders. "I promise. We are here for a very specific reason."

The moment we opened the door to the lobby and walked in, I swore I was having a flashback to a grindhouse movie. The wallpaper—dear Lord, ick—was clearly from before I was born. The brown and green flowers and stripes were faded from time and cigarettes. The stench of long-gone smoke clung to every surface in the room.

The woman behind the desk was focused on her Sudoku book. She was completing the answers in pen, a cup of half-finished coffee close by. Her gray hair was cropped short and a pair of reading glasses was perched on the edge of her nose. "Yes?" She didn't look up.

"We'd like a room." Harrison sounded far too chipper. The woman must have thought so as well, because she looked up and scowled at him. "For two nights," he added.

She sighed and moved over to a computer that looked old enough to have had grandchildren of its own. "Name, address, and phone number. We only accept credit. No cash. Checkout is at noon. You steal anything and I'll charge you double for it on your card."

I had to turn away to keep from looking at Harrison. Because if I made eye contact with him, I'd lose my shit and I got the impression that our hostess wouldn't approve.

"You have rooms with vibrating beds, right?" He asked the question so innocently, I almost believed that he didn't know the answer already.

"You're that weirdo that called the other day? I told you we had one. No one likes that crap anymore."

"We'll take it if the room's available."

I looked in time to see her roll her eyes and shove a room key across the counter. "Do you see any other cars in the lot? It's all yours."

Harrison whistled as he filled out the form, pausing only long enough to wink at the woman as he slid his credit card across the counter. That was it, I was going to start giggling and I would never be able to stop. I was walking out the door when Harrison called out, "Thanks so much. Looking forward to our stay!"

The laughter exploded from me the moment we got out of sight of the windows. "Oh my God, that was insane!"

"I knew when I spoke with her on the phone we needed to come here. It was too perfect."

"This really is the weirdest, best place in the world." I approved wholeheartedly.

The motel stretched out along the highway. White paint was faded and peeling and the trim had begun to separate from the siding. If we were very lucky, the roof was hole-free. If not, I hoped the weather forecast was clear until we headed for home. Our room was toward the end of the motel. I had to assume it was due to the fact that it possessed a vibrating bed and they wanted the types of people who would want a room with a vibrating bed as far away from others as possible.

Harrison shoved the key into the lock, needing to jiggle it a few times before if finally slid in. I held my breath and hoped for the best. The smell of stale air and air freshener greeted us. The floor was covered in thinning brown shag carpet that led to brown tile in the bathroom. There wasn't any dust so I hoped that meant they still cleaned the rooms regularly. The bedding was at least from this century. A tasteful chocolate duvet covered our vibrating mattress, topped with four pillows.

The sight was too tempting to resist. I dropped my purse and jumped onto the bed. The mattress was softer than I'd expected and I didn't bounce nearly as high as I would have liked. "The sheets smell clean. I just hope there aren't any bedbugs."

"I doubt there's been anyone staying in the room since the

eighties." He dropped the luggage, reached into his pocket, and pulled out a roll of quarters. "Want to go for a spin?"

It was ridiculous and amazing and absolutely the most perfect idea in the world. "Fuck yeah. Crank it up."

I rolled over to make room for him to join me. It took us a moment to get comfortable and for him to feed the coins into the small machine attached to the headboard. There was a strange whirring noise for a moment before the bed began to rattle.

You know when you're a kid, and you sneak-jump on your bed, knowing full well if you were to get caught you'd be in trouble? That sense of glee mixed with an undercurrent of danger? That was the burst of joy that shot through me, pulling my laugher as it went. Harrison's chuckles became full out barks the longer the ridiculousness of what we were doing went on.

My head rattled to the side, making it easier to look at him. For the first time since we'd had our fight, he looked at peace. The tension was gone from around his eyes and his jaw had relaxed. His skin was flushed and there was an enthusiasm in his eyes that I hadn't seen before. He really was the most handsome man of my acquaintance.

I could easily have chalked up the funny feeling in my chest to the vibrating bed. It was a strange tingle that radiated out to every cell in my body. Like a weird chain reaction of happiness ignited by a man who'd come into my life when I'd needed him most. I didn't know if it was fate, or simply good timing, but I was thankful that he was here with me.

Our gazes met and that tingle zipped through me once more. His cheeks were beginning to show his stubble, a look that I approved of on men in general and him in particular. I reached up and touched my fingertips to his lips, enjoying how the vibrations made them feel against them. He nipped at the ends before sucking them into my mouth. His tongue teased around my nails and lapped at my joint.

"Kiss me." It was a simple request, one I had no doubt he'd comply with. But yet again, he didn't do what I'd expected.

Rather than kiss me, he sucked on my fingers, pulling them farther into his mouth. His teeth nibbled my skin, sending pleasant little tingles through me. The combination of his teasing and the vibrations made me horny enough to beg. "Please. Kiss me."

My fingers were pulled free with a pop and he rolled on top of me. I hooked my leg around his, loving the feel of his pants against my bare skin. He cupped the side of my face and ran his thumb across my jawline. There was something in his expression, an emotion I was too terrified to identify. But I couldn't escape it, or him; I was frozen in place by his stare and the weight of my longing. I gasped as he lifted his knee higher against my pussy. It grew damp with desire. Then the waiting was over. He leaned in and pressed his lips to mine.

The kiss started off softly, mostly skin against skin as the vibrations did most of the work. But as the seconds ticked on, he grew impatient and began to deepen the contact. His tongue dipped into my mouth to tease mine. It was soft and contrasted the rough scrape of his stubble against my chin. I held nothing back, opened my mouth to him, drinking in the taste and smell of him. His hands were moving across my face and neck, caressing me, holding me in a way that I could feel his love and respect, even if he didn't voice it.

I pushed my hands into his hair, once again marveling at how soft it was. I lightly dug my nails into his scalp and down to the back of his neck. I felt him shiver against me, his muscles tighten and contract as I continued to tease. Harrison groaned and bucked his hard cock against my pussy.

"I can't wait to finally fuck you." He said the words against my mouth. I wanted to swallow them whole, keep them locked inside me forever.

With a little effort, I shifted so I was able to wrap my legs around his waist. The change in position put his cock against my clit, pressure in addition to the shaking bed. If there were a way to package this moment up and sell it, I'd be a billionaire. The tension increased as he bucked in counter time with the shaking. I was beginning to get to the point of no return. My orgasm wasn't creeping up any longer. It was galloping full speed ahead.

As I let my eyes slip closed, about to let my body take me over the edge, the bed stopped.

"No," I groaned. "Fuck, that's not fair."

"Close, were you?" He kissed his way down my neck to my chest, where he placed several reverent kisses to my cleavage.

"You have no idea."

"I think I have some." Rather than stop as he always had before, he continued kissing down across my stomach. It was only when he adjusted himself between my legs and reached for the hem of my dress that I realized what he was about to do.

Oh, bless him.

The black lace panties were my way of compromising for having sex on the day of a funeral. It was clearly the right choice when Harrison pushed up my dress and moaned. Rather than reach to remove them right away, he leaned in and rubbed his nose against my pussy.

"You smell so fucking amazing." Opening his mouth, he pressed it to my cloth-covered clit and blew. The hot air had me press up against him, my back bowing off the bed.

"If you keep doing that I'm not going to last long."

"We can't have that." He pulled back and hooked his hands around the band of the panties. "These are the sexiest things I've ever seen."

Despite everything we'd done to this point, I grew shy as he worked the thin lace down my hips, exposing me to him. It wasn't anything he hadn't seen before, so why did this feel different? He left me long enough to pull the panties free. Rather than toss them aside, he tucked them into his pants pocket.

"What—"

"Shh." He then put his face between my legs and licked across my clit.

The warmth of his mouth on me had my thighs trembling. I dug my nails into the comforter, scared that I'd suddenly take flight before I'd get to enjoy the end result. He ran his tongue around the swollen nub, flicking it every so often before he'd continue with his teasing. It was almost too much after the pressure from the vibrations before. It wasn't until he pressed a finger into my pussy, curling it up to hit something deep inside me I'd never known was there, that my orgasm raced forward.

My back bowed and my hips lifted off the mattress as his hands came up to support my ass. I called out his name before it dissolved into a wordless scream. It didn't take long for the pleasure to overwhelm me and I was pushing at his head. "Stop. Please. God."

He pulled back, his chin wet from my come. "Delicious."

Panting, I turned my face, unable to look at him. "You're crazy."

"Just telling the truth." He ran his hands up the insides of my thighs. "You need a drink?"

Oh no he didn't. "No. I do need a cock though."

It was weird, seeing Harrison look slightly embarrassed. "I didn't want to rush it. This weekend is about you."

"Then consider this an extension of what you just did." I sat up, grabbing his shirt in my hands and giving him a small shake. "We've done *everything* except the one thing I want. Now go get a condom from the sex kit and get your ass back over here to fuck me."

He looked at me so intently I thought I was going to blush again. Whatever it was he saw the moment passed. He gave my thigh a light slap and went in search of the condoms as directed. It was fun to watch him move around the room. The way his arms flexed as he unbuttoned his shirt and pulled it free. The micro-expressions on his face that betrayed the presence of the fleeting thoughts that were racing through his head. I might not know everything about his past, but clearly his ex-wife had hurt him.

The bitch. She better hope we never meet.

I beckoned him with my finger when he started to undo the front of his pants. "Come here and let me take those off."

"I'd been planning on the two of us playing strip poker first, then sex." He stopped at the foot of the bed. "But I've learned to be flexible over the years."

My hands were steady as I opened his fly and grabbed hold of his cock through his briefs. Unlike before, I knew what he liked, those spots that would drive him nuts. The nerves that I'd half-expected to show up, didn't. It was odd, but somewhere in my mind Harrison had shifted from friend-with-benefits to lover. It eased my body and mind, and helped me to fully enjoy the moment.

This particular moment involved me sucking his cock.

I was too impatient to push his briefs all the way down, just far enough so I could take the head of his cock into my mouth. I teased him the way he'd licked at my clit, slow and steady. I wasn't going to have him come in my mouth, not this time. No, that honor was going to be for a different place.

It was a bit of a challenge, but I kept swallowing him down as I worked his briefs and pants across his hips and down his thighs. Thankfully, gravity helped out and I was quickly left with a naked Harrison. Grabbing his ass cheeks with my hands, I used him as leverage to take him deep into my throat.

"Christ, you're good at that." His hands went to my head, resting there rather than helping.

I wasn't about to argue with him. Hell, I'd watched videos on how to give a great blow job over the years. There was nothing wrong with wanting to excel at something and Rob had never complained. It was nice to know that my skills were transferable.

His cock was hot and leaking as I lapped at it. I tucked my teeth behind my lips and bit down on his head. Harrison sucked in a breath and his fingers tightened in my hair, a sure sign that he was enjoying himself. As I played with his balls with my free hand, I felt them tighten, the skin now too rigid to tug. He was close to coming, which wasn't something that I wanted to happen. Not yet at any rate.

It made me more than a little sad to pull away, but I really wanted to have him inside me. The little moan he made when I finally broke contact was immensely satisfying though. "Hush. I just want to put this on."

The condom was slick as I pried it from the wrapper. It had literally been years since I'd had to deal with one of these things. I'd been on the pill after we'd gotten married and we hadn't bothered. So the whole application thing was awkward at best. Harrison was certainly enjoying the show, if the perma-grin he had on his face was any indication. But the moment latex met skin, his eyes rolled up into his head and a full body shudder passed through him.

"You like that?" I made sure to squeeze his shaft extra hard as I rolled it down to the base.

"I like your hands on me." His teeth were clenched as his eyes remained shut. "And your mouth."

"I can tell. I hope you like the rest of me as much." Letting him go, I stretched back on the bed and spread my legs.

"You." He swallowed, his tongue peeking out as it swiped his bottom lip. "You're going to kill me."

"*La petite mort.*" I cocked my head to the side and smiled. "You'll like it."

Harrison dropped to his hands and knees on the mattress and crawled up my length until his mouth covered mine and his cock pressed to my pussy. "You're beautiful." He thrust forward.

I gasped. His cock filled every inch of me, pressing deep into my body. My breath shortened and for a second I was overwhelmed by the gravity of the moment. I was thankful that he held still, letting me adjust to having him there.

"Are you okay?" He tucked my hair behind my ear.

"Yeah." I tried to smile but my lips quivered too much. A tear had formed at the corner of my eye and slipped down my hairline to my ear. "I didn't think I would react this way. It's stupid."

"No it isn't." He wiped the tear trail with his thumb. "Want me to stop?"

"God no. Just. Stay there for a minute."

The wave of unexpected emotion ebbed the longer he held me in his arms. The whole time Harrison managed to keep himself in check and not once did he pressure me to continue. That helped me relax and in no time I started to gently buck my hips, encouraging him to move. He kissed me hard as he started thrusting.

Even though I'd used the dildos in the past month, the artificialness of the silicone had nothing on making love to a man. It wasn't simply his cock; no, it was most definitely the whole package when it came to him. The smell of Old Spice and shampoo, the hint of sweat rising from him as we writhed on the bed. The feel of his skin and hair and muscles against me, solid and reassuring.

And wow he was hot. Waves of heat caused sweat to pool between my breasts and on my belly. We had to stop so I could strip my dress and bra free, leaving me blissfully naked. Now completely free from impediment, Harrison captured my breasts in his hands, suckling first one then the other nipple. Never once in the past had I been able to have multiple orgasms. It just wasn't my thing no matter how hard Rob and I had tried. The fact that the precedent hadn't been set didn't seem to matter.

Harrison would swivel his hip, grinding against my clit at the same time he'd pinch my nipples. The mix of pleasure and pain wasn't something I'd experienced before. Not like this. The faint stirrings of arousal grew higher and hotter, until I was moaning and meeting Harrison's thrusts with some of my own.

"Shit." His voice was muffled as he pressed his forehead to my shoulder. "You're going to make me come."

"Me too."

He bit down on the spot where my shoulder meets my neck. His tongue flicked madly over my skin the same way he'd teased my clit. It was all too much for me; being with him, everything that we'd done that had led us to this moment, it all converged. My muscles seized and I squeezed around him as my second orgasm slammed into me. I bit the side of his biceps and dug my nails into his back as I cried out.

Harrison tensed as well, groaning into the mattress. His hips jerked as he slammed into me twice more before he finally fell forward. He crushed me before I dug my fingers into his sides. "Can't breathe."

He took the weight on his forearms and knees and kissed my collarbone. "Sorry. I thought you killed me there for a moment. Had to make sure I was still breathing."

Out of the blue, I started laughing. For the first time since Rob's passing I was happy. Not pretending to be so, not even *in a good mood.* Joy had been my onetime constant companion, but had stopped visiting with Rob's death. Harrison had brought that back to me, giving me something to move toward.

"You okay there?" He looked confused.

I gave him a shove so he rolled off me. "I'm fine. That was . . . awesome." I kissed him for good measure.

"Don't move. Let me get a cloth to clean you up." Holding the condom, he disappeared into the bathroom for a minute.

Stretched out wide on the bed, I relaxed and let the mattress hold me up. This was what I'd been missing. It wasn't so much about the sex as it was the connection. Rob and I always had fun when we'd made love. It was one of the reasons why his cards really weren't a surprise to me. And yes, they would help me get out of my shell sexually, but they also served another purpose. They were a tool to help me find the right man, the one who could make me happy.

Only someone who could handle these cards with humor and grace would be a good fit for me. Rob must have realized that as well. Too bad the man who was turning out to be perfect for me would be gone in a month.

With my gaze locked on the ceiling, I realized that Harrison and I really did click. Sure we weren't perfect, nor did we have the history that Rob and I did before we got together, but that didn't matter. I loved the adventure, the discovery. I loved the new punch lines we were starting to develop. God, I especially loved the way he could turn me on and play my body like an instrument. It was mind-blowing.

I loved . . .

Slowly, I sat up, my eyes growing wide.

Shit.

I really *was* starting to fall in love with him. Somehow, without me really realizing, Harrison had taken up a small spot in my heart that had nothing to do with sex and everything to do with . . . whatever the hell the two of us had. He'd started to take root inside me and now I had thoughts and feelings for him winding throughout me.

I was going to have to figure out what I could do about that before things ended badly for both of us.

23

When we sat down and really looked at what Rob had intended for me to do with a partner, we realized it was too much for three days. I mean, I was more than happy with the idea of having nonstop sex over the weekend, and while Harrison assured me he'd be more than able to keep up with the demands, we both agreed that we might need breaks. And possibly food. And wine. Definitely wine.

I also realized that as much as the sex-ins were good times, I was starting to get greedy again. Harrison was only going to be here for a little over a month and I still didn't know all I wanted to about him. If he was going to leave me, then I wanted to mine every detail I could from him. Memorize every tidbit and file it in my head next to my memories of Rob. I didn't need to question why he'd become that important to me. It was obvious.

That realization hit me as we were in the middle of a particularly epic fuck session. I was on my hands and knees and Harrison was taking me from behind. His hands would alternate between squeezing my hips and caressing the base of my spine. The two motions were so different in their intensity, it got me wondering what he was thinking about. Or more accurately, who.

"Do you miss your ex-wife?" I asked the question as I reached between my legs and started playing with his balls.

Harrison chuckled as he slammed into me a bit harder than before. "I'm a bit terrified to answer that question at the moment."

I tugged his balls, but not in a way that would hurt him. "Just curious. Have you had sex with other women since her, or just me?"

In a move that I couldn't figure out later how he managed, he flipped me over onto my back and slid his cock back inside me. "Why are we talking about my ex?"

"It's fun to talk during sex." I ran my nails down along the length of his arms. "Don't you think?"

"Not about my ex."

"Sorry. My brain goes all weird when I get horny. Rob used to—"

"Not about Rob either."

I rolled my eyes. "Fine."

Then he did this thing with his hands on my clit and my nipple in his mouth and I was screaming like a banshee. After he'd come and we were stretched out on the bed in all of our sweaty, naked glory, I laced our fingers together and asked again.

"So *have* you been with other women since your divorce?"

He let out this little huff of air through his nose that could have been annoyance, but I took it as him realizing that once I got something in my head I wasn't going to forget about it. He was smarter than most people if he'd figured that out about me already.

He gave my hand a little squeeze. "You are the only woman since Angie. I wasn't all that keen to get into any relationship, even just a fling."

"So what made you change your mind about me?" I wanted

to be flattered by his about-face on his views on women, but I wasn't so naïve to believe I was the reason for it.

"You. Well, you and your situation. Mrs. Le Page talked you up to me quite a bit those first few days. Then there was the incident at the bar. You tweaked my protective streak."

"I tweaked something." I ran my finger up the length of his flaccid cock. "Well, your protective streak is going to have to learn to leave me behind pretty soon."

"Six weeks." He rolled onto his side so our noses were nearly touching. Being this close to him, it was as though the entire world had disappeared and all that existed was this room and the man on this bed with me.

There was something about the look in his eyes that made my skin tingle and my breathing deepen. A spark that I'd seen before, not in Harrison, but on the day Rob had proposed to me. Slowly, he rubbed the tips of our noses together. "I think we have a problem."

"What's that?" I barely managed a whisper.

"I can't get into another relationship. I just can't." He swallowed hard before reaching up to cup my cheek. "And you are still in love with your late husband."

I jerked, but he didn't let my face go. "What does that mean? Of course I still love Rob. I always will."

"I wouldn't want anything less for you." He sighed, his eyes slipping closed for a moment. "I can see that brain of yours working away. You're comparing me to him. Trying things that you used to do for him to see if I'll like them. I'm not him."

"I know. I don't want you to be him."

It wasn't fair, and yet I understood why it bothered him. I pushed myself to a sitting position. Given the position, my belly was all doubled over and my boobs sagged down nearly touching the rolls. Rob would have poked at them, maybe even teased me. I wouldn't have felt embarrassed about the look or his words. Harrison couldn't resist them either, but rather than poking, he ran his fingers across the dips and valleys in a gentle caress.

"You're only the second man to ever see me naked."

"I'm honored."

"You should be." I kissed his forehead. "You're right. In my mind I do compare situations with what I've done in the past. Sometimes your reactions surprise me because they're not what I'm used to. It's actually really exciting for me, which is something I hadn't expected. There's something to be said for a new beginning. I'm not going to lie and say that I didn't wish we could be together longer, see if we could make something work, but I know that's not going to happen. So let's just have fun until you have to leave. Okay?"

Rather than the relief I'd expected to see on his face, I was surprised by the fleeting look of disappointment. "Sounds perfect."

He didn't want things to end.

My lungs stopped working for a moment while my brain processed the meaning of that. Despite everything—his ex, Rob, only being here for six more weeks—he didn't want things to end either.

I didn't know how to feel about that. I mean, it was good. Really good. Sure, now I knew more about his past and that would complicate matters. And no, I probably wasn't ready for something serious. Neither of those facts meant that I wanted him to go.

I wanted Harrison in my life for more than just sex.

Regardless of the whole sure-I-might-be-a-teeny-bit-in-love thing, coupled with the whole Rob-wouldn't-fault-me-but-still-guilty thing.

The moment I sucked in a fresh breath, my heart raced with excitement. If he was starting to have feelings for me, if there was a chance that he might actually fall in love with me, then I was going to take it.

I wanted Harrison. I wanted a much longer chance to get to know him.

By God, I was going to win him over.

Harrison got up and went in search of the sex bag. "If we've agreed on having fun, then we better work on these cards of yours. I'd hate to leave anything undone when I go."

The cards. Well, if that's what was going to give me the time I needed to figure out a way to get him to stay in Toronto, and subsequently with me, then I was going to take it.

"Well then," I said as I pushed myself onto my forearms, "let's make a list and get to work."

Operation Win Harrison's Heart was on.

24

What I really needed was a grapefruit.

When I'd convinced Harrison that we needed a break from our sex marathon to go to the store, I knew he wasn't keen. Getting cleaned up was necessary, as was making our way into the local convenience store where the prices were anything but. When I told him that he didn't need to come in with me, he smiled and turned up the music in the car to wait.

That gave me the opportunity I needed to find the one thing I wanted to use to cross off one of the sex cards.

A grapefruit.

There'd been this link that the girls had sent around work. It was so non-HR friendly that there were a lot of hush-hush conversations about it, only showing people on a smartphone once they'd promised not to say a word. It was that kind of epic.

In it was a woman demonstrating how to give a blow job using a grapefruit. She was a pro and yet came across a bit like your aunt who was giving you sex advice without your parents knowing. She showed me and every other woman in my office how to do this with confidence, and I knew that someday, I'd have to try it. The noises that came out of her mouth as she slid and slipped the fruit over a dildo were obscene. And one hundred percent arousing.

I had to do that to Harrison.

The clerk gave me an odd look when I put down the case of beer, a package of wet wipes, and the grapefruit in front of him. I simply smiled, happy in my knowledge of what I was going to do with everything and not caring what he thought about it in the least. I paid for my items and practically skipped out of the store.

"That didn't take you long." Harrison turned the music down once I got in. "Whatcha get?"

"It's a surprise."

The beer bottles clanked together when I hit the bag with my feet. "Beer. You're an awesome lady."

"I know."

"I noticed there was a park on our way into town. Want to stop for a bit?"

He was being all subtle about it, but having sex in a park was one of the things on the list. There was no reason why I couldn't do my thing and give him the added bonus of a little public display. "That sounds great."

"I don't know if I like that smug tone of yours." He patted my thigh as he pulled out of the parking lot.

"You will."

When we got there it turned out that it was actually more of a boat launch than a park, though there was enough green space that I forgave the mix-up. There was a car parked off on the far side, closest to the water, but that appeared to be it. We were alone.

"Oh perfect!" I jumped out of the car, taking the bag with me. "Come on."

I didn't wait for him, making my way over to a grassy area by a tree. If anyone were to come by, we'd hear and see them before they'd see us. That would give us the reaction time necessary to cover ourselves and make sure we didn't get arrested for indecency or anything. "Harrison, grab some napkins."

My dad had always taught me to carry a pocketknife in my purse. You never knew when you'd have to break into your car, fix a lock, or whatever unforeseeable adventures he assumed I'd have. For this particular misadventure, I needed it to cut the ends off the grapefruit and core it. Not an easy task given my tools, but totally doable.

"I think you're doing that wrong." He dropped the napkins beside me and laid out a blanket. "Come sit over here. It's more comfortable."

"Will do as soon as I finish this." I wiped my hands with the damp wipes, grinning as I did. "Oh can you also take your pants off? Underwear too."

That particular look on his face was way beyond adorable. He kept shooting me strange looks even as he undid his pants. I love a man who can be both confused and still go along for the ride.

Seeing his bare legs in the bright sunlight made me appreciate him as though he were a brand new person. The hair on his legs was far thicker than I'd noticed before. The muscles were far more visible as well. They were thick and well formed, running the entire length of him from feet to ass. I'd touched and been touched by his body, but even that hadn't made me appreciate the whole package.

"You are one sexy man." I lifted the grapefruit up for him to see. "Are you going to ask?"

"What day?" He smiled even as he stretched out on the blanket.

"I think this will count for Days Twenty-one and Twenty-eight." I paused to consider. "We could also throw in Day Fifteen if you want?"

"Sex with food, sex in the park and . . . role-playing?"

"Good memory, Mr. Kemp." I got up onto my knees and

smiled at him sweetly. "Oh sir, I have gone and found all the things you wanted. What shall I do with them now?" I'd failed drama class in high school. My teacher had actually begged me to never take another lesson and focus on business courses. My performing hadn't improved over the years.

The smile on Harrison's face fell away. Gone was the man who'd looked bewildered a moment ago, and in his place was a man who looked cold as ice. "You took too long."

Shit, he was actually pretty good. The whole hard-ass routine was a total turn-on. "I'm sorry, sir. Can I get you a beverage?"

"Quickly."

I put the grapefruit down and went for the beer, using my pocketknife to pop the top free. "Here you are."

"You expect me to touch that after you have with those disgusting fingers."

I was actually getting nervous. Dammit, he was right. "No, sir. Of course not."

"You'd better not. Now, get over here and give me my drink."

I wasn't entirely sure what to do until he lifted up on his forearms and opened his mouth. I pressed the bottle opening to his mouth and carefully tipped it up until he swallowed down several gulps. "Acceptable."

"Thank you, sir." It was only a bit of role-play, but his praise felt good. "Is there anything else I can get for you?"

"Something to eat." His gaze drifted down to the pool of juice that had leaked onto the blanket. "Rather, I want you to eat me. Get down there and suck my cock."

Jesus H. Christ. My body shook as I maneuvered myself between his legs. The sun shone through the leaves of the tree above and was hot against my back. Even through the blanket the ground was cold on my knees. The contrast confused my body and put me on edge. I was horny, scared of being caught, and confused as to why Harrison acting like an asshole turned me on.

There'd be time to question that later. First, I had a blow job to give.

"Sir, if I may, I'd like to try something. To give you more pleasure."

He didn't answer immediately. Cocking his head to the side, he dipped his chin toward me. "Seeing your breasts would give me pleasure. Take off your shirt."

That was easy enough to comply with. I took off my shirt and bra and set them in a smaller pile beside his stuff.

"Good. Now, you may try your thing. If I don't like it, there will be consequences." With that, he stretched back, his hands laced behind his head. "Begin."

Okay. Right. Beginning this thing. Here we go.

I took the grapefruit, eyeing the opening I'd made when I'd removed the core. The width of the hole wasn't quite big enough to accommodate his girth, so I stuck my thumbs in and pried it apart enough that I thought it would be comfortable for him. Positioning it at his erect cockhead, I carefully slid it down the length of his shaft.

"Fuck!" He bucked his hips up as I went.

I had to use my free hand to push him back down to the blanket. "Am I harming you, sir?"

"No," he said through gritted teeth. "Continue."

"Are you sure? I wouldn't want the acid to get into a cut—"

"If you stop, I will tan your hide, wench." There was a sparkle in his eyes and his lips threatened to break into a smile.

So my crazy idea was working. Thank you Internet blow-job lady.

I used the fruit to masturbate him for a few strokes. It took me a few minutes to get the hang of things. This wasn't like the video, the woman far more experienced at using a dildo. No, this was Harrison and me and the last thing I wanted was for an injury to happen and have to explain this to an emergency room doctor somewhere.

But the more I worked the fruit over his shaft, the more the juice began to flow. His skin shone in the sunlight, the smell of male arousal, grass, and grapefruit surrounded me. I couldn't resist any longer. I leaned in and on the next downstroke, took his cock into my mouth.

Harrison's legs shook as his muscles tightened. I moaned, remembering the sounds on the video, wanting to make this as visceral an experience as I could for both of us. Then I upped the pace. Faster I stroked the fruit up and down his cock, while I swallowed down both the juice and his secretions.

"It's like your pussy and your mouth at the same time." He spoke the words to the sky, but I heard them deep in my body. "Holy fuck."

I kept going, knowing that he didn't need a response. The fruit had softened from my grip, allowing me to play with the rind more. Using both hands, I changed the shape of it, flattening it out from side to side like one of those paper cootie catchers I made as a kid.

"Alyssa—" He moaned loudly. "Gonna make me come."

It didn't matter that my own orgasm wasn't currently on the agenda. In hardly any time, I'd pushed him to the limit of his release. I'd reduced him to a quivering mass out in public where anyone could see. I stroked him harder and faster, wanting to push him over the edge. It only took another minute before he cried out. His screams echoed across the water, bouncing off the trees that lined the lake. Come and juice mixed together and filled my mouth. I swallowed it all down, savoring the uniqueness of the taste.

"Stop. Stop, please." His hands were on my head shoving at me to pull back.

I released him with a pop. "That's a first for me. I've never used fruit or had a guy beg me to stop." Carefully, I pulled the grapefruit off and tossed it aside. "You okay?"

Harrison had thrown his arm across his eyes as he took giant, bellowing breaths. "I'm dead."

"Oh that's fantastic." I grabbed a napkin to wipe my mouth. "I've never killed anyone before either."

"You're a menace to all men. You could be a serial killer. Look at my poor dick." He flicked his softening shaft with his fingers.

"Death by blow job. I somehow don't think I'd have too many people report me."

He chuckled. "No. I think you'd be safe. You'd probably have a lineup."

I stretched out beside him, taking a moment to run my sticky fingers across his belly. "You're a mess."

While he'd reacted exactly the way I'd wanted, it wasn't enough. God, I was becoming a greedy sex fiend. I moved my fingers lower, teasing his pubic hair. I didn't think he had any more in him, but the longer I caressed his groin, careful to avoid his shaft, his cock started showing signs of life. Of course, now that I knew a repeat performance was possible, I was totally going to take advantage.

"Here, let me redeem myself and clean you up."

There was something soothing about using the wet wipes on his skin, rubbing and cleaning the juice from his body. His hair squeaked as I rubbed and scrubbed it. His cock was starting to grow hard. It would be easy to pull my shorts and panties off and ride him here in the fresh air. I was so horny I'd probably come within a minute.

It was an idea.

"You don't happen to have a condom on you?" I traced a line up his hardened shaft.

"You really are trying to kill me." His smile was shadowed by his arm still across his face. "I think I have some in the car."

"Ah yes. Day Nineteen." I scratched his balls. "That would be four in one go."

"We seem to be tearing through these cards of yours at a fast pace."

"Would you rather not? Want to save it?" I didn't want him to see my disappointment, but I really did suck at hiding things.

"Hell no. I'm just still recovering. Give me a minute."

I wrapped my fingers around his cock. "You seem pretty recovered to me."

He grabbed my wrist to stop me from stroking him. "The condom is in the center console. Go grab it and get your ass into the backseat. I'll be there in a second."

Okay, so I might have squealed before I threw on my shirt and raced to the car. I was horny! You couldn't blame a girl for getting excited at the prospect of some hot sex in the back of a car. I tried not to look back at Harrison to see what he was doing, but it was really hard. The box of condoms was exactly where he told me it was. I took a strip out and left the others where they were. If things continued to go my way, I would need them again later. I then opened the back door and stretched out on the backseat.

In the movies they make car sex seem hot and easy. There's steam and panting, with hands and feet pressing suggestively against the window. It normally happens at night and occasionally involves a psychotic killer or possibly a werewolf. At least in the movies I've seen. The one thing they forget to mention are the little things—like seat belts. The buckle clips were strategically placed to annoy. One was pressed into my side while—in my enthusiasm to assume the position—I bashed my ear against another one.

I was rubbing at my ear when Harrison came ambling up the hill with our stuff gathered up in the blanket. He tossed it in the trunk before coming around to join me. "You okay?"

"Buckle mishap." I held the condoms out for him.

"Anxious."

"Horny."

"I love a woman who knows what she wants." He bit on the edge of the condom foil, holding it between his teeth while he pulled off my shorts and panties.

"Don't bother with the shirt. I won't be long."

Aww, he looked sad about that.

"I was going to try and come again," he said once he freed a condom from its prison. "That might not work out."

"I'm not in a rush. Come again."

If you'd told me a year ago that I'd be this blasé about an orgasm, I would have laughed in your face.

"So generous." He rolled the condom on, lifted my legs, and positioned his cock at my pussy. "How about we play it by ear?" And then he filled me.

The movies did get one thing right about car sex, that feeling of doing something naughty. With my ankles up by his ears, I was stretched in a way that wasn't natural. The fake leather of the seat began to squeak from the sweat that had formed on my body. Harrison still smelled of grapefruit and his skin held the scent of sunshine. The angle of our bodies forced his body hard against my already swollen clit and his head at an awkward angle against the roof.

He was naked, I was partially clothed, and we were fucking in the back seat of a rental car. The force of his thrusts started the car rocking with the motion. I closed my eyes and took it all in. This was different and strange and exhilarating. I couldn't imagine doing this with anyone but him. Not even Rob.

I ran my hands along his arms, loving the feel of his strained muscles. My pussy throbbed and I knew it wouldn't be long before I would be screaming myself. But as much as I wanted to come, I didn't want this to end. I couldn't explain it, but I knew that this was special.

I knew that maybe, possibly, I was in love with Harrison.

Seemingly out of nowhere, my orgasm swelled and spilled across me. I screamed as I clung to him. I wanted to move against him, but I was pinned against the seat and couldn't get any leverage. It was frustrating as much as it turned me on.

"That's it." He thrust as deep as he could go. "Yeah."

The pleasure faded into the background as my orgasm slipped

away. Not that it stopped Harrison. He'd been serious about wanting to come a second time, and I was all on board with that plan. What I hadn't been expecting was that my body was keen on the idea of a repeat performance. Rather than the overwhelming desire to stop, my pussy remained sensitive and my clit ready for more.

Well okay then.

I draped my legs over his shoulders, which shifted my ass closer to him. The change in the angle let him get closer and deeper. Our mutual groans and moans filled the confines of the car. It was a weird contrast given the expanse of space where we'd just been. Everything seemed more intense, ramped up.

Harrison had his eyes closed. I was fascinated by how his sweat made his hair stick to his forehead. The flush on his cheeks and chest brought out the rich brown of his stubble and accentuated his muscles. As his orgasm approached, the muscles in his jaw flexed and his lips began to tremble. I wasn't quite with him, but I didn't care. I watched, fascinated as this strong, handsome man came apart.

His groan this time was lower, more guttural and it vibrated through me. He surged forward a few more times before finally coming to a stop. Yeah, that wasn't going to be enough. I stopped him from pulling away as I reached between us to finger my clit.

"Let me." His voice was raw.

Thankfully, he knew exactly how to touch me. Keeping his cock deep inside my pussy, he fingered my clit at a frantic pace. My body was a rock, shaking as I willed the orgasm to come. So close. Just about.

"Guh!" I screamed and bucked and squeezed as I came.

It was as though every molecule of air left my body in that moment, only to come rushing back in a powerful gasp.

Harrison pulled back after a minute, slowly lowering my legs to the seat. "Wow."

My body ached from the awkwardness of the angle and the muscles in my thighs were happy to no longer be crushed against the back of their respective seats. "That was. Yeah, wow just about sums it up."

It only took us a little while to get cleaned up and dressed once more. I was happy to crawl out from the car to stretch. I felt fantastic, completely sated and internally at peace. Not only had I just had two amazing orgasms, I was okay with the idea that I was actually in love with Harrison.

As I turned around, taking in all I could from the environment, I realized something wasn't right. There was something missing. . . .

"Oh my God, the truck is gone."

Harrison looked lazily over his shoulder to where the vehicle in question had previously been. "Yeah, the boat had pulled in as I was coming up the hill."

"And you didn't think to tell me?" That was a screech. I was actually screeching at him.

"They gave my naked ass a thumbs-up, so I didn't think they'd give us any grief."

I sat down on the ground, a rock sticking into my ass. "Kill me."

"Naw, they never saw you."

"Not the point! They could call the cops."

He held out his hand. I couldn't believe that he was so calm about the whole thing. "Then we better get out of here."

When I slipped my hand into his, everything felt right. "My hero."

"Always."

We came chest to chest as I stood, which was why I was able to see the flicker of shock cross his face. Whether it was from his comment, or something else, I wasn't about to mention what I saw. But that flicker of hope that had ignited inside me flared a tiny bit brighter.

*   *   *

Harrison was in the shower scrubbing grapefruit from his groin when I thought it was probably time to check in with Nikki. If anyone would appreciate my situation, it was my sister. I opened a bag of chips we'd picked up on the way back to the motel as I waited for her to answer.

"Alyssa! Where the hell are you?"

That wasn't exactly the greeting I'd been expecting. "And hello to you, too."

"It's been two days and you haven't checked in yet. You promised me that you'd do that."

"I sent you a text when we got here. You knew who I was with and everything. It's Harrison." He wasn't some stranger that she didn't know.

Actually, he kind of was.

"Fuck, he could have kidnapped you. You should have called me sooner."

I pulled the phone away from my ear and looked at the display. Yes, I had in fact called my sister who never once cared what anyone thought of her or what she did. "Why are you freaking out?"

"Why am I . . . you went away with a stranger to have sex."

"Nikki, you knew what we were doing—"

"I still don't even have your location. He could take you anywhere and we'd never be able to locate you. You're pretty naïve when it comes to shit like this."

"I'm not naïve—"

"God only knows what this man could have done to you."

"Nikki!" I wasn't one to get upset at her, but this was a bit much. "I don't know what your problem is, but you need to calm the hell down."

"You're not thinking with your head. You're always too trusting and people take advantage of that."

The thing about sisters is that early on in your relationship you embed an invisible knife in each other's hearts. Then over the years, you twist it just to get at the other person. Nikki just twisted mine hard.

"I'm not a child. I know what I'm doing. And forgive me, but you were the one encouraging me to go ahead and have some fun with him. You told me I had nothing to lose and experience to gain. You were the one who said I needed to move past Rob."

"Rob. Yeah, you've clearly moved past him. On to the next guy before you know it."

"Hey! That's not fair." My throat tightened. "Rob has been gone a long while now. I'm trying here."

There was silence on the other end. I could hear her breathing so I knew she hadn't hung up. "Nikki, what's wrong?"

"Nothing. I was scared. I'm glad you're okay."

"Hon—"

"Call me when you get back so I know you're home." The line went dead.

What the hell had just happened?

I was still sitting staring at the phone when the hiss of the shower stopped and Harrison emerged naked in a billow of steam as he toweled his hair. "I would have offered shower sex, but I need more recovery time than that."

There was nothing I could do about Nikki, not at the moment. I'd spent my whole life doing the things that others expected of me. I was sorry that I'd upset her, but when it came right down to it, the only way I'd be able to move on with my life, to get the things that I wanted, was to go out on a limb and grab them.

"Hey, you okay?" Harrison cupped my cheek, rubbing his thumb along my jaw.

"Yeah. I was just checking in with my sister."

"You sure? You look upset. If we need to go back—"

"No." I covered his hand with mine and trapped it against my face. "She's having a bad day and took it out on me. It's nothing she won't bounce back from."

I'm fairly certain he knew I was lying, but he didn't call me on it. "Okay. There's still a dry towel in there if you want to shower."

"Awesome. Then how about we find a place to get some supper."

His smile lodged itself behind Nikki's knife, a balm to the wound.

25

I was exhausted and slept well that night, despite the pointy springs that composed most of the mattress. When I woke, I stretched out, expecting to come into contact with Harrison's warmth. Instead, I was met with cool sheets. Instantly awake, I sat up and scanned the room. The suitcase wasn't visible. Neither was the sex bag.

"The hell . . ."

Nikki couldn't have been right about him. While I might not have the experience with men that she does in the sex department, I do know people. What the two of us had might not be love, but there was respect. He wouldn't leave me here in the middle of nowhere with nothing to show for it.

Would he?

I sat in the bed with the sheets pulled up to my chest waiting for something to happen. When I heard the car pull up and the door slam, the tension bled from me. Harrison opened the door, a carrier with two cups of coffee and a Tim Horton's bag resting on top.

"Good, you're up. I got us breakfast."

It was corny, but the moment he smiled at me it was as though the sun had come out from behind the clouds. Warmth spread through my chest, fueled by the joy I felt. "Tim's is a much better option than I thought we were going to get."

"Here you go." I took the coffee and breakfast sandwich from him. "I got muffins, too. For later."

Without rocking the bed or spilling the coffee, Harrison leaned in and kissed me. It was a lazy kiss, one that could have gone on for hours and I wouldn't have minded. He'd had a sip of his drink already, and the taste of it urged me to keep going, to try and suck it from him. If it weren't for the interruption of his cell phone ringing, we probably wouldn't have gotten to breakfast at all.

Don't answer it. Stay here and keep making out with me. . . .

"Sorry." He kissed me once more quickly before fishing the phone from his pocket. "Hello?"

It was amazing to watch him go from relaxed and happy to tense and pissed off. There didn't even seem to be a middle ground. One moment he was great and the next, *poof,* insta-pissed.

"I told you not to call me."

It didn't take a genius to figure out that it was his ex on the phone. My heart sank a tiny bit, but I wasn't so vain as to think this was any of my business. I took my coffee and sandwich and indicated to Harrison that I'd be outside.

The air was heavy this morning as large gray clouds filled the sky. It had been so hot and humid recently, the obvious upcoming rain wasn't much of a surprise. It seemed to be holding back for the moment, so I took my breakfast over to an old picnic table. The gray wood dug into the backs of my thighs, forcing me to adjust several times before I got comfortable.

This was actually quite pleasant. A nice hot cup of coffee and warm food to occupy me while I waited for my guy to come out. Mentally, I cuddled up around the term *my guy,* loving the way it felt. Sure, I was probably reading too much into it, but

Harrison was starting to act the way Rob had before we'd gotten engaged. While yes, there were certainly some barriers we would have to face if we were going to make things work between us, I couldn't imagine that they would be too insurmountable.

His needy ex-wife would be the biggest concern. Well, that and the fact his job was going to take him away soon. If that move turned out to be Montreal, or somewhere else in Ontario, then I could work with that. Maybe there was even a chance he could ask his office for a more permanent posting here in Toronto. There were lots of possibilities that we could discuss.

You've clearly moved past him. On to the next guy before you know it.

The sandwich turned to lead in my stomach as I forced down the last bite. It wasn't a bad thing for me to move on. Rob had told me he didn't want me to be alone. Hell, Nikki had said that too. Now her words revived the guilt that I'd thought I'd gotten past. Was what I had with Harrison a bad thing? I didn't think so, but maybe I was blind to what was really going on.

God, why did life have to be so complicated all the time?

I'd gotten halfway through my coffee before Harrison finally joined me.

"Everything okay?" I turned around to look at him when he didn't immediately answer. "Harrison?"

He gave his head a little shake. "Yeah, it's good."

It clearly wasn't, but I didn't want to press matters. "Come sit. I think this thing can support us both."

It wasn't a sure bet. When he sat down on the opposite side, the entire table shifted in a not-so-reassuring manner. "Scary," he said once everything stopped shifting.

"Hey, it was stable with just me here. I'm not saying you're the problem, but ya know."

"I'm used to being the problem. Don't worry." He smiled, but it didn't quite reach his eyes.

His mood had clearly changed and long slow kisses weren't

going to be back on the agenda until I improved things. I slid my hand across the table to cover his. "So, I was thinking maybe we could do something today that didn't involve sex. Well, at least for the first part of the day. I'm sure we can slip a card or two into the mix." I grinned. "Like I said, I was thinking. I saw a sign when we were driving back yesterday for zip lining. Rob and I used to do that a couple of times a year. It's a lot of fun if you haven't done it. We could go, get our hearts pumping."

He pulled his hand away as he leaned back. "Not really my thing."

"Oh. Sure." Maybe he was scared of heights and didn't want to admit it. I racked my brain trying to think of something else. "I know. We're pretty close to Lake Simcoe. We could drive up and maybe rent a speedboat. Rob and I did that a few times too."

"No."

"Yeah, you're probably right. I don't think my boat license is valid anymore anyway."

There had to be something. I knew Harrison was an active guy, but I didn't really know if he was an outdoor active guy. Not that Rob had been, but we always managed to find something to do. "The only other thing I can think of is to maybe check out some of the little antique road shops along the way. Rob hated when I dragged him along to those, but they're pretty cool and you can always find something—"

"Alyssa!"

He'd shouted my name so loud that I jerked back hard enough to send the picnic table rocking once again. "What?"

"I'm not Rob."

Whoa. Shock bled into annoyance. "What's that supposed to mean? Of course you're not Rob. I buried him two years ago."

"You'd never know it from the way you talk. You mentioned him three times in thirty seconds."

Had I? Sure Rob wasn't far from my thoughts most days, but I'd gotten better, moved on to bigger and better things. Was trying to move on to him. "So what if I did?"

"And that's why you're going to have a hard time finding anyone else. You're in love with a dead man."

My head swam and my stomach felt as though it had filled with blood. My mouth watered and for a moment I thought I might actually throw up. I had to cling to the edge of the table to keep from swaying. "Pardon?"

"Every day when I talk to you I can see it. That little flash that passes through your head when you think about him. *How would Rob react? Would he like this? This used to be my favorite thing to do with Rob so every other man I'll ever be with will have to like it too!*"

I couldn't speak. Even if words were able to come out of my mouth, I didn't even know what to say. How does a person respond to something like that? I couldn't very well deny it. I was in love with Rob and I always would be. But did that mean I'd be forever condemned to living the rest of my life alone?

He'd balled his hands and his breathing was coming out in short gasps. "*Maybe if Harrison does everything I want him to it will be good. But not as good as Rob.*"

"You asshole." Tears streaked my face, but I made no move to wipe them away. "I didn't deserve that."

His red face slowly drained of color. "No."

"This wasn't about a relationship. You'd said that from the beginning." I wiped my nose with one of my napkins. "You agreed to have sex with me. You've been the one to stress this wasn't anything more than that. How dare you get mad at me for . . . for being who I am."

"Alyssa, I'm sorry."

"You damn well should be."

Harrison slowly got up and moved around to my side. When he reached out to touch my shoulder, I couldn't help but flinch. He pulled back before making contact. "I shouldn't have said that." His voice had gone quiet. "Any of that."

"No. You shouldn't have." I wasn't going to cry anymore. I wouldn't give him that. "I would like to go home now."

"We should probably talk first."

"No." I got to my feet, careful not to touch him. "You're right. I do still love Rob. That must be a hard thing for you to be faced with. I'm sorry you're having a hard time with your ex-wife. You broke up. It didn't work out. You both have gone your separate ways."

It was hard to face him, to look him in the eye and see what he was feeling, but I did. Which was apparently not much based on his blank expression.

"But at least you have the option to still talk to her if you want. I don't. All I have are my memories."

"That's the problem. I'm with you and I feel as though you're using me. I'm not Harrison, but a Rob stand-in."

"You offered. I didn't need you."

"Bullshit. I saw you at that dance club. You looked like a deer in the headlights when that guy came up and started grinding on you."

"And you thought I needed saving?" I might be a lot of things, but even Rob knew that I was more than capable of looking after myself.

Rob again. Maybe he's right.

No. Fuck that and fuck him.

"Harrison, I know this is hard for you to believe, but I managed to get my husband through chemo, watched him rebound, watched the cancer come back, buried him, handled all of the details surrounding his death *and* kept going. I might not look like a fighter, or strong, or anything else modern women are supposed to me. But. I. Am."

"I know." His words were gentle, almost sad. "I never thought you weren't."

"The sad thing is that despite you warning me about your aversion to relationships, I thought maybe we might have a chance. That's what I was thinking about before you came out here, how I could convince you that it might be worth a shot,

you and me. Thank you for putting me back on the right path."
I walked back toward the room. "I'm going to pack."

"Our bags are already in the car. I was planning on taking you back to the city. To spend a night in a five-star hotel instead of this dump."

I couldn't even look at him. "I assume you left me some clothing?"

"Yes. In the bathroom."

"That saves me a step then. I'll get dressed and you can take me home."

Those were the last words we said to each other for several weeks.

26

Today was the first condo association meeting since we'd laid Mrs. Le Page to rest. Pierce had skipped last month's session out of respect, but business couldn't be delayed indefinitely. We were notified that this month's meeting was on. Full speed ahead.

For the first time since I'd move into the building, I'd arrived at the cafeteria early enough to help set up. Walking in brought more than a few strange looks from the other tenants as I wheeled out one of the chair trolleys and began to set out the stack. Even Pierce did a double take when he came in, though he knew enough not to come talk to me.

Apparently the rumor mill was working full steam ahead.

I'd been in a foul mood since the moment my alarm went off. I could only blame part of it on missing Mrs. Le Page as much as I did. The other part . . . the other person I was missing but didn't want to admit it, was Harrison. That revelation had brought on a five-minute pity party before I got my shit together and left for work. My day hadn't gotten much better after that, and the last thing I wanted to do was mope around my condo. So, I'd eaten and made my way down to help set up.

Which, based on everyone's reactions, was the first sign of the apocalypse.

I started fixing the rows, making sure there was more than enough legroom when people started arriving. Everything was normal until a hush descended on the room. I turned and saw Mr. Le Page standing in the doorway. I honestly hadn't expected his attendance tonight. God, I hadn't been able to show my face at these meetings for nearly a year after Rob's passing. I too had been greeted with the same awkward silence when I'd arrived. It hadn't been until Mrs. Le Page marched over and guided me to sit with her and her husband that I felt as though I might make it through.

Standing straight, I walked over to him. My throat ached and I was scared to talk. Instead I looked up at him, gave him a shaky smile before pulling him into a hug. His arms were weak around me at first as I rested my face on his shoulder, but soon they tightened around me. We stood there clinging to each other, knowing the other understood how we felt.

Finally we broke contact and I looked away just long enough for him to wipe a tear from his cheek. "Well, my dear. What's the news?"

"I got us the best seats, Mr. Le Page. At the back and close to the door."

"Excellent. Never know when we'll need to escape old Pierce's ranting."

I hooked my arm around his, ignoring everyone as we made our way to the seats. "I suspect we'll have them tonight. I heard that someone put garbage into the recycling bins outside."

He chuckled, which brought back some of the life into his eyes. "Lord, who would have been dumb enough to have done that?"

"I say we blame Harrison. It's not like he'll be around much longer."

Mr. Le Page cocked his head to the side, watching me as we sat. I did my best to ignore his silent question.

The last thing *in the entire universe* I wanted to talk about was Harrison. Or my nonexistent relationship with him. Or how despite pretty much hating him and doing everything in my power to avoid seeing him over the past few weeks, I maybe sort of missed him so much that my heart ached.

Or how I really had been comparing him and Rob and that I felt like shit when he pointed out what I'd been doing.

No way I'd talk about any of that.

The rest of the people shuffled in and a few even came over to offer their condolences to Mr. Le Page. I held his hand the entire time, offering him reassuring squeezes when I thought he might need them. Eventually, the seats were full and Pierce called the meeting to order.

"Thank you everyone for being on time. I'd also like to thank our volunteers who helped set up tonight, Oliver, Michael, and Alyssa."

The smattering of applause and the small smile Pierce offered me felt pretty good. Maybe I'd have to come early more often.

"On to business."

Someone came in late, the heavy thud of the old cafeteria door opening followed by footsteps echoed in the room. Pierce eyed whoever it was, shooting them his all-too-familiar glance of disapproval, before continuing. The latecomer pulled up a chair behind us and I didn't think anything more of it.

While I'd been keen to help out, the meeting itself was as tedious as ever. I'd enjoyed having Harrison with me shortly after his arrival, even though he'd been more than a little annoying. And while I knew Mr. Le Page wasn't against a little lighthearted kidding around, one look at him and I could tell he was currently reliving his own memories of meetings past.

My chair shifted when the person behind me kicked it accidentally. I scooted forward an inch to give them a bit more room. Next month I'd add even more space between the rows just to make sure that didn't happen. We had room for it, might

30 DAYS / 223

as well take advantage. Another minute and the person started tapping their foot against the leg of my seat. I let it go for a bit until it became unbearably annoying.

"Stop," I said as I turned to glare at whoever it was.

To see Harrison sitting there.

Yeah no.

I turned forward, crossed my arms, and stared straight ahead. I'm sure Pierce was saying something. I knew he was because I could see his mouth moving. The only thing I could focus on was the weight of Harrison's stare on the back of my head and the steady kicking of his foot against my chair.

I wasn't about to give him the satisfaction of a reaction, so I resigned myself to being annoyed and continued to ignore him.

Clearly, that wasn't to his liking. The next thing I knew he'd leaned forward and his mouth was next to my ear. "I need to talk to you."

"Shh."

"Lyssa."

Oh, now he was doing that to get a reaction from me. "Three. Syllables."

"Is there a problem there in the back?" Pierce said loudly enough to show his annoyance.

"Not at all," Harrison said. "I was just asking Ms. Barrow if she would mind shifting over so I could see better."

I scraped my chair loudly to the side. "Better?"

"Thank you, Ms. Barrow." Pierce looked at Harrison from over the top of his glasses. "Mr. Kemp, I do realize you're leaving next week, but do please try to be respectful of the other tenants."

"Wait, you're leaving?" I turned fully around to look at him. "I thought you were here for another few weeks?"

"I told you I needed to speak to you."

Pierce cleared his throat. "I'm sure you can both discuss things at the meet and greet. *After* the meeting."

"Sorry." I turned back around in my seat. There was no chance I'd be able to pay attention now.

Harrison was leaving.

I'd be all alone again.

The last thing I wanted was to go to the roof for the party. It didn't matter that this was our last one of the summer and that always meant margaritas, or that I'd overheard Mrs. Castor mention that she'd made homemade salsa and chips again this year. If I went upstairs, then Harrison would be sure to follow. If Harrison followed and started talking to me, then we'd end up getting into a fight. While I might have thrown a beer in his face last time, I sure as hell wasn't going to waste good tequila on the likes of him.

Though I might punch him.

In the end, the decision was taken out of my hands. Mr. Le Page had slipped my arm through his and was using me as a bit of a shield. While Pierce hadn't said anything directly during the meeting, his gaze had kept flicking to the widower. That had made everyone else pay more attention and the end result was an influx of well-wishers when things had wrapped up.

"Do you want to go back to your condo?" I'd whispered.

"No. I . . . I think I still need to be around people. I've missed the company."

I knew exactly how he felt. Sometimes the possibility of being alone was worse than the actual condition. If he wasn't ready to handle that quite yet, then I wouldn't abandon him. When we started to make our way up, I realized that Harrison was nowhere in sight. Good, maybe he'd gotten the hint and left. He'd told me that he was leaving far sooner than his original plans had indicated. It didn't matter if I knew the reasons why or not. It's not as though we were a couple. He didn't owe me an explanation—or anything else for that matter.

Pushing down my disappointment, I stayed linked with Mr. Le Page as we made our way to the roof.

The margaritas were cold enough to make the plastic cups sweat. I had to wipe my hands more than once to dry them off. I thought I'd feel awkward standing here, as people offered their condolences and made odd conversations to avoid talking about anything that might remind Mr. Le Page of his wife. After twenty minutes, people finally stopped coming over and left the two of us alone.

He finished his drink, staring at the bottom of the empty cup. "How did you manage this with such grace?"

"The margarita? Believe me, there's been more than one tequila incident."

He smiled. "People. I know in my heart they mean well. But as they speak I . . . I want to . . ." The smile fell and he looked back into the empty cup. "I need another drink."

I took it from him, stacking it beneath mine. "No you don't. It doesn't help. And I know exactly what you want to do. You want to hit them. Or scream at them. You want to rage and show them how angry you are. Why can't they see how unfair this was? It wasn't supposed to end this way. She wasn't supposed to go first. She wasn't supposed to die at all." I put my drink on the ground so I could take his hands in mine. "You're angry. It will pass in time."

"I keep thinking I should have noticed something wrong with her." He was crying without making a sound. "I can't believe she was sick and I didn't see."

"And you've officially entered the bargaining stage." God, it was weird seeing someone reliving the thoughts that had bounced around in my head. "That was worse than the anger for me. Because I blamed myself. But it wasn't our fault. Not mine and certainly not yours."

He nodded slowly, but I wasn't fooled into believing he was okay. He would be, but it would take time. "The one thing that drove me nuts when I was first dealing with everything after Rob died was the advice everyone tried to give. That said, I'd like to give you some if I could?"

His smile was a bit more genuine this time. "Of course."

"Don't fight the emotions. It's okay to be angry, sad, happy, and lonely. It will take time for you to work through them all, but don't fight them. You have to go through them all, as painful as they might be. When you do, you'll wake up one morning and the air will be a bit easier to breathe and the sun will shine a bit brighter. It will be then that you'll know everything will be okay."

He pulled me into a crushing hug. "My Charlotte always said you were far too wise for your age." He let me go and reclaimed our cups. "How about I get us both another drink?"

"That would be wonderful."

I never thought my own experiences would be useful to anyone else. If even a little bit of what I'd learned could help ease his pain a tiny bit, then I'd do my best to be there for him. After all, he'd done the same for me.

Harrison stepped beside me. I didn't need to look at him to recognize his aftershave and shampoo. Sad that I'd come to recognize his unique scent after such a short period of time.

"How's he doing?"

His question caught me off guard. It shouldn't have. I knew he'd struck up a friendship of sorts with the older man over his time here. "As well as can be expected."

"It's good that he has you to talk to. Someone who knows what he's going through. My dad didn't have that when we lost Mom. I think it made things harder for him."

"What can I do for you, Harrison?" With everything else going on, I couldn't handle idle chit-chat with him. It hurt too much.

"I need to talk to you. Alone."

"Not happening. You can say what you want here."

A group walked past us and said hello. I felt him tense beside me and I knew he was annoyed about not getting what he wanted. Well, too freaking bad. He lost that privilege back at the motel.

"I wanted to tell you that I'm sorry. Before I left, I wanted you to know that."

His apology should have meant more to me than it did. "Fine. You're sorry. I believe you. Now you can go."

He sighed, breathing heavy through his nose. "Don't you even want to know why I'm going?"

"Work? Another client matter across the country? Does it matter? In the end you're running away." Leaving me behind. Just like everyone else.

The muscle in his jaw jumped. "You know nothing about what I'm doing. What's happening."

"You're right I don't. Because you keep that stuff away from me. This was just about sex, after all."

"Alyssa—"

"No. Just stop." My throat tightened, making it hard to swallow down my anger. "You were right about me comparing you to Rob. He is . . . was a huge part of my life and that won't change. I won't change, won't deny that part of my life."

"I never asked you to."

"Maybe not, but you made it clear that you didn't like it either."

"Can you blame me?" He stepped in closer, so I could feel his body heat against me. "You had this perfect fucking life. Do you have any idea how hard it is for someone to step in after that? That's why this had to be about sex and nothing more. You're not willing to change? Fine. But you can't expect your lovers to change for you. I'm not Rob. I will never be Rob. I'm *me*, Alyssa."

"Why would you think I'd want you to change?"

He blinked. "You really have no idea, do you?"

Mr. Le Page chose that moment to finally return, handing me my newly refilled cup. "Ah, it's nice to see the two of you talking again. I was beginning to worry that you'd had a falling out."

I knew I had about five minutes before the tears were going to come. I had to get out of here. Away. Turning to Mr. Le Page,

I gave him a hard hug. "I'm not certain we ever had a falling in. You know that anger thing I mentioned. It has a tendency to come back at the weirdest times. I'm really sorry to leave you alone, but I need to head home."

"Okay, my dear."

"I'm sure Harrison here will keep you company." And with that I left.

No more. I was done. The idea of trying to change who I was to fit into someone else's preconceived notions of what a relationship should be wasn't going to work. Harrison was simply a reminder that I'd had my one shot at love. It was over now and I had better accept the fact that I was now on my own. I had no doubt I'd make similar mistakes with other men.

So no more.

This singular Alyssa was here to stay.

Part 4

New Beginnings

27

Moans and the sounds of fake kung fu filled my bedroom. I was stretched out naked beneath my sheets, my laptop strategically placed on the unused side of the mattress as I played a porn movie. This was one I'd picked out the day before at the sex shop and was quite excited to see. It was done by the same production company who'd put together the pirate movie I'd liked, so I figured this one would be as good. Boy, I wasn't disappointed in the least.

Who knew ninjas could be so hot?

I slipped my hand between my legs and gently fingered my clit. It had been awhile since I'd had an orgasm. I refused to remember the last time I'd come, seeing as it had been with he-who-shall-remain-nameless. I needed to start over and make some new memories that I could use for future fantasies. So good-bye pirates and hello ninjas.

In the current scene, the male ninja master was creeping through the window of the captured princess. The story had tried to explain why the ninja master was a middle-aged white guy with a big cock, but it had far too many plot holes for my liking. Thank God . . . big cock.

"Oh dear! How did you get into my room?" The princess was the same woman who'd played the princess in the pirate movie. Who knew it was possible to get typecast in a porno. I wondered if she'd had aspirations to be in other movies, or if she really enjoyed her job? I hoped it was the latter.

"Quiet or they'll hear." He pulled his mask off to reveal a clean-shaven jaw and thick black hair. "I'm the ninja master here to rescue you."

"But I was told you were a villain. That I'm here locked in this castle because of you."

"I would never. You are to be my promised wife. And we shall rule all of Asia."

Yeah, they weren't going for historical accuracy with this one. They'd done better with the pirates.

"Marry me? But my captors have threatened to take my virginity. I shall never make it to the wedding." She leaned back against her pillows, exposing her breasts.

"Then I shall fuck you now and claim you as my own." He grabbed the front of his silk pants and ripped them off.

Bingo, there was the cock.

I increased the pressure on my clit, rubbing small circles to increase the stimulation. The ninja master had torn off the princess's nightgown in one easy rip, leaving her fully naked. He then grabbed her by the waist and pulled her flat onto the bed. When he began to lick her pussy, I started fingering myself in earnest.

It felt good as my body warmed up to my touch. My nipples grew hard and my pussy nice and wet. As the moans from the movie increased, I let my eyes slip shut. I didn't need to watch it to use it as motivation. The sounds were enough to keep me going.

My mind took over when my eyes lost their stimulation. I became the princess, naked against the sheets, the ninja between my legs. His black hair was soft as I ran my fingers through it.

His stubble on his cheeks was rough against the insides of my thighs as he sucked my clit into his mouth. He'd tormented my clit, flicking it rapidly with his tongue while he squeezed my thighs with his hands. He'd move his fingers closer to my opening, running the tip around it so I knew exactly what he planned to do next.

I pushed my finger into my pussy, fucking it in and out slowly. This time my moans joined in with the pair in the movie. I could see his face as he devoured my pussy, but when he looked up it wasn't the ninja master, but Harrison between my thighs.

Even in my fantasies, I knew I shouldn't be thinking about him. Knew it would only lead to disappointment and heartbreak. But this was the one place I couldn't lie to myself. Where I couldn't escape him even if I wanted to. The one place I gave myself permission to dream.

"I'm going to fuck you now, my love."

Yes. I shoved a second finger deep inside, frantically fucking myself on my hand. Thoughts of Harrison's hard body pressing down on me generated some sort of weird muscle memory. My pussy clamped down on my fingers as my thumb pressed hard against my clit. Coupled with the screams from the princess in the movie, I was done for. My orgasm came hard and fast erupting in lightning flashes. I bucked my body trying to recreate the feeling of having him in me, with me, but it wasn't quite right.

Finally the pleasure faded and I was left somewhat sated, guilty, and slightly weirded out by my ninjas.

This wasn't fair.

I slapped the cover of my laptop down, threw back the covers, and went to get cleaned up. I was meeting Nikki for lunch and I'd never hear the end of it if I was late again. So pushing my fantasies to the back corner of my mind, I raced through my Saturday morning routine.

Nikki was already there, but her coffee order hadn't come yet. That meant that I wasn't in trouble. "Sorry I'm late." I fell into my seat and draped my purse over the back of it. "Have you been waiting long?"

"You're not actually. Late that is. I actually was early."

There was something in her voice that grabbed my attention. "What's wrong?"

In a very un-Nikki-like fashion, she didn't deny that there was a problem. "It's kind of the reason I asked you here. I think I owe you an apology."

"For what?" The last three times we'd gotten together everything had been fine. We even agreed on what movie to go see last week without bickering.

"For telling you not to trust Harrison."

My hackles went up. "No reason to apologize for that. You were right all along. He couldn't handle our agreement, which had nothing to do with me. He was a dick and I'm much better off without him around."

"No you're not." Nikki sighed and slumped back against her seat. "You've been miserable."

"Bullshit. I was miserable when he was around." It didn't matter that in the two weeks since he'd moved out I'd walked down to his condo and knocked on the door in the hopes he'd still answer. That was nothing but my own childish obsessiveness and I really needed to grow up and move on.

"Lyssa—"

"Alyssa. Three syllables." The response was a reflex.

"Since when has that nickname been an issue?"

"It's not. It's fine. I'm fine." *I just might possibly be heartbroken.*

"You *have* been miserable. This is exactly the same as when you found out about Rob's cancer."

"Don't compare the two. Losing Harrison was nothing like losing Rob. How could you even think they were remotely the same?"

"I don't. But the fact that you said *losing* Harrison, rather than Harrison leaving, or anything else, proves that I'm right. You were in love with him and I was too jealous to notice."

There were so many things wrong with her sentence that I wasn't sure where to begin. "You were jealous? Of what?"

Nikki sighed and pressed her forehead to her placemat. The waitress, on her way to our table, took one look at Nikki and indicated that she'd come back. I'd make sure to leave her a good tip.

"Nikki, please tell me what's going on?"

She lifted her head enough to look like a toddler who thought they were about to get into trouble. "I told you. I was jealous."

"Of?"

"I've been through three marriages. Three. All of them have ended, not all horribly, but they have ended. I was with Michael the longest and we only managed two years." She sat back up and fixed her hair, her gaze averted. "I used to look at you and Rob and think, wow, they are so in love but that's totally the exception. I didn't know anyone else as blissfully happy as you. Then you met Harrison and I saw that same joy wash over you again. I wanted to know why you seemed to get all the good guys. Why couldn't I find the good ones? One man. That's all I wanted. Someone for my own who liked me the way I am. When I found out that Harrison had whisked you away for a sex weekend, I got jealous. I'm sorry that I put that seed of doubt in your brain about him."

I rarely find myself stunned, but Nikki managed to knock me speechless. My older, far more successful sister, who never seemed to have a care in the world, was jealous of my two relationships. The world very well might be coming to an end.

"Well you can rest assured that I don't have weird sort of man-wooing juju. Harrison was an ass and he's gone."

"But would he have left if you didn't have it in your mind that he was a jerk? I mean, things started to go downhill for you right after my phone call. Maybe without really meaning to, I'd influenced you." She pressed the palms of her hands to her eyes. "I never wanted to hurt you. I certainly didn't want to break the two of you up."

"You didn't. Harrison had been clear right from the beginning that he had no interest in getting into another relationship. He hated that Rob and I had been so happy. Too much pressure on him or something. It had nothing to do with you, or even me." I picked up my menu and started to read over the specials. "But since you're feeling guilty, you can pay for lunch."

"Are you sure?"

"About you paying? Certain."

"No, about me not being responsible? I don't like to see you so unhappy. Not after I'd finally gotten my little sister back."

I tightened my grip on the menu, but smiled as brightly as I could. "I'm still here. Now, what's good to eat?"

I returned to the condo with a full stomach and an even fuller mind. While Nikki and I hadn't talked any further about him, I couldn't get my mind off Harrison. It was maddening. No, Nikki hadn't said anything that would have influenced my decision. It was simply really bad timing. Or good timing, as it gave me a buffer to get over him before he actually left.

Without realizing, I walked past my place and was halfway to Harrison's. God, this was stupid. I needed to get over him. He was gone, off to wherever his business had sent him, and I'd never see him again. Still, since I'd come this far, I couldn't resist the urge to complete my futile task.

The wood was cold against my knuckles as I knocked. This was dumb. He wasn't there. I didn't bother to wait, and started plodding back to my place.

"Hello?"

I spun around, greeted by the sight of a small blond woman. Her hair was cropped in a neat bob and she was wearing dress pants and a blouse that screamed businesswoman. "Hello."

"Did you just knock?" She looked back into the condo. "I'm

just moving in and I keep hearing things. I thought that was the door. This building is weird."

"I did." I marched back and held out my hand for her. "I'm your neighbor, Alyssa. I live in the next unit. I thought I'd come over and say hello." *Nice cover-up. Gold star.*

"Maranda. Hi. I'm only here for a few weeks to finish up some work that our last guy left."

"Harrison?" I couldn't believe that he would have left a job unfinished. Not after how seriously I knew he took things. "I thought he'd finished with his clients and the company moved him back home?"

Maranda frowned. "He shouldn't have been talking to you about work or our clients. That's confidential."

I so didn't like her already. "He didn't. Just casual conversation stuff. I don't even know who he was meeting."

Her frown told me that she didn't quite buy it. "I don't know him. I was told he had some personal matters to attend to. His wife was sick or something." She looked back into the condo. "I'm sorry, I have to finish getting ready for a meeting. Was there something else you needed?"

Harrison's location. "Nope. Just wanted to welcome you to the building." I gave her my little wave. "Hello."

"Thanks." She smiled weakly at me before shutting the door.

I tried to piece together the events of the last time I'd seen him. I didn't let him talk, or give him a chance to tell me what was going on. As far as I knew, he'd been moved for work as planned, just a bit ahead of schedule. All I'd cared about was myself, that he was leaving me behind, when I should have been worried about him.

What kind of person did that make me? I didn't really want that answer.

There was one person who might know what was going on. It was time to pay Mr. Le Page a visit.

28

The scent of old smoke and new construction was present as I stepped into Mr. Le Page's condo. This was the first time that I'd been here since his wife's death, a fact that I felt terrible about. The bottom of the pie plate I'd brought was sticky and still warm from my oven. I knew he loved apple pie, and with his kitchen still not fully functional, I figured he'd enjoy the treat.

"I see you know the way to a man's heart." His smile chased away my nerves. "Let me take that and we can have a piece."

"I didn't know if you were busy, but I wanted to see you."

"I appreciate it. I love my son, but he's grieving as much as I am. It's nice to have a break from all that. Plus, I could use your input into some redecorating choices."

The kitchen was in better shape than I'd expected. The contractor had already put new cupboards and a countertop in place. "Wow, they've moved fast."

"Bobby, my son, he pulled a few strings for me. His friend owns a company and well"—he held out his arms—"this is the result."

There were color palettes and tile samples on the table. I immediately started mixing and matching. "Oh this is nice."

"Charlotte was always the one who did all that. I don't have the eye or the inclination for it." His voice caught, forcing him to clear it. "Can I offer you some tea?"

"Yes please."

Within a minute, I had three options for his kitchen worked out and a piece of pie as my reward. "These are the best combinations. I'd say pick which one speaks to you."

"Thank you, my dear." He took a bit and sighed. "And this is delicious."

"I figured you could use a treat."

"Indeed. Now, what's bothering you to bring you up here?"

"Bothering me?" I hated that I blushed so easily. "Can't I just come and check on a friend?"

"You can. Did you know that Charlotte always said you were the sweetest girl she ever knew, but that you couldn't lie to save your life?"

I laughed. "I'm pretty terrible at it."

"You are. So I'll pour the tea and you talk."

I stuck my fork into an apple piece and twirled it around my plate. "Harrison is gone."

"Yes he is. You're bothered by this?"

"I . . . I know I shouldn't be. But yes, I am."

He placed a small cup in front of me. The tea was weak, little more than flavored water. I remember Mrs. Le Page complaining once that she never let her husband make the tea because he never let it steep long enough. She claimed that he did it on purpose to annoy her, that it was one of her few pet peeves. Now, I couldn't help but wonder if he simply liked it brewed this way.

Maybe Harrison was my weak tea. He thought I'd been trying to change him into Rob, make a copy so I had what I'd always had before. I hadn't been, not consciously. If anything, the longer I spent with Harrison, the more I realized that the things I liked most about him were the things that were completely different from Rob.

Rob and I had been a natural couple. We'd grown organically together, filling in each other's cracks. Harrison and I weren't like that, we didn't develop into a pair, but that didn't mean that we were any less of one. We were more puzzle pieces that, after a bit of mutual adjusting, slotted into place.

He'd become my preference.

"That's a lot of thinking you're doing over there, my dear."

I looked up startled. How the hell could I have forgotten where I was? "I'm sorry. I'm just . . . I'm trying to work a lot out. I just saw the woman who moved into Harrison's condo."

"I see. What did she say to you to bring all this on?"

"That his wife, his ex-wife was sick and that he'd gone off to help her." I couldn't be mad at him for wanting to help the woman who he'd married. While they might not be together any longer, she'd meant something to him once and it was admirable for him to want to be there for her.

"He told me as much at the meeting. He also asked me not to tell you."

I shouldn't have been surprised, but I was. "I didn't give him any reason for him to want me to know."

"It wasn't that." Mr. Le Page drank his tea, wincing as he looked down into the cup. "I made that weak. Habit. Sorry."

"It's fine. What wasn't it?"

He put the cup down and sighed. "Charlotte was much better at this sort of thing than I. He didn't have a lot of details at the time, but he said that his ex-wife had been diagnosed with cancer."

Oh God. "Why wouldn't he tell me that? I could have helped." If he was going to be there for his ex, he would need a support network of his own. That was something I'd learned the hard way.

"I think he didn't want to remind you of what Rob went through."

"Of course. Idiot." Typical Harrison, always trying to fix the situation whether he understood what was broken or not.

"I should also tell you something else. Before your Rob passed, he gave Charlotte a letter. He wanted her to give it to the young man who would eventually win you over. I'd forgotten about it until I was going through her things. I gave it to Harrison when I heard he was leaving."

Tears welled up in my eyes. "What did it say?"

"I don't know. We never opened it and Harrison didn't read it in my presence."

I couldn't imagine what Rob could possibly say to someone in a letter. God, if Harrison thought this whole situation was weird before, he'd be glad he ran away now.

"He's never going to want to talk to me again." I dropped my face into my hands. "I screwed this up so bad."

"I don't think you did." The sound of him sipping his tea was soothing. "That boy cared for you. Anyone with two eyes could see that. I think he was scared of making the same mistakes that ruined his marriage. He wanted you, but he didn't know how to win you."

I peeked up at him. "Do you think?"

"I know. More importantly Charlotte knew and love was something that she was rarely wrong about."

He'd been scared and I'd been angry. Those two things, coupled with his ex's phone call and Nikki's freak-out, had been enough to make us both overreact. He'd tried one last time to reach out to me before leaving for good and I'd shot him down without so much as a backward glance. I'd walked away from a chance at happiness and had been miserable ever since.

Mr. Le Page set his cup down and leaned closer. "I know it's not my place, but I noticed something when Harrison was talking to me before he left. He seemed annoyed that his ex-wife had reached out to him. Not that he'd come out and say it with her being ill. He did mention that it was hard for him to go back. They'd ended things. He'd wrapped up that part of his life. Unlike you and I and our losses, Harrison was ready for something new."

Oh.

A person's perspective is shaped by their life's experiences. My outlook had been shaped by losing Rob. I had no doubt that if he hadn't gotten sick and died, we would still be together today. Harrison's life hadn't worked out that way. He'd closed that chapter, chosen to end his marriage. While it was natural for me to keep Rob close in my mind, it wasn't the same for him. His ex-wife would be the last thing he'd want to compare someone to.

"I'm such an idiot." I closed my eyes and let out a groan.

"No you're not. You're a kind woman with a big heart. There is more than enough love in you for both of them. More than enough for you to fix this particular situation, if that's indeed what you want."

"Thanks for the tea." I downed the rest of my cup and stood. "I should probably go and . . . yeah, go."

"Do you have his number? To check on him?" There was a sparkle in the old man's eyes. "I have it written down somewhere if you don't. He wanted to make sure I could call him in case I ever needed anything."

"I do. I just wanted to know what was going on before I called him." I hugged Mr. Le Page. "Thank you."

"I'm just finishing what my Charlotte had started. She was convinced that he was the perfect man for you."

"If you need anything—"

"I'll come down."

With one final hug, I headed out. I needed a plan if I was going to get Harrison back.

29

I was more determined than ever to win Harrison back. I ran my plan past Nikki to make sure it had enough smut factor to be effective, but not enough crazy to scare him away. With her approval, I launched Operation Star Wars, otherwise known as Get Harrison to Talk to Me.

Cell phone. Check.

Blank cards. Check.

Lingerie. Check and double check.

Dildo and duct tape. Oh yeah, baby.

I was good to go.

My plan was twofold. First, I had to get Harrison to speak to me again so I could earn his forgiveness for not giving him a chance to tell me what was going on. Second, I needed to woo him. I didn't have the first clue how to woo a man, but I knew Harrison well enough at this point that I could at least take a reasonable stab at it.

There was a chance that this would all be for nothing. He could be by his ex-wife's bedside right this moment declaring his renewed love for her. Illness did strange things to a relationship and I'd seen couples reunite more than once in similar circumstances. If that was the case, if I'd lost my chance to be with him, then I'd have to accept it. I had an opportunity and I'd blown it.

But if I hadn't, if there was a sliver of hope that maybe the two of us could make something together, then I needed to try. I owed it to both of us.

I started the Saturday morning of the Labor Day weekend. The air was cool and the breeze had picked up, typical for a late August day. I had a cloth grocery bag filled with my items, ready to go in case things worked out. My cell phone was sitting on my coffee table, the display screen currently blank. I took a fortifying breath, picked up the phone, and searched my contacts for Harrison's number.

Hello?

It was hard to wait for a response. There were any number of reasons why he didn't get back to me immediately. He could be out running errands, or at the hospital with his wife, depending on what they were doing for treatments. Anything. I shouldn't pressure him into responding. That wasn't the tone I wanted, nor was it how I wanted to regain his trust.

Still, I needed to say my piece.

Hi. This is Alyssa (in case you deleted me from your contacts). I wanted to let you know that I heard about your ex. If there is anything I can do to help, ANYTHING, let me know. I've been there. I know how hard it is to deal with things and still try to stay strong for the other person. You need someone there for you. If not me, then please find someone else.

I pressed send and a weird shaking crept up my arms. It was almost enough. Almost. But there was one last thing I needed him to know. There was no sense in chickening out now.

Oh, I also wanted to let you know that I think I love you and if it's too late for that it's okay. I screwed up. You didn't deserve to constantly be compared to Rob. You were right. I think I was feeling guilty for wanting to move on. For being ready to move on. I just needed you to know that. And that I'm sorry. Have a good day!

There. The ball was officially in his court.

Leaving my phone on the table and the bag on the couch, I got up to go scrub my toilets. Because why not. I spent the better part of the next hour washing down every inch of every surface I could find in my condo until I couldn't clean another thing. Then I vacuumed. Then I organized my shoes. I was about to start on doing the laundry when my phone started playing "Born To Be Wild," my Harrison-specific ringtone.

I never considered myself particularly athletic, but I jumped over the arm of my couch to get to the phone, landing bouncing on the cushions. Taking a moment to steel myself against the myriad of possible answers that could be waiting for me, I ignored my pounding heart and picked up my phone.

Just woke up.

Well that was anticlimactic. I then looked at the clock. *It's nine o'clock. You're normally long up by now.*

I'm in Calgary.

Wait. *What?*

Home. Calgary. That's where my ex is.

That was something I should have known. *Sorry.*

It's good. I'm up now.

I was getting a little antsy that he hadn't mentioned anything about what I'd said. It's not as though I declare love via text message every day. Still, I knew Operation Star Wars wouldn't be won that easily. I had to push on.

How is she making out? What kind of cancer?

Mr. Le Page?

Yeah. Don't be mad at him. He only told me after I bugged him. Not exactly true, but I didn't want to get him in trouble.

I'm not. A pause. *She'll be fine.*

Now he was being stubborn on purpose. *I'm sure she will. Lots of cancers are easily treatable if caught early enough. What does she have? Breast? I hope not, but there are a lot of excellent treatments now.*

Another pause, much longer this time. *No, skin cancer.*

I wasn't about to belittle any sort of cancer, but if a person was going to get one, that was like winning the lottery. What confused me was Harrison leaving town to be with her. He could have handled things long distance and with the occasional visit. Then I remembered the phone calls, his frustration, and some of his comments.

She didn't tell you how bad things were before you came out, did she? You thought it was something more serious than it was?

Yeah.

Ouch. *I'm sorry.*

Don't be. You weren't the one lying to me.

No, but I didn't give you a reason to stay either. Well, I'd gotten him to talk to me and for once I wasn't screwing things up. It might be too early to start the wooing phase, but it would give me an idea of if this would work.

I grabbed one of the blank cards from my bag, wrote down my message, and took a picture.

Harrison, I miss you.

With a few button presses, the image was sent off. The delay for his response took longer than I'd hoped, but when it came the butterflies in my stomach took flight.

☺ *I miss you too.*

Yes! Operation Star Wars was underway. I shoved my phone into my pocket, grabbed my bag, and went to my bedroom to get ready. When I left my condo, I knew I wouldn't stop until I won him back.

30

The next phase of my plan involved a little visual teasing. I decided the best place to start was at my coffee shop. I didn't realize how busy this place was on a Saturday morning, but wasn't
going to let that stop me. I took a picture of the outside of the
building before going in and getting in line. Len, the barista
who'd put a little extra punch in my coffee the last time I was
here, was taking orders. Thankfully, there were too many other
people around for him to do anything more than smile and wink
at me.

I smiled back as I paid for my drink, bolting the moment I
could. It took a minute to find a table that wasn't next to a family. I sat, put my drink down on the table, and put my bag on my
lap. Now for some fun. I shuffled through the sex cards until I
found the one I wanted. I placed it on the table and snapped a
picture and sent it to Harrison.

Day Thirteen
Heat up your mouth with hot liquid
and then give him a blow job

I had to be careful before I did the next part. Waiting until I was certain no one was looking, I pulled the dildo from the bag, put it next to the coffee cup and card, and took another picture. Grinning, I shoved it back in the bag, just as one of the other baristas walked by. She gave me a weird look.

Shit. "I'm doing something for a bachelorette party. Dildo about town."

That seemed to be the right thing to say because the woman laughed and nodded. "Been there done that. My friends chickened out and I was the one with the toy. Have fun."

"Thanks!" *I'm a lying liar who lies.* At least it was for a good cause.

Not wanting to look too obvious about what I was going to do next, I drank my coffee as quickly as I could. I then got up and went to the bathroom. It was one of those small, single-stall rooms, which was why I figured it would be perfect for this next card. All it needed was a little alteration.

I took the dildo out once more, along with the duct tape. Using a little ingenuity, I taped it to the wall about waist height. Perfect. Dropping my gear to the floor, I got undressed as quickly as I could so that the only thing I had on was the lingerie I'd bought for this occasion. I stood beside the taped up dildo so it was still visible in the mirror and took a picture.

Oh yeah.

It took a bit longer to get dressed again, but I managed it in short order. There was a knock on the door, which caused me to drop the cards that I'd been sorting through.

"Just a minute." Aha! There it was. Resting it on the dildo, I snapped another quick picture before ripping it off the wall and shoving it into my bag.

Day Twenty
Have sex in a public bathroom

I sent it, along with the picture of me and the dildo, off to Harrison, before making sure that I'd removed all evidence of what I'd done and left the room. There was a young mother and her toddler standing there waiting for me to leave. *No guilt, no guilt*... "Sorry. All yours." I bolted from the coffee shop.

My phone had buzzed several times after I'd left, but I was too chicken to see what Harrison was saying. At worst, I'd hoped he was enjoying the humor in my little adventures. At best, I hoped he was getting turned on.

The next stop on my little sexventure was the CN Tower. It seemed slightly ridiculous to pay money just to get a picture, but I wasn't going to do Operation Star Wars half-assed. It was all or nothing.

Not that Harrison would appreciate the meaning behind this, but being terrified of heights, the CN Tower was the last place in Toronto I tended to go. First, it was a big, honking, concrete tower. Second, you had to go up said concrete tower in a glass elevator. Last, the bloody thing had a glass floor. No. And yet, here I was, fee paid and climbing into the elevator to go up to the top of this monolith so I could get the perfect dildo picture.

Who said romance was dead?

When the elevator doors slid open I noticed there was a group getting ready to do the edge walk. Those idiots paid money to get strapped into a harness and go on the *outside* of this thing. They were nuts. And yet...

I went up to the guy who looked to be in charge. "Excuse me? I have a very odd request."

By the time I'd explained what I wanted him to do for me, the dude was laughing his head off. "You want me to take a picture of your dildo by the door outside?"

"If you could. It's a bit of a joke. My boyfriend is out of town and ... well."

"It's cool. Just, don't tell anyone I did this. I could get in trouble." He held out his hand and I gave him the bag. "Give me ten minutes."

Fifteen minutes later I sent Harrison two pictures.

Day Twenty-three
Have sex on a balcony

The second was the image of the dildo in front of the door that led to the outside of the CN Tower, the Toronto cityscape behind it.

With those done, I thanked the guide and went back down to solid ground. Needing a distraction from the elevator scenery, I took a moment to scroll back and see what he'd said earlier. The first one was simply a smiley face. But with each subsequent picture I sent, his comments got more verbose.

☺

Cute.

A hot mouth would feel weird.

Is that a public washroom? How did you get the tape to hold that thing to the wall?

LOL it is! Where is that? I'll have to add it to my list of places to visit.

Holy fuck, you're in lingerie. In the . . . shit girl. My cock is a rock right now.

Where are you off to now? Hello?

Is that . . . are you at the fucking Tower?

LOL!!!! How did you manage to get that picture. I can't believe you're doing this.

By the time the elevator reached the ground, I was a grinning fool. It was working. I had one more stop before I could head home. On the way to the subway stop, I popped into the bookstore. Having spent more hours than I could count here over the years, I knew exactly where the book I wanted was. Originally, I planned to simply take the picture of the dildo next to the Kama Sutra, but as I picked it up and flipped through some of the pages, I realized I might actually want to have a copy. You know, just in case I ever found myself in a situation where I needed a hot-ass sex move and didn't have any good ideas.

I paid for it as quickly as I could before shoving it in my bag along with the other things. The rest of the pictures I wanted to take I could do back at my place, so I hopped on the subway and headed back.

With the running around I'd done, it was already late afternoon. I was starved and in need of food. The timing worked out perfectly with what I had planned next. As I made myself an egg and cheese sandwich, I pulled out a few things that might be fun to play with: a wide-faced spatula, my bottle of honey, and a rolling pin. I didn't quite know what we could do with the rolling pin, but I knew Harrison would have more than a few ideas. I lined them up, this time positioning them with the card, and snapped the picture.

Day Twenty-five
Use three items from the kitchen

This time I waited for Harrison's response. I stared at the phone's screen as I ate my sandwich and then continued on with a bag of chips. When it came, I had to read it a few times before it registered.

I would spank your ass with that and then fuck you with the rolling pin. When you didn't think you could take any more, I'd turn you over, pour honey on your pussy and lick it off until you screamed.

My hand was between my thighs before I knew it. How was it possible that he could turn me on that fast? I had one more picture left to send him, and after that comment, I wanted to take things to the bedroom. I positioned the Kama Sutra against my pillow and set the dildo and the card beside it.

Day Eighteen
Try a move from the Kama Sutra

I was surprised when I didn't hear back from him right away. There are a number of logical reasons why he couldn't respond. It was noon there. Maybe he had to meet with friends, check on his wife, work. Still, when an hour went by and there was still no response, I decided that I couldn't wait around any longer. Operation Star Wars would have to go on hold and I'd keep my fingers crossed that things would work out.

31

After things had been going so well Saturday, I grew more and more concerned when Harrison didn't respond. I waited until close to bedtime before I tried sending him another text. At this point I'd been honest enough with both my feelings and desires that at the very least he owed me something.

Even if it was to simply say good-bye.

I fired off a quick, *Hey are you okay?* and then went for a shower. When I got out, towel wrapped around my head, the indicator light on my phone was flashing. Rather than an apology, or the dick pic I'd been silently hoping for, there was only a quick *Ttyt* on the screen. Talk to me tomorrow? But what about tonight?

I fell into bed and called Nikki.

Nikki didn't bother to say hello. "So, how's it going? Any word from him?"

"We talked."

I pulled the phone from my ear when she squealed. "And?"

"And I sent him the dildo pictures."

Another squeal. "Did he love it? Of course he did. Probably thought it was freaking hilarious."

"He did laugh." I sighed. I didn't mean to, but it came out on its own.

"What happened? Do I need to beat this guy up?"

"No. He's in Calgary anyway."

"Why the hell is he there?"

"That's where he's from and where his ex is. He went back to help her through her cancer scare. That turned out to be not as bad as I thought. She has skin cancer and he said she'll be okay."

"She was using it to try to get him back. I've seen it before with certain obsessive types. He's going to need to make a clean break from her. Maybe he should move. I know! He can come back to Toronto and marry you. I bet his company could even move him here."

The thought had crossed my mind as well, but I refused to get my hopes up. "I'm not going to put that pressure on him. It makes me no better than his ex if I do. If he wants me, wants a relationship with me, then it has to be his decision."

"Yes. Just keep sending him dildo pictures in the meantime."

I laughed. "I love you. Thanks."

"Love you too. I need to make sure my baby sister is happy. You deserve to be happy."

"So do you. You'll find your Mr. Right someday."

"No doubt. I'll have a lot of fun living vicariously through you in the meantime."

I hung up and did my best to sleep that night. Instead of rest, I found myself caught in the throes of a series of erotic dreams. Harrison and me naked on a beach, making love by the water. Harrison sitting in the backseat of a convertible with the top down. I climb onto his lap and begin to ride him. Me captured by a pirate and Harrison bursting in wearing army pants and no shirt to rescue me. I had no idea where that last one came from. Not that it mattered, because each dream ended the same. Just as my orgasm approached, I'd wake up and be left with nothing.

I couldn't even have a proper wet dream anymore.

I gave up trying to sleep at six in the morning and instead

made myself a coffee and began to read through the Kama Sutra. Some of the positions were things that looked natural, a few that Harrison and I had even tried. There were others though that you had to be a bit of a contortionist to be able to pull off. Yes, Harrison was in pretty awesome shape, but even he might find some of these challenging.

The human body wasn't meant to bend that way.

With the book turned on its side so I could better wrap my head around the position, a realization hit me.

I hadn't thought about Rob in days.

The book became heavy in my hands and I set it down hard on my lap. I'd been so focused on figuring out how to win Harrison back that Rob hadn't entered my mind once. Not for a moment. Even in the times when he normally would have been my natural reaction. Instead Harrison had quietly come into my thoughts and gracefully took over center stage.

Guilt pushed tears up into my eyes, but I blinked them back down. There was no reason to be guilty for thinking about another man. If anything, I should be proud of myself. Finally I was starting to move on, to live my life once more. I found someone who I knew could make me happy, just as happy as I'd been with Rob. He wasn't a replica or a replacement; Harrison was something new, different. He brought out a different side of my personality, encouraged me to grow in different ways.

Harrison had brought joy back into my life. I just hoped I'd be able to repay the favor.

Sunday passed slowly. There was still no word from Harrison. I sent him a few messages over the course of the day, and I saw that he did get and read them, but he didn't respond. I even took one of the blank cards and drew a frown on it and sent him the picture. That did get a response, but it was only a quick, *Tomorrow. Promise.* Well, I'd waited this long for him, what was one more day?

Torture, that's what it was.

I'd slept like crap that night, my mind playing out the

weirdest scenarios. In half of them I was making love to Harrison. In the other half he was breaking my heart. It was clearly the uncertainty of not knowing where I stood with him, but it pissed me off nonetheless. I deserved some happiness after everything I'd been through. Didn't I?

My phone buzzed, causing me to open one eye to look at the clock. Shit, I'd put it on vibrate instead of mute. It was five forty-three in the morning. It was probably just a spam e-mail or something. I closed my eye and hoped I could get back to sleep. Another buzz, followed by a third and I reached over to mute the phone. Someone would die once I was awake. Later.

When I woke up it was almost nine-thirty. My muscles ached from having spent far more time in bed than I normally do. I stretched long and stayed that way until I rolled onto my stomach. My phone was precariously balanced on the edge of my nightstand. Scooping it up, I flopped back into my pillows to delete the spam.

Except it wasn't spam.

It was a text from Harrison. *Good morning!*

Wow, that would have been two in the morning for him. He must have been up really late working on a project for a client or something. I scrolled down and realized that there were more than three, but over a dozen texts and images. What the hell was he doing?

It's time for a scavenger hunt!

The next one was actually an image. I had to turn my phone around to see that it was an image of a dark room, lit by what I thought was a laptop. That's . . . strange. I kept scrolling, reading, and looking, trying to figure out what the hell he was up to.

A picture of a car parked at night.

The lit-up console—oh an Audi, nice—of the car.

A highway? Maybe?

Finally I got to another message. *It's really quiet this time of night. Gives me lots of time to think.*

Thinking was good, at least I hoped it was. The message was

followed up by another image. This one made me sit straight up in bed. It was the sign for the Calgary airport. I swung my legs out of bed and stood while I scrolled down to the next image. It was an airline attendant holding a ticket. That was followed by a close-up of the ticket. Calgary to Toronto, one-way, arriving at five forty-three in the morning.

"Oh my God, he's here." I looked at myself in the mirror and screamed.

It was a happy scream. Except for the part of me that was horrified at what I saw reflected back. I needed to get cleaned up and figure out what to wear. I had no idea where he was or when he was coming to see me. If he was coming. He had to be, right? That was the whole point of flying to Toronto, to see me. God, I hoped so.

I mentally flailed around as I snatched my phone and ran into the bathroom. While I was in the shower, my phone buzzed several more times, and each one sent my heartbeat up another notch. My skin was still damp after a quick toweling off, but I didn't much care. My fingers shook as I looked through the texts.

The inside of an airplane.

A cup of airplane coffee. I mentally cringed, knowing how crappy those normally were.

The next picture was of the Toronto skyline from the plane. I stopped moving and simply stared at it. Holy shit, he was really, really here.

As I was staring at the screen, another message came through. *I assume you're awake now.*

I had to type my response three times to correct my typos. *Yes, I am. Where are you??*

Not telling. You have to find me. He followed it up with another picture. This one was of the lake. No, not just the lake, the bench by the lake where we'd stopped after the funeral. I hastily got dressed and ran to the subway.

The crowds on the streets and subway were still dense given

it was a holiday. There were lots of things going on downtown, which made it that much slower to get where I was going. Without being too much of an impatient bitch, I maneuvered my way out of the underground and walked as quickly as I could to our bench.

Except Harrison was nowhere in sight.

I was tired after running to get here, so I sat down. Maybe he had to step away for some reason. He'd be back. My phone buzzed.

Talk to the man.

Talk to the who?

"Excuse me?" I spun around on the bench to see a man who looked to be in his midforties was standing behind me. He was decked out in running gear, not the type of person who'd be waiting around. "Are you Alyssa?"

"Yes." My heart skipped a beat.

"These are for you." He jogged over to a garbage can and picked up a bouquet of flowers that had been hiding on the ground behind it.

They were daisies and they smelled wonderful. "Thank you."

"You're welcome." His grin was infectious. "I get the feeling you're going to have a good day today."

"I think so too." I clutched the flowers to my chest as he continued on his run.

They were beautiful. I buried my nose into the tops of them and breathed in deep. My head filled with their scent and my heart with his love. This was what had been gone from my life for so long now. Passion and fun and silliness and love. I wanted more. More of it, more of him, more, more, more.

My phone buzzed again. *Like them?*

I love them. Where are you??

Soon. Talk to the woman.

I was on my feet spinning, looking for the next piece to the puzzle. There were lots of people walking around, but none that seemed interested in talking to me.

My phone buzzed. *She is working. I think.*

Working? There weren't many people working on Labor Day around here. It wasn't until I spun around a second time that I caught sight of an elderly Chinese woman who was searching for bottles in a garbage can down the path. Going on assumption only, I walked down the path toward the pier to her.

"Excuse me?" She didn't respond. "Excuse me. I'm Alyssa."

She looked up at me, checked me out, and in the next moment grinned widely. Nodding several times, she reached into the top bag from her cart and handed me a ticket. It was for the ferry over to Center Island. It was a holiday so that meant it ran every half hour or so. I had about fifteen minutes to get where I was going.

"Thank you!" I placed a kiss on her cheek for good measure and ran.

The ride from downtown to the island is only minutes long, but it could have been days given how impatient I was to finally see Harrison again. It didn't help that he was continuously sending me messages.

The ferry on this side has left.

It's really quite beautiful on the island. Though it would be more so with you here.

Are you on it now? Now?

Wait, I can see the ferry. I want you to go to the bow of the boat and wave for me. I want to see if I can pick you out.

Did you wave??

I raced over to the front and waved as frantically as I could, but I doubted he'd be able to see much of anything given how many people were standing around me. But I looked for him, and with each passing minute my anticipation and excitement grew.

There!

He was close to the edge of the dock and the moment our gazes connected, I saw him grin. His shoulders straightened and he rose up on the tips of his toes for a moment before he turned and walked away.

No! *Don't leave, you jerk!*

I'm not going far. Come get me.

I was able to behave myself until I disembarked and stepped foot onto the docks. I tried to see him past the throng of people milling around, trying to get on and off the ferry. I couldn't, so I decided to head off in the direction I'd seen him go.

Harrison was standing at the end of the pier at the opposite end of the ferry. He stood there, his hip leaning against the metal gate at the entrance. I dodged through the crowd, slipping past everyone until I finally reached him. I didn't stop until I was nearly pressed against him. How I held back, kept from throwing my arms around him, I'll never know. Instead, I looked into his eyes and I smiled.

"Hi." I had to swallow past the ball of emotions that threatened to block my throat. "You're here."

His hair had grown longer in the few weeks since I'd seen him last. I couldn't see his eyes because of the black sunglasses currently perched on the bridge of his nose. It didn't matter. From the curve of his mouth, that little smirk he'd perfected, I knew the eyes hiding behind those glasses were sparkling. Harrison was up to no good, just the way I liked him.

"Alyssa, Miss All Three Syllables. Would you be interested in joining me for a walk?" He turned and offered me his elbow.

I shifted my bouquet to the other side and slipped my arm through his. "I would love to."

The moment we started walking, all the tension that had built up in my body over the last two days melted. He was here and I was with him. I stepped closer so our bodies were pressed at the sides.

"I missed you," I said after a few minutes, needing to get that out of the way. "More than I thought I would."

"I missed you, too. Honestly, I didn't think I'd hear from you again."

"Me either." The breeze tickled my face, and the smell of fresh cut grass was around us. "You're really here."

"Yes." He chuckled. "Still here."

"This isn't going to come out right, but I'm going to ask it anyway. Why? We fought, again, and I walked away from you. I'd been mean and pigheaded. I thought that was it and you were gone for good."

He stopped our walk and wrapped his arm around me. "If you really thought that, then why send me the pictures? Why reach out to me at all?"

He really had a way of getting to the heart of the matter. "I found out about your ex-wife. And I remembered how hurt and alone I'd felt when I went through that with Rob. How angry I was at him, at the cancer, how guilty I became for feeling angry. I didn't want you to go through that alone."

Groups of people walked around us, spreading like water around a rock in a river. We stood there, and as far as I was concerned, we were the only two people in the world. I'd come this far, understood the consequences of not being one hundred percent honest about my feelings. I couldn't stop until I said it all.

I took a breath and placed my hand on his heart. "I also realized that I'd made a mistake. You were right. I had been comparing you in my head to Rob and that wasn't fair. The funny thing is when I thought you were gone, that there was a chance that I'd never see you again, I couldn't get you out of my mind. I wasn't thinking about Rob at all. Then when I talked to Mr. Le Page I realized that I'd been seeing you and your relationship with your ex through my own 'widow' perspective. I was reading things into it that weren't there. It wasn't fair to you. I knew that I'd had another chance at something special, something that my sister reminded me doesn't come around that often, and I'd blown it."

"No, you haven't."

I wanted to laugh, but I knew he'd take it wrong. "Thank you for reminding me of something too."

"What's that?" His voice was hushed, but it didn't hide the crack.

"That love is too precious, too rare to just let it go away. I'd convinced myself that what I had with Rob was my one and only shot at love. That while sex is great, that was all I really had to look forward to. I needed more than that. I need a friend as well as a lover."

We stared at each other a while longer before continuing down the road. When he spoke, it was the first time since we'd gotten together that the self-confident mask slipped. His grip on my arm tightened, as though he was scared I'd run away. *As if.*

"When Angie called me, when I finally listened to her, and she told me she was sick, I went. She'd cheated on me, used me so she could move in certain social circles, but she didn't love me. Not the way you and Rob loved each other."

A group of children ran past us, balloons chasing behind them. He watched them go, his stride slowing. "I didn't think I could give you what Rob had. The more I listened to you talk about him and the things you did, I didn't know if I had what it took. My only long-term relationship had been tainted and ended horrifically. I didn't want to hurt you, but in my mind I was bound to screw things up like I had with her. So I went back."

"But she'd lied to you."

"It wasn't much of a surprise. It was her way of forcing me to listen to her. And I did. Listen. The problem was she wasn't saying anything new. It was about *her* wants and needs. She didn't ask me what I wanted or needed. Funny thing was I nearly fell for it." He took my face in his hands and bent forward until our lips touched. "Until you sent me that first picture. Then I knew what I had with her had never been real. Not like what we'd shared. I had to get you back. If you'll have me."

"Yes."

I couldn't tell you who started the kiss, not that it mattered. He held my face, his thumbs caressing my skin as his fingers massaged my scalp. His lips were demanding softly, unyielding in their desire for more. I didn't deny him, or myself. I slid my hands around his neck, pressing my body hard against him until no one would be able to see that we weren't one entity.

It was in that moment I became a plural once more.

Alyssa and Harrison.

When we finally came up for air, I caught the sounds of some giggles and catcalls in the distance. "Seems we have an audience."

He cocked an eyebrow and looked around. "I don't remember that being on the cards."

"I think we can forget about the cards now. We've officially moved past them." I patted his chest and toyed with one of his buttons. "I do wish we had a bed though."

"Funny you should mention that." He turned me to face a charming little house. "Ta-da."

"What's this?"

"This is a bed and breakfast that just so happened to have their last guests leave a day early. We have a room for a night. If you want."

I squealed and jumped up and down. "I want! Now. Sex now, please."

He pulled me back against his side and led me up the walkway. "Calm down or else they might change their minds."

"Did they not know about the impending crazy-monkey-sex? That's bad form not to warn them, Mr. Kemp."

"I'm a bad man."

I kissed the back of his hand. "No you're not. You are a very good man. And I look forward to showing you exactly how I feel about you."

32

The owner of the B&B was a charming middle-aged woman who wasn't at all naïve to the fact that we were about to go bang like bunnies.

"You two are lucky. We're normally booked solid for most of the summer. My last booking had to leave early due to an unexpected change in their flight."

"Luck seems to be on my side these days," Harrison said before placing a kiss to my temple. "Thank you for fitting us in."

"I've changed the bedding and left the menu on the nightstand. Normally I need an hour warning about supper. If I don't hear from you by seven, then I'll assume you're not hungry."

The sparkle in her eyes as she directed us to the room at the far end of the house had me blushing like a madwoman. Yeah, I knew that *not hungry* was code for fucking. Thankfully, she didn't call us out directly. I probably would have melted into the floor if she had.

I took a breath before I opened the door and stepped inside. The room was absolutely beautiful. I spun in a slow circle so I could take everything in. "Wow. This place is . . . wow."

"Couldn't have put it better myself." He wasn't looking at anything except me.

And there was that blush again. "Oh stop."

"I'm not stopping until I hear you scream." He shut and locked the door.

"No. No way. Screaming is totally vetoed. Did you see the look she gave us?" It would have been slightly less embarrassing if we were newlyweds or something. But only slightly.

"Well then, we can do Day Twenty-two then." He started taking off his shirt as he kicked off his shoes.

Not wanting to be left behind, I pulled my T-shirt off and tossed it aside. "How do you remember all the cards? I only know a few of them."

"I'm a guy. They're sex cards written *by* a guy. I also have an excellent memory." He unzipped his fly and pushed his pants down. "Plus I took pictures of them all."

"You *what?*" I threw my shorts at his head. "Why would you take pictures of them?"

"To impress you with the size of my memory." He smirked then pushed his briefs to the floor.

I looked at his erect cock and licked my lips. "Consider me impressed. But remember what they say. It's not the size of the memory, but what you can do with it." I made quick work of the rest of my clothing, not stopping until I was as naked as he was.

"That sounds like a challenge." He came closer a step.

"It is." I took a step as well.

He took a side step toward the bed. "Then I better make sure I live up to expectations."

I took a side step to match him. "You will."

"You can't make a noise." Then he reached down and pulled something out of his pocket. "I'd taken this off earlier. I think it might come in handy now."

It was a black silk tie.

My body was very pleased to see it. Rather than verbally give

266 / Christine d'Abo

my consent, I sat down on the bed and opened my mouth. Harrison sighed as he lifted the tie to my lips, slid it into place, and tied it around the back of my head. "That is the hottest thing I've ever seen."

I could have responded, the tie wasn't on that tight, but the game had already started and I wanted to try to do this as best I could. Because me and being quiet really wasn't a combination that went well together.

"Slide back on the bed. Get right in the middle."

I scooched back until I was in the spot and then stretched out. My nipples were already hard and my pussy was wet from my eagerness. I'd been dreaming about this, about being with him again for days now. With the moment finally here, I didn't know if I could wait a second longer to feel him against me.

Unfortunately, Harrison didn't have the same game plan that I did. He walked around to the side of the bed, took my hand, and stretched out my arm. He then moved around to the other side, looking at me the entire time, and repeated the action with my other arm. Moving around to the foot of the bed, he adjusted my feet so I now resembled some human-shaped starfish.

A month ago, this position would have made me feel embarrassed, exposed, more naked than I already was. But not now, not with him. The only thing I could think about was Harrison and wanting him to touch me, to lick me, to make me come so hard that I forgot I wasn't supposed to make a noise.

Harrison returned to the foot of the bed to look down at me. Lifting his finger to his lips, a reminder not to make a noise, he quietly half-laid on the bed so his face was hovering above my pussy. He leaned in and kissed the inside of first one, then the other of my thighs. His breath came out in a hot rush, which set my body shivering.

The kiss of his tongue against the dip between my body and leg almost had me moaning from the headiness. Instead, I bit down on his tie and hoped he didn't want this back. He shifted his face and repeated the kiss on the other side, before he trailed up, kissing across my hip and to the bottom of my ribcage. I tried to squirm away, but his hands held me still. I was forced to grip the duvet cover, squeezing it between my fingers as though my life depended on it.

Harrison continued to tease me. Kissing the underside of my breasts. Licking the space where my cleavage would be if my breasts weren't splayed apart. Kissing just below my armpit, which almost caused me to giggle. I kicked my feet on the mattress, a silent demand to get on with it. He ignored me, continuing taking inventory of my body.

He sucked on my nipple lazily, flicking the tip with his tongue in a manner that was more loving than arousing. It wasn't until he switched breasts and took the dampened peak between his forefinger and thumb that the real pleasure started. He pinched and rolled it, the pleasure coming from it slowly at first, building as the minutes moved on. I began to buck my hips, wanting him to lick me, fuck me, anything that would help me come.

He didn't.

After a torturous amount of time, he started to make his way back down the other side of my body, mirroring every kiss he'd made on the way up. He added a few extra licks and kisses for good measure, especially when he returned to my belly. He paid extra attention to my belly button, licking around the hole several times, before he finally started kissing a trail down to my pubic hair.

Rather than simply head right for my clit, Harrison lowered his nose to the thick patch that covered my pubis, and breathed me in. I'd done that to him before, loving the way his natural scent made everything seem that much more real in my head. The coarse strands moved the skin beneath as he played, the area becoming more and more sensitive with each passing second.

I loved it.

I hated it.

I really *was* going to scream if he didn't get on with it soon.

I might have sighed when he shifted down lower and reached up with his hands to expose my clit through the hair that protected it. His thumbs parted all that was in the way, until the air kissed at the heated skin. I looked down and my heart melted a bit at the look of joy on his face before he leaned in and covered my clit with his mouth.

At first, he didn't lick, just sucked. The pressure grew stronger the longer he continued on. As the pressure increased, so did the pleasure. I pressed my hips up, forcing my pussy hard against his mouth, hoping he'd give me what I wanted. It must have worked, because the next thing I knew he began to flick my clit with his tongue.

The whole keeping-silent thing was getting really difficult. I squeezed my eyes shut as my body tensed. I was so on edge, so aroused, I didn't know if I was actually going to be able to come. Was it possible to be too horny? Maybe. But in the end, this wasn't the way I wanted to feel my release. I reached down and tugged at his head, motioning him to come up.

I wanted him inside me when I came. I wanted to enjoy the sensation of his cock sliding in and out of my body, of having his hands hold me as I rode him. Yes, that was the image I couldn't get out of my head.

Ignoring his frown, I pushed him to the side and started to climb on top. When he understood what I was trying to do, he smiled and went onto his back willingly. I grabbed a condom from the nightstand where he'd so wisely put a box, and rolled it down his shaft. Unlike him, I wasn't capable of teasing caresses. I threw my leg over him, positioned his head at my opening, and sank down until we were joined together.

Fuck. Me.

My clit came into contact with hot skin, sweat forming on us both already. The duvet was soft under my knees, making it a comfortable ride. Bracing my hands on his chest, I lifted my hips, slowly rising up the length of his shaft, before falling back down into place. Harrison sucked a breath in through his nose and gritted his teeth. Oh yeah, this was going to be fun.

Again I rose and fell on him. Then again. And again and again until I thought I might lose my mind. Each time my clit kissed his body, my pussy tightened around his cock. His hands tightened around my hips, his nails digging into my skin, encouraging me to go again. We continued this little dance, the rhythm and speed increasing on each thrust. My breasts swayed with the motion, my nipples tingling, wanting to be touched, tasted. I leaned forward, pleaded with my eyes for him to do just that. His eyes were closed, so I leaned up as much as I could to hit his chin with my breast.

He smiled and without opening his eyes, did what I wanted.

I had to bite the damp silk of the tie to stop from moaning. I missed making noise. Missed begging and pleading, and moaning and sighing. But as much as those things aroused and stimulated, the quiet had an appeal of its own. I was able to hear the sounds of our lovemaking. Hear the beat of his heart when I lowered my head to his chest. The smell of our arousal and sweat made my mouth water. Even the feel of his hands on my body, his tongue on my breast was amplified. This was possession of a different kind.

We owned each other.

My body was close to release and I wanted to squeeze every last bit from it that I could. I started grinding down on his cock, forcing his body to rub my clit until I knew there was no going back. I wanted to keep playing the game, keep the noises bottled up as much as possible. I doubled my lips over, biting on them from the top and bottom at the same time. The air I sucked through my nose wasn't coming fast or deep enough. I grew light-headed, which only served to intensify the rising pleasure.

The first waves of my orgasm snuck up on me. I was surprised by them, not even having a chance to tighten my muscles. My hips stuttered on my next downstroke, which had Harrison opening his eyes. The look of surprise on his face was only fleeting, because in the next moment the next wave of my orgasm forced my eyes shut and every muscle in my body to contract. I bit down hard on the tie in my mouth, not quite able to contain my orgasmic scream. It was a low, guttural noise, primal even. Not something that would normally come from me.

As the waves seemed to go on, I felt him tense below me. His hands flexed on my hips, holding me still. I was too weak to argue and let him do what he needed. He fucked hard, slamming into me with a force that nearly blasted another orgasm from my exhausted body. All I could do was look down and watch his face contort with pleasure as he came. The tendons in his neck bulged and his face flushed as he tried to stop his own cries. With a final powerful thrust up, Harrison collapsed back onto the mattress and silently pulled me down to rest on his chest.

Once we'd recovered, he reached up and took the already loose tie from around my mouth. I had to swallow a few times, and wiped the lingering drool that had gathered at the edges of my mouth on his chest.

"Sorry about the tie. That's pretty much ruined."

"I'll add it to the sex kit. We can use it again."

I loved the fact that there would be more times. "Good idea. Think they heard us?"

"No doubt. The bed was squeaking."

"Was it?" Clearly, I was more out of it than I realized. "Oh well."

He wrapped his arms a little more securely around my body. "Alyssa?"

"Yeah?"

"I really want to tell you something. But I'm not sure if it's too soon or not."

I lifted my head so I could look him in the eyes. "If it's what I hope it is, then no, it's not too soon."

"I didn't want to get into another relationship after my marriage ended. I didn't want to get into a rebound and end up hurting the other person." He brushed my hair from my forehead. "But sometimes things don't go the way we anticipate. And love comes when we're not expecting it."

Tears were in my eyes even as my heart pounded.

"Alyssa, I love you. I want to stay here in Toronto with you."

"I love you, too," I whispered. I had to clear my throat before I could continue. "What about your job? Will they let you transfer here?"

"I don't care. If they don't, I have more than enough contacts in the area. More than a few have already offered me a position if I ever decided to relocate."

"Really? This is really going to happen?" My grin was so wide it hurt my cheeks.

"It is. If you'll have me."

"Oh yes. You're stuck with me now." I laid my head back down on his shoulder with a sigh. "Stuck like glue."

"That's good. Because I think we still have a few more of those cards to get through."

It was funny, but the idea of going through them had started to lose some of the appeal. "You know what? How about we make up some cards of our own. Something that both of us want to try."

The fingers that had been playing with my hair paused mid-twirl. "Really?"

"Yeah." He kissed the top of my head. "By the way."

"Yes?"

"You can call me Lyssa if you want."

33

The graveyard was awash in sunlight. The buzz of a lawn mower chattered away in the distance, competing with the sounds of a minister conducting a service not far away. Gravel crunched beneath my feet as I made the long walk toward Rob's plot. It was no longer one of the newer graves, the grass having been there long enough for it to be even with the rest and a part of the surroundings.

My steps slowed as I drew closer to my destination. It wasn't that I hated coming here, or that it was a reminder of my own mortality, but it was that rising emptiness that came every time I saw his name etched in the stone.

I placed the bouquet that I'd brought into the small stone vase that was a part of the base. Rob had never been much of a flower guy, but he'd insisted on the vase, knowing it was something that I'd want to do. It was. Just another way that he was still helping me out.

"Hey." I knelt down and picked at some of the grass that had grown too close to the stone. "I miss you. And I still love you."

I'd finally come to terms that I could still love Rob without it having an impact on my growing love for Harrison. Love wasn't an either-or situation. It was a limitless entity that grew in strength the more it was shared.

"So these damn things." I pulled the sex cards from my pocket and held them out in front of the grave. "These turned out to be a good idea. I know you said that I shouldn't hook up with the first guy who I met. I know you said I really shouldn't fall in love with that person either. That I should take some time to get to know myself and what I want."

I'd placed the cards into a plastic bag so they wouldn't scatter. That was the last thing I needed. Sex cards going amiss at a graveyard. Though the stories that would have come from that happening might have be entertaining.

"The thing is, I did have time before I jumped into another relationship. And while I might not have had a whole lot of experience when it came to sex, I did have a lot when it came to love. What you and I had was special. But it wasn't my only chance. I understand that now. And I have you to thank."

I placed the cards on top of the gravestone, watching as the wind blew the empty part of the bag like a flag.

"I think you would really like Harrison. He's not a computer guy like you were. Or a gamer, though I managed to teach him how to play Settlers and he's pretty good. And Nikki actually likes him, which is saying something. He's serious, but knows when to have a good time. He likes action movies and makes me go to the gym. Mostly he loves me and all my quirks."

The wind blew a bit harder and when I looked up I saw that the cloud cover had thickened. "It wasn't supposed to rain today, but I think it might. I better go." But I didn't stand.

"I miss you. It doesn't hurt anymore, but I do still miss you. Harrison helps with that. He loves me and I really do love him. Thank you for knowing, for understanding. Thank you for being one of the most amazing men I've known."

I did stand then, kissing the cold stone on my way up. "Harrison is waiting for me. We're going out for dinner and a movie. We're celebrating his new job. Oh and he's moving into the condo with me. That will take some getting used to, but I know we'll do fine."

I gave Rob one more smile, turned, and walked back to the parking lot where Harrison was waiting. When I got there, he gave me a big hug, holding me until I was able to get my emotions back under control.

"Okay?" He kissed the tip of my nose.

"Yeah. I'm good."

"We can skip supper if you want."

"No. Rob wanted me to go on with my life. That's what I'm going to do."

Harrison hesitated, looking down the path where I'd just been. "I should go pay my respects."

"Not that you can't, but why?" I appreciated him accepting Rob as a part of my life that wasn't going to fade away, but that didn't mean he had to force it either.

When he reached into his pocket and pulled out a letter, my breath caught. "Mostly because of this."

I didn't need to ask what it was; I'd never really forgotten about Rob's letter passed on to him by Mr. Le Page. "What does it say?"

"When I was back in Calgary and you'd started sending me the pictures, I remembered about this letter. I hadn't read it, but knew I needed to before I made a decision about us."

He held it out for me to take, but I couldn't. "Tell me?"

He nodded and put it back in his pocket. "Dear whoever you are. She's the best thing that will ever happen to you. Yes, she's worth it."

Tears rose in my eyes, but I was able to hold them back. "So are you."

He smiled, patting my hand before opening the car door for me. "I'm taking you someplace special."

I laughed as I wiped away evidence of our moment from my face. "Oh? Where?"

"The revolving restaurant at the top of the CN Tower." He leaned down and kissed me hard. "I hear they have a great big bathroom."

I laughed as he shut the door. The sun came out through the clouds to warm my face. Everything was going to be wonderful.

Epilogue

The wind picked up, blowing at the bag as it lay on the top of the cold grave maker. There was very little weight to it and the wind was persistent. Leaves helicoptered down from the trees above, brushing past the bag.

The service down the lane from the grave was just ending. A trail of solemn attendants filed past in small groups. Each group commented on the life of the ninety-two-year-old woman who they'd just laid to rest. Many of the groups spoke of the good times they'd shared with the lady. Others spoke about the minister, the reception afterward, the weather.

At the end of the group were the young people. The great grandchildren, those who barely knew the woman but had fond memories of cookies, Christmas presents, and twenty-dollar bills slipped to them when parents weren't looking. They weren't children any longer, all of them now making their own way in the world.

As the group approached, the wind grew even stronger. The bag containing a stack of handwritten cards was no match against its force, try as it might to stay where it had been placed. They had nearly all passed by when the wind gave one final gust, sending the bag with the cards tumbling to the ground.

A young woman looked over at just the right time to notice their fall. "Hold up!" she called out to the group.

She bent down to retrieve the cards, intending to put them back on the stone where they'd been. That was, until she caught sight of what was printed on the lined paper.

Day One
Masturbate

"What the hell . . ." Curious, she opened the bag and quickly looked at the contents. "Holy shit."

"Glenna, you coming?"

On impulse, the young woman shoved the cards into her pocket. "Yup."

"What was that?"

Glenna wasn't like her cousins. She wasn't a go-getter. Sure, she knew what she wanted, *who* she wanted, but he didn't know she even existed. Maybe these sex cards could help her become the type of woman who would be noticed.

Not that she'd tell the others of her plan. "Oh nothing. Just some garbage."

She could wait until she got home to look at the cards. After all, she had all night.

Acknowledgments

How can you properly thank people, show your appreciation for all of the support an individual has given you, with only a few simple words? You can't, not really. However, I will attempt to do my best.

To my readers. Your support over the years has meant the world to me. Thank you for continuing to pick up my stories and for coming along for the ride.

Thank you to Kristina and Kim. When I was writing this book, my life took a challenging turn. You were there to hold my hand, give me hugs, and keep me going when I needed it most. My friends and partners in crime, I love you both.

To my wonderful agent, Courtney Miller-Callihan. Man, we've come a long way in a short period of time. Your support, advice, and friendship are more than I would have anticipated when we started together. A simple thank-you will never be enough.

To Esi Sogah, my editor and the woman who didn't run screaming when she read the premise for this book. You took a chance on this story and for that I'll be forever grateful. Plus, I'm fairly certain we might have been separated at birth. We need to explore this possibility over a glass of wine. Or two.

And finally to my husband, Mark. There are no words. But thankfully, you know me well enough that I don't need to worry about forming them. I love you.

Experience Glenna's story in

30 NIGHTS

Available in 2016

from

Christine d'Abo

and

Kensington Books